The Trail of the Reaper

The Trail of the Reaper

PETER FOX

St. Martin's Press
New York

Library of Congress Cataloging in Publication Data

Fox, Peter F.
  The trail of the reaper.

  I. Title.
PR6056.0865T7   1983   823'.914   83-2949
ISBN 0-312-81366-X

First published in Great Britain by Macmillan London Limited under the title Kensington Gore.

First U.S. Edition
10 9 8 7 6 5 4 3 2 1

PART ONE

Though this be madness, yet there is method in it.

William Shakespeare

ONE

Nelson Hogan consulted his watch (a Gucci, naturally; solid gold, thirty jewels, I don't wear just anything on *my* wrist) and then let his left hand slide down the leather grip of the driver working its way around the shaft until it was just touching his right. Then he eased it back a fraction.

Six forty-five. He was due at London Weekend at ten which left plenty of time for breakfast and a shower. Right now it was golf so switch everything else off. Hogan extended his arms, shook his hips.

A fabulous morning. They had talked of rain later but right now the morning sky was a near unbroken blue, fading into a haze on the horizon over to his left and right. Dead ahead of him was the number eight fairway with its green beyond the patch of trees, and further on, the rising and dipping contours of the course with its small stands of conifers here and there and the clubhouse in the distance, small from here but very neat when you got up to it.

Hogan hadn't teed off from the first hole, of course, he never did when he slipped in from his estate for his morning practice. Number eight was the nearest hole to start from. Looking up again before hauling back he decided he had time for a good hour today, at least, because . . .

Funny. He'd imagined there was nobody about.

Hogan stared hard at the end of the four-hundred-and-fifty-yard long par four. Well, maybe not. If there was somebody near the green they'd stopped moving now. But he could have sworn somebody or *something* — moved, just as he looked down at his ball; something dark, something black, a figure possibly.

To hell with it. If they got a golf ball in the ear they'd better be members.

The most wonderful chat show person in world history let go with what was honestly a very nice drive. It knifed out, long and low, hugging the ground for a good fifty yards before it lifted and

9

soared, not a trace of slice in sight. Always the same of course; when you're alone, you're beautiful. Hogan sighed, almost, and started to stride after it.

Just get that air, just *get* that air. Nelson Hogan breathed in hard, getting that air.

He greened in two and holed in four, which made him feel slick, par or not, because it's one thing to hole in par and it's another to pull out superb shots and that drive had been superb.

His next two holes were superb too, so that by the time he teed up for the eleventh he was a happy man, and his thoughts were sliding smugly into other areas, like this ultra funky programme they wanted all of a sudden.

All about fame, they said, how people handle it, how it handles them, and like, all that. Not just another show, something more documentary they said. Hogan had liked the idea right off because fame was a thing he could wax deep and lyrical about, having had such unique exposure to it. He could play being a philosopher, right? Show them all that dispassionate and far-seeing eye that he always knew he had. Pad out the image too. Already he was thinking titles. Something snappy but highbrow it had to be, along the lines of 'Nelson Hogan on—' or 'Hogan and the nature of —' or maybe . . .

Something moved. That made twice. It was gone now but it had been up there ahead again. It was human and it was clad in black, but now it was gone.

Or hiding.

Hogan got ready and took up his stance. This time he looked fixedly up the fairway, longer than before, just in case some silly kid was fooling around out there. The green was out of sight this time, on the other side of a small copse, so you had to know the line, although the copse was small enough at this distance to provide a pretty good line on its own. You couldn't go far wrong if you just sighted on the copse.

Dammit, if there was a flaming kid messing about he was going to get an earful. He knew how to handle kids, don't worry about that.

Wham. Another nice one. That was going to clear the trees, no problem.

Hogan started walking.

The nature of fame? No. What about the nature of stardom then? Hmmmm, maybe.

10

Having a small mind that fitted easily into a small groove, Nelson Hogan stayed on the same phrase all the way up to the green. The nature of . . . Oh, *no*.

It was an inch from the hole. One rotten inch.

They'd never believe him of course, Hogan thought cheerily as he strolled up to his ball. He might as well claim a hole in one for all the credit he'd get, no point tapping it in. He bent and picked it up and rubbed the moisture off it with his thumb and forefinger. A blade of grass, not more than half an inch long, stuck to it, and this he scraped clear with the fingernail of his index finger. Still rubbing the ball, he transferred it to his other hand and then tossed it up in the air a couple of times as he headed for the twelfth tee. His bag was over his shoulder. He pinched his nose. He looked at his nails. He hooked a nail over his lower front tooth and ran it along, cleaning it. It was an absent gesture that millions had seen on TV.

Oh, yes, millions.

He'd have to make this the last hole, he decided, after a slant at his Gucci. Still getting that air, he took out the driver and brandished it like a club with both hands as all the best golfers do before lowering it to the ground and bowing forward to sink his tee. Suddenly he thought of the joke about the rich toff who stopped at the garage in his Rolls and started fidgeting with a tee while the dope of an attendant filled the tank. Maybe he should work that one into a show; it wasn't one you met all that often. How did it go now? Oh yes. 'What's that for?' says the attendant. 'What, that?' says the toff, 'Why, that's for resting your balls on when driving off.' 'Amazing,' says the attendant, spilling petrol on the floor. 'Rolls think of everything, don't they?'

Hogan chuckled as he spread his feet. Yes, that was suitably rustic. He could hear the squeals from the audience now, they always . . .

Hold on, hold on.

Something was going on inside his goddamned mouth.

It had started right on the very tip of his tongue, a sharp tingling sensation like a myriad of little hot needles, only now it had spread back along the *whole* of his tongue and it was moving into his cheeks and lips as well.

Hogan stood up straight and started working his mouth from side to side like a man who has just bitten into a lemon.

But it was getting steadily worse, if by worse you mean more

11

intense, because the whole of his mouth and throat was alive now and he was starting to salivate and slobber over his lips.

Shit, what *was* this?

Nelson Hogan dropped golf ball and clubs as the prickling in his face began to subside and was replaced by a numbness. It was like coming out of the dentist with your lips full of novocaine, only far worse than that, because the whole area around both jaws just felt dead, as if he could have bitten into his tongue, his lips, his inner cheeks, anything, and just not felt a thing. God, even his teeth couldn't feel each other. And the whole thing felt *huge*, immense, as if the lower half of his head was swollen out like a pear so he had this sudden crazy urge to look at himself in a mirror.

Then he tried to swallow.

He managed it once, but when he tried again it just didn't work because his throat was constricting. It seemed as if he was trying to swallow his own head; it was impossible. And then his throat would lurch open on its own so when his head tilted back he could feel oceans of saliva pouring down there in a continuous trickle.

Dear God help me, thought Nelson Hogan, but that was the last formulated thing that went through his mind because that was when his knees gave way and he started to vomit. On his knees, trying to crawl forward, he could feel the tingling building up again in his arms and legs, only this time it brought wild terror instead of curiosity, and a desperate urge to scream. But there was no scream, just an open gagging mouth and popping frightened eyes and a sudden rushing weakness that consumed his whole body all at once and sent him rolling over on his side, his mouth still yawning and his cheek resting on the short grass. He started twitching quietly.

There were pains in his extremities now, but he couldn't move, couldn't even turn his face around to look up. With a great effort he managed to rotate his eyes so that he could see above the trees, which brought one last horror because he was still completely lucid and would remain so until circulatory failure shortly killed his brain.

The sky was green. And so were the clouds. Everything was green.

He was still lucid when he heard the footfall by his ear and the rubber-gloved hand reached down to force open his mouth although by then he couldn't even move his eyes any more . . .

More or less at the same time that the celebrity was getting into his final spasm, you'd have found Superintendent Tickle reading the note. It irritated him slightly, you'd have noticed.

Detective Chief Superintendent Arthur J Tickle had not been in frolicsome mood even before he arrived at the Yard, what with his damned wife and her damned nagging about the damned holidays all over breakfast. He had come in early, partly to get out from under the verbal flak and partly to cut into the pile of work that had been sneaking up on him for a week now, so what he needed at the moment was to be left alone, right? He did not need lunch with the sodding commissioner, thank you very much, he did not need the giggling WPC behind the door that his desk constable was trying to chat up (Arthur J Tickle had never been a big giggler, surname notwithstanding) and he did not need *this* thing.

This thing being the note.

What was holding Superintendent Tickle's reptilian gaze was a piece of notepaper about six inches by five, containing three lines of type. Paperclipped to it were an envelope, similarly typed with the words 'Homicide. New Scotland Yard, Broadway, SW1' and a memo from somebody or other from downstairs giving a list of officers' names, one of which was Tickle's and a request for everybody on the list to make any comments they felt they could. The typing on the note said:

1 down
Porker not a definite article in this Indian dwelling
Reaper

Tickle perused the memo. Hrrrrrumm. Came in four days ago. Nobody knows what it is. Please comment. Well great.

The Chief Superintendent furled his simian brow and scraped his big meaty mitt across his chin as he shifted his sweating rump forward a fraction. The chair creaked under the strain as his bulk sagged backwards. Tickle slouched uncomfortably and glowered at the thing from a distance, to give his mind some elbow room.

Crossword puzzle almost, formatwise, but then it's been signed like a note. Reaper? Hrrrrrm. Name or title? What the hell is it? A hoax? A threat? A warning? Why 1 down? Does that mean

13

there's going to be a 2 down, or a 1 across? All of a sudden Tickle felt ridiculous, and then immediately angry at having his time wasted by this damn garbage when he was up to his neck in it as it was. Bloody stupid it was, they got scores of these sort of things every sodding week, so why pick on this one? Bloody stupid.

Tickle grabbed a pad and scribbled *Could be others. Else ignore* and then tore off the sheet, added it to the paperclipped note and memo and pushed the whole thing to the corner of his desk.

Tickle didn't feel any different then, of course, because there was nothing to feel different about.

Not so far.

TWO

Detective Sergeant Alison Prendergast stood on the edge of the blue mob of coppers with her thumbs in the pockets of her jacket and kept her eyes on the hazy figure in the distance.

She'd just got here, but according to the pathologist who was still busy doing something or other, Nelson Hogan had been dead between four and six hours. It seemed like a long time to lie on a golf course, undiscovered, but things like that happened; you had to live with it. Nobody was playing much today, that was all. But for the fact he was lying on a green for people to trip over, you could almost have put it down to poor visibility. A thin mist had come down since the early morning, or so one of the local bobbies told her; it had been clear around breakfast time but had gone murky since then.

The figure was moving across from left to right now, and Sergeant Prendergast smiled as it stumbled and staggered. It was true what they said about Lamarre, she thought, he *was* scruffy, you could see it from here, even in this fog. He was carrying the usual shabby blue raincoat folded and slung over his shoulder like a blanket, his hands were as usual in his trouser pockets, elbows sticking out sideways and his jacket trailing out behind him like a sail.

He was heading this way now, otherwise she'd have gone out there to join him in whatever he was looking for, which would have been a laugh for anybody who cared to take one because whenever Prendergast walked anywhere with Lamarre she always upstaged him on account of her longer legs. People had laughed to see them together, but discreetly.

Detective Sergeant Prendergast had shapely legs, too, when she wanted to display them, although today it was corduroys and boots. The rest of her wasn't bad either, a bit on the slim side maybe but then it was a matter of taste; she certainly didn't lack structure. Her hair was strawberry blonde and she kept it shoulder length when working but let it hang longer when off

15

duty. Lamarre could never fathom out how she did that, even though he saw a good deal of her off duty and had plans to see more. Underneath her fringe was an elfin face and a pair of teasing blue eyes and a nose that crinkled up and made you just *ache* whenever the mouth below it parted into a laugh.

She could have been a model, but she was a cop. A good one too, and a dedicated one although nobody could understand why because it didn't seem the kind of job she ought to have fallen into. Heeled-up family, father an estate agent, mother a JP, she had been to Roedean or somewhere similar and university to boot, all of which made people — especially other cops — wonder why she was what she was.

I like it, she would tell them, I like the job, honest. But they would usually just shake their heads and be polite.

Lamarre was trudging up to her now, his breath coming in evenly spaced long white puffs. Very even and very long, because Lamarre might have been on the short side for a copper, but he was fit as a butcher's dog and a walk around a fairway wasn't going to start him gasping like half the other dicks you could name on the Metropolitan force. Not a chance.

Sergeant Prendergast logged in the ensemble. Par for the man, she decided affectionately. The green tie, which in no way complemented his crumpled grey lounge suit, was loose and twisted, its tails hanging separately from the open neck of his shirt as if somebody had tried to wring his neck with it, and the shoes, originally brown brogues, had probably been used for playing football with the local kids on the street outside his flat in Wandsworth. She had dropped in on him and found him doing that once. It had been a sight for sore eyes.

'Now then, Al. Just arrived?' His eyes were of such dark brown that they were almost black. Could ten years in a hot climate do that Prendergast wondered.

'Just this minute. Getting the lie of the land, Jack?'

'Nah. Humped my arse around for sod all. It wants a damned good brushing with the thin blue line.' Jack Lamarre pointed in the direction from which he had come. 'His house is over there. He'd have been playing in this direction. I'll organise a sweep backwards when the body's gone. Had a look yet, by the way?'

'Yes,' Alison Prendergast said quietly. 'I saw it.'

'What do you make of it then, Al?'

'The picture?' Lamarre had always called her Al; she liked it.

'Could be a nutter.'

'Right,' Lamarre said and thought 'right.' He sank his neck deep into his shoulders and looked off into the mist, subconsciously cringing from what he only vaguely imagined could well be a bad scene. He looked like a vulture standing there. His dark eyes scowled out from under his dark eyebrows that sloped up and down across his face like the sign for a humpbacked bridge, separating the shock of tousled black hair on his head (hardly ever combed) from the perpetual shadow that covered his chin (frequently not shaved). Sometimes, when interrogating suspects or goading superiors, those eyebrows would rise up quizzically in the middle, emphasising their natural slant.

Lamarre had a reputation for goading superiors, along with his pithy approach in general, and secretly, Detective Sergeant Prendergast was quite keen on those eyebrows. She was admiring them now, actually. Secretly, though, secretly.

Detective Inspector Jack D Lamarre — some said J.D. but most said Jack, and a few said he should never have been let out of Hong Kong. Right now he felt strangely unsettled for at least two reasons that he knew of and maybe others besides. Two was enough anyway.

The obvious one was bloody Tickle sending him down here in the first place, right? It always happened if a big shot got killed in the sticks somewhere, they sent in a couple of Yard people because it looked better in the P.R. Let an old tramp get rubbed out in Richmond and that wouldn't need P.R. would it, so Jack and Al would still be in town and the tramp job would get done just as well by the local dicks of district X area Y whatever it was for frigging Richmond, Jack couldn't or wouldn't recall. God, but it riled, especially when you reckoned that they'd sent him and Al and not the mighty Fabian and his squad so they weren't all that keen on it, they being Tickle and whoever else was behind it. So far he'd got one local sergeant called Taylor who looked like bloody Heydrich and wasn't on the sodding scene right now, and a lot of dirty sneers from the others.

It made you . . .

'. . . ideas, Jack?'

Lamarre sniffed and blinked and arched up his eyebrows so you couldn't tell from the outside that he was sulking, though he did have that other beef on his mind and that was showing a little.

'Right,' he muttered again. He turned to face the fateful twelfth green with its squirming mass of constabulary and the shrouded shape on the ground.

Prendergast turned with him but looked back over her shoulder to the fairway.

'No ideas at all?' she repeated, because she knew he hadn't heard.

'No,' Lamarre was answering mechanically, and he kept looking at the covered body, his forehead lined and tight. 'Could have been anyway you want. Could have followed him from the house, could have been waiting here. Could even have been walking next to him for all I can tell at the moment.' Something was troubling him badly.

'What're we going to tell the press?' Prendergast asked, getting nervous. She didn't want to bug him because he looked kind of fierce at the moment.

He didn't answer for a minute so Sergeant Prendergast cast about for the species in question. Not here yet, but they would be, without being hailed. They could smell blood, those people.

Good thing on the whole, though, Prendergast reckoned, the press were OK. It was the others she couldn't take, the TV types. They got her down some.

'I'll give 'em something later when I've had a chance to think,' Lamarre told her finally. 'Anybody comes at you, tell 'em that.'

'Will do,' Al said, smiling, but there was that cloud again, all over his face.

Try it then.

'What's up, Jack?'

'Come again?'

'You look like something just bit you. What's up?'

Lamarre tried a grin, but it came out like toothache, and then he heaved a kind of sigh.

'It's a funny thing,' he said softly, 'but I never met a maniac in Hong Kong. Not once in ten years on the force there. We had contract killers, drug rings, pimps, you name it, we even had slave traders, but never a single maniac. It's just not a Chinese thing, Al. It never struck me till right now. Hell's bells.'

'What are you trying to say, Jack?'

He looked at her; she never called him by his rank, he wouldn't let her, except when brass was about. She didn't need to be told the answer, but she waited.

'I think this looks like a homicidal maniac,' he said quietly, 'and I'm not sure I know what to do. How the hell do you like that?'

She bent forward a fraction, cocked her head and said, 'Jack . . .' which was when Leech appeared and interrupted.

A spherical little man was Dr Leech, with an almost bald head. His head, in fact, was virtually as round as the rest of him, shiny and round, and crossed by a very small number of hairs, maybe seventeen in all, that travelled all the way over from east to west and appeared to be held down by varnish. His face was very rosy and jolly and covered by a lattice of tiny red veins, especially around his pug little nose.

Everybody knew Dr Leech. Dr Leech was a pathologist and coppers, who know more clearly than the rest of us what pathologists have to do, tend to remember them.

Leech was brandishing a plastic bag around in his hand. Inside it was a mixture of grass, soil and Nelson Hogan's vomit.

'Finished,' was all he said, which meant the police could go poking about the body, bagging up pocket contents and so on, before it was removed to the mortuary where it would meet him again.

Lamarre nodded and asked for a report as soon as poss.

Leech went away humming something classical, a fragment of *Carmen* actually, although only Al Prendergast could have named it. Leech was always humming bits of some music or other. Whether poking his fingers into an axe wound or peering up a rape victim, he was never stuck for a tune.

Sergeant Prendergast gave Inspector Lamarre a watery smile as if to say 'go on, Jack, go on from where you were', but he just squeezed her arm.

'Want another look?' he said.

'No.'

Jack Lamarre walked over to the corpse on the ground and squatted beside it. The sheet was off it now and back in the squad car whence it came. He looked at the bulging eyes still staring sideways along the ground, and the open mouth, and the golf ball rammed down inside, just visible.

Madman's work? Not necessarily, until you looked at the picture and then you got the feeling and you became convinced. It was still there, pinned on his chest because Leech wanted it left there for now. Something about the paper, he had said, shiny sort. Might have something human on it; a flake of skin maybe.

19

Anyway, he wanted it untouched until he'd looked. Then it was due in forensic.

They would identify the picture soon enough. It had been quite badly crumpled and creased at some point in time and then subsequently smoothed out. And judging from the ragged edge it had been torn out of something, a book of prints possibly, or a colour supplement perhaps. It showed a mounted human skeleton on a devilish horse, wielding a scythe and surrounded by others. The ghoulish classic image of death claiming final dominion over all. The profane Reaper.

THREE

'It just seems incredible,' the man called Sherman said, putting on a moderately good display of grief and shock, complete with shaking of head and biting of lip, except that incredible wasn't the right word if you were full of shock and grief. You generally stayed on a more elemental level, wordwise. Incredible was a word that went with amazement, not grief and shock.

Piss artist, this one, was what Lamarre decided.

Sherman was a theatrical agent, the late Nelson Hogan's agent in fact, and Lamarre had just informed him that his client was no more. Ordinarily, Jack wouldn't have come to this man first off, but Hogan didn't have any family that he could talk to and uniformed men were crawling all over Richmond, so . . .

Anyway, the man at London Weekend who Jack had informed was not now about to have his long overdue meeting with Hogan — ever — had mentioned that the late great was pretty tight with his agent and that the said Mr Sherman was the person to talk to about Hogan the man as he really was. So to speak.

Check that.

'You knew him very well, I gather?'

Sherman increased the stoop of his shoulders by means of an increased wringing of the hands. It really was good.

'To tell you the truth, Inspector . . .?'

'Lamarre.'

'. . . Lamarre. To tell you the truth we were damned close. God, I just can't believe it.'

Sherman surrendered himself to a gasp and a shudder and a screwing up of the eyes. Lamarre tried to keep his face straight.

No, not callousness. It was just too much to be true.

'Listen,' Lamarre said, leaning forward earnestly in his easy chair so he was reduced to literally peeping over the rim of Sherman's acreage of desk. 'Listen, I must ask these questions. You seem to be the only person who can give us some answers quickly.'

'Yes, yes of course, Inspector,' Sherman said bravely, breathing deeply as an aid to composure. 'You must ask whatever questions you think fit.'

What the hell does he think I'm going to ask, Lamarre suddenly thought. I mean, he's coming on like he was married to the clown or something.

'Clearly, we'd like to know if he had any enemies that you know about,' he ventured gently.

Sherman pondered that.

'None,' he said after a minute, 'None at all.'

'None?' Jack said incredulously. 'Surely, everybody's got a . . .' What the fuck was the word. Bête-noire? Alter ego? What the hell do you call it? 'I mean, didn't he ever argue with anybody? Did he never annoy anybody? Get up anybody's nose?'

Sherman looked at Lamarre for a few moments and then picked up his horn-rimmed glasses from his blotter and put them on his face. Clearly this was a prelude to something so Lamarre sat upright again and waited for it.

'Inspector,' Sherman started, 'it was not in Nelson Hogan's interests to get up people's noses, as you put it. Surely you know what he did on television? You must realise that charm and affability were the tools of his trade.'

'Charm?' Jack said 'Affability?'

'His whole image was carefully presented to make people relax in his presence.'

'Image?' Jack said. The detective's temper was rising very, very slowly. First an act, now this crap.

Sherman glared at him now.

'Are you trying to be abrasive, Inspector?'

'Abrasive?' Jack said.

'Dammit man . . .'

'I'm trying to find out who could have killed the bloke,' Lamarre snapped. 'And you're just giving me a stream of horseshit. Did he have any possibly mortal enemies that you are aware of or didn't he?'

'No, he did not!'

Sherman jumped to his feet and went stiffly over to what turned out to be a drinks' cupboard. All the way over, he didn't look at Lamarre once, not once.

'Would you like a drink,' he said, still not looking, 'or shouldn't I ask, since I presume you're on duty?'

'I'm on duty. I'll have a whisky.'

Sherman swung round and grinned.

'With water,' Jack added.

That kind of broke some ice, somewhere. The agent came over to the other easy chair, handing Jack his whisky and then sat down opposite him. He crossed his knees and let his body slide sideways. Suddenly he looked completely cured of his grief and shock.

Lamarre waited, patiently now. All he wanted were some simple answers.

'What did he do with his money?'

Sherman cocked his head. 'Lived well. Had a lot of luxuries. He was fond of his comfort.' The man's face went dead again, as if he had just then remembered the reason why he shouldn't be smiling.

'Investments?' Lamarre asked.

'Oh yes. Plenty of investments. Property mostly, I think. I can give you the name of his stockbroker. He made far too much money to spend, of course, Mercedes and mansion notwithstanding.'

'Had a lot, did he?'

'A millionaire,' Sherman said, apparently surprised that the policeman didn't know that. 'At least.'

Jack just rolled his tumbler between the palms of his hands. He made a point of studying the agent's face for a few seconds and then went down to the whisky and beyond it to his outstretched legs and his battered shoes. They needed cleaning, he decided. Or renewing.

'Was Mr Hogan into anything criminal?' he said amiably, at length.

'Pardon?'

'Anything criminal? Involving criminals. Perhaps somebody may have wanted to harm him for some reason?' Sherman stared at him, seemingly aghast. 'If you know of anything like that, I do advise you to tell me,' Jack added very quietly. 'And I do mean now.'

Sherman kept gaping a little longer and then seemed to break out of it. His face collapsed back into its former mask of ribald reverie and he started snickering nervously.

'Oh no, no, not at all,' he said. 'Oh no, I'm sure of it, Inspector. There was nothing like that. Oh no.'

23

No, Jack thought, there wasn't. I can see that. All right, all right.

What else?

Lamarre took a drink. 'I believe Mr Hogan was a keen golfer,' he said. He took another swallow, right on top.

'He was a damn fine golfer,' Sherman said, as if in defence of the dead, deprived of their dues.

'Just so. What I was wondering is, er, did he have a regular partner?'

'He had several. I happen to have been one of them.'

'Do you know the others.'

'I suppose so. I can give you a list if you want. Why are you interested in that, may I ask?'

Lamarre thought he might as well tell him. Had to be part of what the papers got anyway. You can't have a hundred coppers combing a golf course line abreast without the whole neighbourhood knowing.

'He was killed on a golf course. The one near his house.'

'Dear God,' Sherman said, as if the fact was peculiarly horrifying. 'I was assuming it happened at home or something.'

'No,' Lamarre said, standing up, 'On the golf course.' He put his empty glass on the desk in front of him and picked up the notepad that lay to one side. There was a pen on top of it.

'Was Nelson Hogan interested in Art?' He asked, as he shoved the writing equipment under the agent's nose.

'Art?'

'Painting. Pictures, I mean. Old pictures. Classical or whatever you call it.'

Sherman shook his head. 'No, I don't think he had any interest in that kind of thing at all. No, I'd have known. Why?'

Oh no, not that. That wasn't for public consumption. Not yet anyway.

'Never mind,' Jack said. 'You were going to give me his stockbroker as well.'

While the other man scribbled, Lamarre went over to the window and stared out with his hands in his pockets. It was a thing he often did when thinking; he never watched what was going on outside. You could have gone up to the glass on the other side and looked into his face and if he was thinking he would have seen straight through you.

This was shaping up for a psycho, all right. They had all

24

begun to fear it as soon as they saw that Godforsaken picture. Al had said it, as soon as she saw it. He himself had said it, but you could bet that, deep inside, both of them had hoped otherwise, whatever they had said. Well, he damned well had, anyway.

But it was shaping up.

They could check, they *would* check, but odds on there was going to be no reason why anybody should have wanted to kill Nelson Hogan. There would be no rational cause, no excuse, no purpose in it. Lamarre was starting to bet on that now. There was only a motivation, and whatever it was it lay deep in some lunatic mind, where it made perfect sense and was perfectly justified, and where the picture of death was its perfect expression.

Or was it just a signature? Yours truly, the grim reaper.

Till next time, Lamarre thought. I know, I know.

Sherman stood up, but it was the sound of the sheet being torn off the pad that shook Jack Lamarre out of his blossoming nightmare.

'Where is he now?' the man inquired, after a pause and a cautious little cough.

Jack dexterously took the piece of paper from the agent's hand, folded it with two fingers and his thumb and popped it into his shirt pocket, all in a single fluid movement.

'Autopsy,' he said cheerily, and headed for the door. 'I may want to speak to you again, all right?'

Sherman wished he hadn't asked.

So did Tickle, truth to tell, because he'd much sooner have worked it out for himself and grabbed the credit, but the damage was done now. He had asked. He *had* waved the mystery clue under the nose of the constable behind the desk outside, just to give the whelp a feel for the sort of mind-bending thing real detectives have to cope with, and the Hogan thing *had* got round by then, and this particular lad *had* turned out to be full of the kind of unrelated fragments of gen that crossword buffs are full of so the little worm *had* got it straight off, hadn't he?

'Porker is a pig, see, and that's a hog,' the kid had told him, 'For "not a definite article" read an indefinite article, which is the "an" bit. Get it, sir? Hog-an, see?'

'What about the Indian dwelling then?' Tickle had challenged beerily. 'Where's India come into this?'

The constable had smirked then, actually bloody well smirked, as if to say 'you ignorant old toad' and then he had pulled out his great big thick dictionary.

Which Tickle now perused again, with eyes as black as night.

Hogan, it informed him coolly, *American Indian dome-shaped house of mud and logs (Navajo tribe).*

'Fuck,' Superintendent Tickle said softly, and then, apart from deciding to have Lamarre tracked down pronto, his mind kind of keeled over and collapsed.

FOUR

The man in the lab was starting to wonder.

Fiddle diddle dee, Leech mused, it's something cute. He was running out of starters, because it wasn't cyanide, it wasn't arsenic, it wasn't strychnine and it wasn't any of the barbiturates. Nor was it any of the other favourites that you tested for as a matter of course, so *what was it*?

Leech hummed a bit of Sousa while he had another think.

He wasn't beaten yet.

Not by a long chalk.

Bobum, bobom, tara-rara . . .

It had been Strauss for the autopsy proper. A selection from Johann the younger for the fluids and externals (samples of skin, blood, saliva, urine, cerebral fluid, teeth scrapings, nail clippings and pubic hair) merging into Johann the elder for the actual cutting (removal individually of heart, lungs, larynx, spleen, liver, kidneys, intestines, stomach, skull-top and brain). There was nothing particular to note, such comments as he had to make having gone, along with fragments of *Die Fledermaus* and the *Radetsky March*, into the tape recorder that was fed by the mike hanging over the dissecting table. The cause of death, the brain told him, was cerebral anoxia, and the cause of the cerebral anoxia, the blood sample told him, was circulatory failure. All crushingly routine, boys, he had informed his unseen listeners, no sweat.

The cause of the circulatory failure was a poison. Had to be, Leech was in no doubt whatever of it. There was no violence done to the man and the golf ball in the throat certainly hadn't killed him, however ugly it looked. On the other hand there were signs of paralysis: there was the vomiting and now there was that faint brown stain inside the stomach wall. It was winking at him now, from its stainless steel dish on the bench.

Leech studied the organ in question for a few seconds and then flashed a sly look at the beakers.

Diddley-dee, tralalala . . .

It was something very fast, and very strong.

Probably on the golf ball. There was definitely *something* on the wretched thing because when he dropped it into its beaker he had seen something come spraying off it. A white powder at a guess. Could have been anything; a bit of the ball, a bit of chalk from a tee-marker, anything.

However . . .

He had a whole row of beakers, each containing a mixture of very dilute acids, similar though less complex in make-up to those found in a human gut. In one he had washed the golf ball, in another he had dropped the vomit, in a third the stomach contents. If the stuff was still around then one of these beakers contained it, maybe all of them did.

But it wasn't . . . coming . . . out.

Leech quadrilled over to his chromatograph, stooped in front of it with his hands on his knees and squinted inside. Not a lot going on in there, was there? A few traces, all normal. Hmmmm.

Rotten technique anyway. Waste of time.

What on *earth* was this stuff?

Leech turned back to his beakers. There was five hundred mil of fluid in each, so whatever he'd picked up had to be dilute.

Fol-di-rol-dol-. . .

He let his finger hang over the beaker that the golfball had been washed in. It was labelled 'ball'. Odds on, the strongest sample was in there assuming it *was* on the ball as he surmised. His finger moved down the line to 'vom' and then to 'gut'.

Dum-di-dum-da, dum-di-dum, too-ra-lai-aaaay.

Best to get on. Some toxins went off with time.

In for a penny . . .

Leech dipped the tip of his finger in 'gut' and placed it in his mouth. He kept it in for a moment or two while he pushed it over the tip and sides of his tongue and down on to the back surface, seeking out the gustatory cells.

Watch out now.

Leech stood there with his forefinger up in front of his lips like a kid caught in the act of something, and waited. The acid he picked up right away, a sour taste down at the back. That was nothing. He was looking for something else. Something sweet perhaps, or something bitter.

Many poisons had enormously strong tastes that could be

picked up even when the toxin was not enough to harm you. And the tastes could be very characteristic, real clinchers in fact. Why, Leech had cut many a corner in this way, and saved a lot of time and . . .

Leech went diving for the sink.

This wasn't a taste, he told himself as he sluiced his mouth out under the jet, this was some kind of attack.

He kept on rinsing and spitting, sloshing the water round his tongue and teeth and gums, forcing himself not to swallow, until the tingling started to subside. Then he turned around with his hands up by his sides, resting on the sink drainer, like a bum at a bar. He stared about him a trifle madly.

God almighty, but he was going to do that once too often.

What in the name of heaven could do that?

Hang about.

Leech broke into the *Campdown Races* as he skidded out of the path lab and along the corridor to his office. A swift flash through one of his tomes (*Ass. Anal. Chem.* 8th Ed.1955. Ch.5. P.543) gave the confirmation he sought, and with it the right tests. The paper chromatograph should have worked but blow that, there were two others. One live animal and one chemical. Right. First off, wire up a rat.

Leech darted back to the lab and wired up a rat.

A delicate procedure, not accounting for the rat's disinclination to participate. It consisted of inserting small wires into the animal's cardiovascular system in just the right places to monitor not just its heart, but the different parts of its heart. Not easy, but Leech was equal to that, no problem.

He gave it a five mil shot of 'ball' and then watched the scope. Doo-dah, doo-dah . . .

Nothing for ten seconds, and then everything. Leech watched with more fascination than he had known in years.

It started with the pulse rate, slowing down to begin with and then accelerating. Then the extra ventricular systoles, then the ventricles started to beat faster than the auricles until peristalsis set in. That lasted twenty seconds or so and then it passed off and the whole muscle started to slow down, slower and slower, until it just stopped, ventricles first, then the auricles.

Just like the book said. Marvellous.

Leech blinked in awe, shook his head and gently touched the dead little creature's smooth white fur. Its eyes were shut tight from the convulsions, and its tiny paws drawn up to its belly as if in prayer.

All right, so far so good.

Now for test Number Two.

The pathologist syringed some more of the stuff into a test tube and then went over to his shelves. Kay-em-en-oh-four, he mumbled softly, scanning the rows of bottles before him. He didn't want to hum anything just at the moment.

When he found the permanganate he took a single drop on a glass rod and let it fall into the tube. Shaking it, he took another rod and extracted a single drop of the mixture. This he smeared on a glass slide, and the slide he inserted into a microscope, set to five hundred times mag. Then he looked.

Yes, they were there already. Very tiny crystals, even at this kind of blow-up, but crystals all the same, flat and red and square-edged, and more appearing all the time.

Just like the book said again. Sssplennnnndid!

Leech repeated it in his mind, verbatim almost, because he had a great memory.

Aconitine. An organic alkaloid. One of the deadliest of all poisons. Kills by depression of cardiac trigger impulses, leading to ventricular fibrillation and circulatory collapse. No known antidote. Lethal dose not more than two milligrams, but death known to have occurred from one milligram.

One milligram? Leech muttered. One little thousandth of one little gram? God, you couldn't even *see* a milligram, hardly. Regular little cocktail, wasn't it, *this* stuff?

The mind stays clear, it had said, perfectly clear. Only you start to see things go green. Something repulsive in that, something horrendous.

He looked at the jar marked 'ball' and then he looked at his forefinger, although he was trying not to think about it any more . . .

FIVE

Al Prendergast leaned against the wall for a while, then she took a stroll around the room, prodding bits of equipment here and there, and then she went back to the wall. The two young boffins kept slipping in sly glances at her while they worked.

But of course she knew that.

'Are you really a copper?' the one with the acne said.

'Yes. Of course I am.'

'Straight up?' Stupidly persisted the other, for the sake of joining in.

'Want to see my card.' She took out her warrant card. 'See. That's me, there.'

'Huh? Oh, listen, we didn't think you weren't really. It's just, well, we don't get many lady coppers, do we, Brian?'

'No,' Brian agreed. 'Not in here Ron.'

'Is this going to take long?' Al said.

The two scientists or technicians, or whatever they were just looked at each other.

'Nar,' Ron said. 'It's all set up.'

Detective Sergeant Prendergast nodded and bestowed them another smile. They both grinned like a couple of retrievers.

The flashlight went on and off with a snap, leaving her with a fading blue after-image of the bench top with the white sheet of paper on it and the Reaper picture in the middle of that.

'I'll just get this developed for you,' Ron told her as he unscrewed the camera from its stand. 'Won't be long.'

'Right,' Al said.

'It'll be nice and clear. Guarantee it.'

'Lovely,' Al said.

While his colleague with the pimples was in the dark room, Brian started messing about with other things. He seemed to be collecting things together; mysterious looking things with wires coming out of them. Boxes with warning labels and holes in the front and cables on the back. For all she could tell he was

31

roughing up some kind of secret bomb.

Al went over to the picture. They wouldn't let her take it away of course, being a possible exhibit A, so she had to have a photo of it. That was fair enough, but another look at the original wouldn't hurt. She switched the lamp on, flooding it with light.

'Creepy, innit?' Brian said.

Al agreed it was creepy.

'What is it anyway? I mean, where's it come from?'

Prendergast glanced at him. He had stopped bustling about; he was just staring at her, waiting for a reply. She didn't want to reply to that one.

'Have you asked anybody else what it is?'

'Yeh,' Brian said. 'I asked the boss, but he wouldn't let on.'

Al wondered who the boss was.

'Well then,' she just said.

Brian humped his shoulders, see-if-I-care-style, and went back to his preparations. Sergeant Prendergast went back to the picture but her thoughts stayed vaguely on him. He was a graduate, certainly. They both were, but God, what a couple of louts. It wasn't that she was a snob, not really, not truly, and it wasn't that she couldn't see a certain beauty in technology or whatever the in-attitude was, it was just — well — these two seemed completely elemental.

Or something.

What the hell *were* all the creases, anyway?

Al bent closer, leaned sideways to bring up the angle of the light. Yes, there were quite a few creases. The Reaper even had a little one across his scythe.

Leaning back on the wall again, Al ruminated on the creases. It could be significant, couldn't it? It *was* real, because nobody from Hogan onwards was responsible for those creases, they were too careful for that. But what was in creases? You could go crease mad.

'You going to dust this for prints?' she asked Brian.

'What? The skeleton?'

'Yes, the skeleton.'

The other technician came back in then, holding the still-wet copies of the photo by the corners, (one for her, one for Jack). He was better looking than Brian, Al thought; pity about the spots.

'You were quick.'

'Lightning, that's me,' Ron said.

'Officer wants to know if we're going to dust that picture,' Brian said. He was grinning away, as if dusting for prints was a subject with potential for unlimited mirth.

'Nar,' Ron said, leaving his mouth open for a moment. 'Nar. You can't dust prints off paper. Paper doesn't hold a print that well. Not unless it's really glossy stuff. That's not glossy, it's just a bit shiny. You couldn't dust a print off that.'

'Get 'em with a laser,' Brian said, patting one of the boxes with a warning label on it, obviously a laser. 'If there's a print on there, we'll pick it up with laser light.' Brian grinned again. 'New technique,' he added with a hint of pride, no doubt pleased to be on the frontiers of science, 'Dead modern!'

'How long's that going to take?' Al wanted to know.

'Not long,' Ron said merrily. 'Probably have had done it by now if you hadn't wanted your photograph. We'll use the same rig, only we'll scan it over an arc using that laser he's leaning on. If there *are* prints on it they'll show up. The laser beam is very intense light, see. It energises all the tiny bits of muck that fingers leave on things and that makes 'em fluoresce.'

'Amazing,' Sergeant Prendergast told him wondering what it meant, and now, typically for her, she warmed to him and his friend because when you thought about it they were a couple of very intelligent and very nice young men who would probably do anything for you, absolutely anything, and they probably helped old ladies over the road and it was probably she who was turning into something unpleasant if the truth were told, only maybe it was happening without her knowing about it. Maybe she should ask Lamarre.

Jack, am I turning into a rotten minded cynical copper? Like you are, and the Deputy Assistant Commissioners and Commanders, and all the others? Tell me it's not true, Jack.

'Nearly dry,' Ron said, offering her the photos, 'It's actual size, like you said.'

Al Prendergast stayed on the wall for a minute, because in her mind she had an image. It was an image of a person, not a man for sure but probably, and this person was creeping furtively around a public library, or perhaps it was a bookshop. The figure had found a book and had turned to a certain page and was about to tear it out. Looking around to be sure nobody was watching, it did so, and then it quickly stuffed the torn-out page into its pocket before anybody saw what it had done. And the page got

33

crumpled in the process.

Crumpled and creased.

Find the book. Then find the bookshop, or the library, or whatever.

'Thanks,' Al said.

They were helpful in Trafalgar Square. A bit stuffy, but helpful.

'Couldn't say for sure,' the first authority informed her. 'At a wild guess I'd say Bruegel, possibly Bosch. One of those Flemish masters at any rate. Anyway, it's old.' He turned the photograph over as if he expected her to have slyly written the name on the back, as a kind of initiative test. 'The person you want is Mr Windropp. He's our resident Flemish expert. Would you like to follow me?'

Love to, Al thought.

He kept hold of it as they went up the stairs.

Al Prendergast had a feeling they'd know. She was no art expert herself but the painting, whatever it was, had a quality about it that you could sense, which meant it was something famous probably, so they'd be bound to suss it. She started wondering if the original could be right here in the National Gallery. Not out of the question was it?

Windropp turned out to be a tallish ponce with a cravat. He reminded Sergeant Prendergast of somebody she used to know in her schooldays, one of *those* boys.

'Well of course it's Bruegel, darling,' he announced, 'Who else could it possibly be?'

'Bosch?' Al said, because that was what the other one said, and this poof could do with an answer or two.

'Pish, dear,' Windropp said, huffily. 'Whoever told you that? This piece owes nothing to Bosch. Whoever says so is a fool.' He held the photo up and brandished it like a tambourine. 'This is a detail from *The Triumph of Death* by Bruegel the elder, painted in 1562, seven years before his death. All right?' He said the last two words as if he were addressing a child.

Al squirmed, either at the picture, or him, or both. She had this urge to take him on. 'How old was he then?' she said, trying to stop herself because God knows it hardly mattered.

'No idea, darling. Nobody seems to know when he was born, do they? Has Mr Bruegel committed some felony then, ha ha?'

'It's just something we need to know about,' Al said.

'Urgently.'

'Ah yes, need to know. Well then, now you do know.'

Sergeant Prendergast tucked a strand of yellow hair behind her ear. She *could* try and be nice, but this one looked as if he wasn't capable of a response. Ugh!

'What I was really wondering,' she began again, 'was whether or not you could suggest the book that this print might have come from.' She put a good deal of beseeching into it, so he'd think he was keeping her alive. 'The photograph is the same size as the print, if that helps.'

Windropp still had it at arm's length. He kept it there while he gazed at it again.

'Well, let's see. It's about quarto size, isn't it? Right.' He jumped up and went out, Al trailing, and across the corridor into another room which was mostly bookshelves. There was just one table and one chair, both bare. 'I used to keep all my books in the office, but one just gets swamped.' He was looking up at a shelf about level with the top of his skinny head, running his slender paws across one book after another. 'Bruegel, Bruegel, Bruegel, here we are.'

He found it on the fourth try.

'Here you are, Sergeant. *Bruegel the Elder — Later Works* published by Macfarlane. There are a variety of authors contributing to the text. Quite a good book actually, and the reproductions are excellent.' He laid it open on the desk at the right page. 'Rather better than yours, wouldn't you say?'

Al said it was, although she could only see that the colours were slightly different in the photo than in the book, but it was the same thing, definitely.

This was the book. This was it. Keep breathing in.

Windropp flicked back a couple of pages to where there was a whole double page spread showing the picture in its entirety. He pointed to an area below and right of centre.

'That's the detail you've got,' he told her. 'The grim Reaper. As you can see, the whole thing is much larger.'

Prendergast stared at it. It was infernal. A landscape of terror and chaos, an army of skeletons crushing the defeated remnants of mankind, slaughtering and destroying in a hellish vision of the final end of everything. The Reaper was in a pack near the centre that seemed to be pressing home some kind of assault on some kind of bastion. They were winning.

'God,' breathed Al gently.

'Powerful, isn't it?' Windropp said. 'As I say, it has nothing of the fragmented allegory of Bosch. This is a single, unified image of the end of man.' He seemed really narked by that Bosch thing, the crumb. 'The original is in Madrid, at the Prado. Don't you think it's wonderful?'

'I prefer the Impressionists,' Al told him quickly, which was half true, because she could prefer just about anything to this thing.

Windropp took it as a barb. '*Chacun à son gout*, darling,' he pouted. 'Was there anything else?'

'The book,' Al said. 'Is it a common text? I mean, are there lots of copies about?' Say no, she thought madly, say it's rare or something, please.

'Oh, I should think so,' the ponce said. 'It's almost a standard work, given its price. Yes.' He seemed to be wondering if there had been any point in that question, and if so, what point?

Rats, Al said to herself, rats and more rats. There was no quick way in to it, then. She was going to need manpower, find the shops and libraries power, phone 'em all up power: Lamarre-type power.

Rats.

SIX

Brian shaved off early by his usual standard, because he wasn't prone to duck out much, even though it was easy. The Metropolitan Police lab is a big place so you could be anywhere for an hour; developing stuff, checking in new gear, whatever. Just because you weren't at a bench didn't mean you weren't here. All Brian needed was a nod from Ron and out through the loading bay, no problem.

The tubes were filling up though, even now.

Brian kept thinking about the picture and smirking to himself as he sat there swaying in the seat with his knees apart and his hands in his black leather jacket, so people opposite him kept glancing up and away all the time, even though Brian never noticed. His mind stayed on it all the way up the Exhibition Road as he minced along with his head down against a faint but sharp wind blowing down from the park. By the time he reached the place he was going to he was cold but he didn't know it.

Brian trudged up a short flight of steps into a main entrance by which the sign said *Department of Botany, Imperial College,* and then straight through an entrance hall and up the marble stairs opposite for two floors. Then right at the landing to a pair of large swing doors (elegantly finished in oak, no expense spared at I.C.) which bore the funky title *Plant Chemistry.*

Daph was sitting on a black bench with her elbow on a faucet, chattering like hell to another bird that Brian knew to be her flatmate. Brian sort of rippled.

'You're early,' Daphne chirped. She had one of those soft Scottish accents that sound like they have to be rehearsed for years. 'Airly,' she said, 'Yoor airly.'

'Got fed up,' Brian threw out. 'Hello Elaine.'

'Brian,' Elaine went demure on a single word, and Brian's inner skin shifted again. Just recently he'd been fancying Daph's flatmate a bit, though he could handle that all right, because Daph was a goer. 'Boring, is it?' Elaine added. 'Told you work'd be boring.'

Now there was history in that one, because like the two girls Brian was an I.C. graduate himself, though his bag was Physics whereas with Daphne it was Botany and with Elaine it was Maths ('sums' she'd say). They had been in the same set together before recently graduating, but whereas Daph and Elaine had gone onto postgrad, Brian had gone forth into the world, to earn money and enjoy town he'd claimed, though they'd all laughed and told him he was wasting his education, especially on the cops.

And, of course, Elaine had said it would be boring.

'Oh it's not boring,' Brian said quietly, after a coy pause. 'I just got fed up, that's all,' and then because they obviously didn't find his coy pause quite coy enough, he went back on it and said again. 'No, it's not boring. Not today especially.'

They were both listening then.

This is boring, Taylor thought, and he leaned against a pillar box and lit a cigarette.

Detective Sergeant Taylor of the Richmond Police couldn't decide if he was lucky or unlucky, so he took time out on the street corner to take stock. While he did so he unhooked his rimless spectacles from below his ears and started to rub the lenses with his handkerchief using his forefinger and thumb, round and round, giving them far more polishing than they needed because what he was thinking took more than the polishing time to think it. All the while he was squinting through the cigarette smoke because with both hands busy the tube stayed in his mouth.

Lucky if you look at it from career, right? That Beau Brummel of an inspector came down from the Yard and he had one sergeant in tow already and he had wanted but one other working in close. Taylor was the one who had gone to the golf course when the body was found, so Taylor was the one he asked for and got. No illusions there, mind, one's charisma didn't glow even unto Broadway yet, it was just luck, but if this thing turned out to be big (*if*? Taylor *knew* it was big, he just *knew*) then, like we say, careerwise it couldn't be bad news.

On the other hand, the job the fucker had given him was definitely bad news. Find out all Hogan's local haunts, was the line, that's like pubs and clubs and charitable soirées and frigging amateur operatics and whatever else, plus the ones nobody else

38

was supposed to know like your friendly gal next door or next street and like that, and *study* the *people*. Hard it was, Taylor ruefully had to concede, because you had to think of the questions yourself, not like door to door where you always asked the same ones anyway.

Still, Taylor circled back again, it could have been door to door. It could even have been a hands and knees job across three holes of the damn golf course, so maybe it's another plus after all.

Sergeant Taylor refitted his nazi officer-type giglamps and ran his hand over his short Aryan white hair. What with his polo neck sweater he only needed a blue jacket and a cheek scar to pass off as the commander of the U47. Taylor reckoned he needed a drink. Sweet Pea couldn't be far.

The Sweet Pea was a small pub, deservedly ill frequented and dingy by Richmond measure, so Taylor reckoned he was OK for an on-duty belt, not that he actually had delirium tremens over the prospect of not being OK, though the little man by the bar gave him a slight turn.

'Higginbotham,' he said suddenly, extending a paw from the end of a tweed sleeve, and displaying a fabulous array of caps. '*Hounslow and Richmond Gazette.*'

'Get away,' Taylor said, noting that this runt was a white as well, only he wore it curly, like a rotten doll.

'You're a police officer, aren't you?' Higginbotham said, stating it rather than asking it. 'Working on the Hogan case I believe.'

'Am I?' Taylor said, sideways, having his turn. 'What case is that, then?'

The newspaper man smiled indulgently while he quaffed a little more of his pint.

'I was passing,' he said.

'Passing?' Taylor came in. 'Nobody's ever passing.'

'Oh but I was. And I heard sirens. And I saw a squad car, and I saw you. I'd say you're a Sergeant at a guess.'

'Been following me, have you?' Taylor grizzled.

'It's all over town by now, you know.' Higginbotham said. 'I didn't join the unwashed throng on the green, didn't need to. My office told me who the victim was on the phone. I mean there had to be a victim, didn't there, the speed that yardman got down here.'

'What yardman?'

Higginbotham sighed.

'Well, I *say* yardman. What I mean is the senior one with the tan that I've never laid eyes on in Richmond before in twenty unbroken years of crime reporting. And his glamorous assistant. Well, I'd have remembered her.'

'You know me, then?'

'Seen you about,' Higginbotham gave it a second and then added, 'how would you like to exchange views.'

'How would you like to answer my question.'

Another second.

'Yes. I have been following you.'

'That's naughty. That's what gets a bruised knee.'

'You should have sussed me out.'

Taylor had a swallow then. True enough. Should have.

'What views?'

Higginbotham grinned with a big hint of relief in his face. This was going to be smooth, provided the bleeder didn't go over budget.

'Let me top you up first . . . er . . . Sergeant?'

'Yeh, Sergeant,' Taylor said.

SEVEN

Back inside his office in the very famous Yard, Lamarre rubbed his eyes and tried focusing on his watch and thought, it can't be . . . Already? He swore a mighty oath in his mind. They'd be gnawing at the door soon, screaming about their morning editions.

Lamarre looked at the capsule. It was in two halves, and they were lying side by side on the flap of the envelope where the young constable had shaken them out for him to see. What looked like a white powder was visible on the inside, even from here. In fact, it could even be yellowish white, like it said on the report.

Lamarre's eyes flicked over to the path report on his desk.

'Bit of luck, finding that, eh, lad?' he said to the constable as he picked up the report. The boy was still there by the wall, because Lamarre had told him to wait.

'Must be going dark on the golf course by now.'

'Yes, sir.'

'I hope nobody's touched that white stuff in there.'

'No, sir.'

'If I told you to get that over to forensic, would you know where to go?'

'Yes, sir.'

Lamarre grinned. 'Off you go then. Be careful with it.'

The lad was off like a whippet, dead keen. Jack Lamarre nodded to himself as he opened the report. He wanted to be sure he had it straight in his mind.

Aconitine. Jack toyed with the pronunciation of the word, which reminded him of nicotine. An alkaloid poison obtained from the Aconitum plant, which is a genus of the family Ranunc . . . Ran . . . hellfire, of the genus Ranunculaceae, better known as Monkshood or Friarscap or Wolfbane. Well, well.

Lamarre skipped through the chemistry . . . very pure, so not home-made . . . amorphous . . . yellowish white powder . . .

41

violently poisonous . . . OK, OK. Probably on the golf ball, so inadvertantly self-administered via touch. Hum, very nasty, very slick.

How did the killer know he wouldn't have gloves on? He needed that to be true, didn't he? And golfers often wore gloves didn't they? Lamarre jotted the questions down in the margin by the word 'touch'.

. . . Not much call for the stuff these days. Formerly used for reducing fevers but not so much now. Main use in veterinary applications. Nobody makes it commercially except on a small scale . . .

Lamarre wrote 'check that anyway' in the margin.

. . . Places to look, veterinary colleges, hospitals, and Zoology-stroke-Botany departments of academic institutions. The last of the three was underlined by the pathologist, and then there followed a paragraph of explanation, indicating Leech's strongly-held view that poison security had suffered in such places in the interest of academic freedom. He seemed to have a hardish opinion on the matter. He should know, though, right?

Lamarre put a ring around the paragraph and commented 'try there first then'.

He leaned back in his rotating chair and crossed his knees and started revolving from side to side using his ankles. As he did this he flicked through the rest of the report, which was concerned mostly with cause of death, and let his mind mull over the capsule.

Could well be a break, could well be.

Lamarre knew a great deal about drugs and suchlike from his time in Hong Kong, a hell of a lot in fact, more than most of the cops in London and more, possibly, than whoever was stalking about out there calling himself the Reaper. They tended to degrade slowly with time, lose their strength, or at least that was what he remembered, and the great thing about that was that it helped you tell one sample from another. And if *this* stuff did that, and the muck in the capsule was the poison used, then they could have just a chance of getting to a particular bottle on a particular shelf in a particular place. But if it was just any old capsule . . .

Don't bank on it, Lamarre counselled himself, just hope.

He looked around his office, trying to keep his mind off his aching back, wishing he could get in a pool and swim for a while, trying to imagine cold water over every square inch of his body.

Not for a while, maybe. But then, why the hell not?

Promising himself a swim or a run or a blowout, of some kind, Reaper or no Reaper, Lamarre let his face turn to the glass partition that separated his office from what he hadn't quite decided yet could be an incident room. There were any number of rooms in the Scotland Yard building that you could turn into an incident room. Large rooms, full of telephone points, which was all that was basically required. The rest of it — desks, tables, filing cabinets, blackboards, typewriters, typists, telephonists etc, etc, etc — you could draft in easy just by moving things and people around, no wiring actually needed.

Normally you'd run a murder hunt from the district involved, even if you weren't local yourself. That was just the usual procedure because your usual murder was a homespun affair. The reason for Lamarre thinking that maybe this wasn't the thing to do here came partly out of the poison report he'd just read — which didn't point anywhere near Richmond, and what with the late departed being without family or foe, it could just be nothing to do with the locality at all — and partly out of the brickbat that Tickle had dropped on him about an hour ago.

The notification, that was, the serving of notice. It pointed all ways, that did. It pointed to a maniac, it pointed to a devious bleeder, and it pointed to another killing.

Or two, or . . .

Couldn't blame Tickle though, to be fair. Nobody could have homed in on that, let alone a man like Tickle. I mean, a record he might have, true, long as your leg, more scores under his belt than Nancy Drew, but Einstein he wasn't . . .

'Ready Jack. Can't hold 'em any longer.' Tickle was hanging from the doorjambs like a drunk at a bus stop. His breath rolled across the three feet between them in noxious waves and his chin wobbled at an angle as he spoke, on account of the tilt of his body.

Jack stifled a groan.

Just now the incident room possibly was full of press hounds, milling about like bees at a dance, waiting for him and Arthur J to pop out and getting more rabid by the minute. They'd be breaking in soon. Morning editions. One or two of them were showing their teeth at the partition, and some of the cops out there looked worried.

Lamarre decided.

Yes, that was going to be an incident room, and as for *them*, they could have murder and they could have poison and they could have lines of inquiry well in hand. But they couldn't have the Reaper, they couldn't have maniacs, and they couldn't have another killing on the cards.

Not till it happened, anyway.

Lamarre forced himself towards the door.

Reaper floated along Kensington Gore on the south side, hands in black coat pockets, going nowhere in particular, just breathing in and out and thinking.

It had rained briefly, but that had stopped now and the air was fresh-cleaned, with the pavements drying out in patches and over the road in the park, the trees were glistening and dripping as the light faded. Reaper could smell the park and could see the strollers in twos and threes. Not many people walked alone these days, though Reaper often walked alone.

Reaper did it all the time, though nobody knew.

'I could kill any of you,' Reaper told the strollers silently. 'Any of you. At will.' And then the idea hung unfinished for a moment before the words 'like a plague' drifted into mind all by themselves, and Reaper smiled a small, private, short-lived, mischievous little maniac of a smile.

Because the strollers were safe of course, it was only a loose thought, drifting unattached. Victims had to be chosen carefully, Reaper had known that already.

Still watching all round, Reaper began to reflect on methods. There would be no *modus operandi* for them to latch on to, that was another thing that was fixed. In fact, given the multitude of ways you could kill, given the legion of interrupts you could put into a human organism's complex vortex of interdependent vital functions, Reaper found it almost a puzzle that anyone should have a *modus operandi* for such a thing. It spoke of ignorance, did it not? And lack of imagination? Another little smile there. Reaper had stolen two capsules full of Aconitine (little plastic capsules in two sliding halves that you get the hundreds of coloured balls in for instant relief from cold symptoms, right? Well Reaper just emptied the coloured balls out, see) and with one capsule used on the golf course that left one for later.

Not yet though, Reaper thought, that would smack of an M.O. Something else first.

Big smile then. Absolutely Huuuge.

44

EIGHT

Pissing down again, Monk thought, watching it driving down at an angle outside the window, another shitty morning. Monk had a fragrant way with words when he was talking to himself, though now his mind was mostly on the girl.

Monk knew she was going to jump him before it happened. He just sensed it, long before she looked across and noticed him squatting there all by himself, watching her like a toad eyeing a gnat. He knew she was going to have a go at him well before she knew herself.

Heading this way now.

Monk didn't look up until she was right by his shoulder.

'Hello. I'm from the Sceptics Society.'

'Good for you.' Nice tits, Monk thought. No bra.

'Would you like to join?'

'Would I like to join what?' Don't grin. Yet.

'The Sceptics Society.'

'No.'

She hesitated, but confidentially. She had a set piece for refusals.

'Why not?'

'Why should I?'

'Well you surely don't agree with *everything,* do you?'

'Hmmm . . . nnno.' Slick, Monk thought, but not enough.

'Then you must be sceptical about something.'

'I'm sceptical about the Sceptics Society.' Mate in one. She laughed, so Monk laughed as well although he was going to have to join the rotten thing now, of course. Still, there could be worse ways of rubbing against the buxom Elaine Sweet, for that was who she was as every postgrad in Maths knew by this time. Monk had had her pointed out to him several times already. Short red hair, slate grey eyes, full lips, curving in and curving out nicely front and back, very maxmin and saddlepoint like geometry on legs, you just couldn't go wrong with little Miss Sweet. The very stuff of fantasies was Elaine. What the hell was

45

this sceptics thing anyway?

'We're against the practice of being gullible,' she explained succinctly, handing him his receipt cum membership form and receiving his quid and a half. 'Practically everybody is passively gullible. People like politicians take advantage of it. People should learn to be sceptical. I'm the treasurer by the way; Elaine Sweet.'

'Sounds a riot,' muttered Monk, who had been persuaded to join the Society not so much by the originality of its concept as by the nipples of its treasurer. He dipped his snout in his coffee. 'I know who you are.'

'Do you? Why's that? I don't know you.'

Monk was suddenly bewitched by the way she had cocked her head to one side, like a little dog suddenly intrigued by a television screen. Oh yes.

'You're one of the new postgrads in Maths,' he announced.

'Saw your picture in the Prof's office. My name's Norman Monk. I'm one of the old postgrads. Everybody calls me Norm.' Seemed like a good enough time to try pawing her a bit so he held out his hand. 'Pleased to meet you.' And what a smile! Aaaaargh. Monk had never seen teeth so white before, or so even. Go on, go oooooon! Get in there, dammit.

'Listen, why don't you have a coffee. I mean . . .'

'OK. I'll get it. Hold these.' And she was off to the refectory counter, leaving her papers in front of him. Monk watched her from his table, unconsciously kneading invisible mammaries with his fingers.

Let me buy you one, was what he had been about to say, but she hadn't let him get it out and now he felt like a prick. This one didn't look like one of your libbers that always bought their own coffee and paid their end at the flicks and stood their rounds in the pub along with the lads. This was the sort you opened doors for and gave up your seat for and things like that. The sort you bullied in bed and . . .

'I got you one too, OK?'

'Uh. Oh right, thanks. Look, let me pay for these. I . . .'

She flapped a hand in his face as she sat down and took a sip. 'Mmmm . . No. You buy them next time,' she said, and Monk thought, 'Fucking hell, next time? Who fancies whom?'

She was sitting opposite him, elbows on the tabletop, with the cup dangling between the forefingers and thumbs of both hands, peeping at him from over the rim.

46

'By "old",' she suddenly asked, 'I suppose you mean you're in the final year? You did say Maths didn't you?'

'Yes and yes,' Monk told her. 'I'm trying to start a thesis but . . . um, well . . .'

She flashed those fangs again. 'Bit of a grind?'

'Yeh, right,' Norman Monk nodded ruefully. So far he had written the title page and nothing else, which wasn't exactly an orchestral event considering all title pages were the same, apart from the title, viz *A thesis submitted in candidature for the degree of Doctor of Philosophy in the University of London* etc, plus sundry additional dross.

'I'm dreading it already,' she said, and this time he got a sexy little shudder to keep him interested.

Something oozed across his mind then.

Was he being toyed with? There was something about her, just something. She was about one millimetre on the flighty side, as if she had . . . had what? Experience?

Don't let the conversation flag, Norm, old boy.

'Met your supervisor yet?' he enquired lamely, loathing himself already for keeping up the shoptalk. Hellfire, they'd be on to number theory next or complex analysis maybe, or something really risqué like Lagrangian dynamics.

'Only briefly,' she said, tossing out, 'I saw him last Thursday but all he did was to give me a couple of books and about *that* many papers to read.' Miss Sweet showed him a gap of about three inches between her thumb and forefinger. 'I haven't read any of them,' she added mischievously.

Monk bestowed his most condecending chortle as if to say 'we were all the same at your age. Dead keen.'

'Got mixed up with freshers instead, eh,' was what he actually dribbled out with.

'What?' Elaine Sweet was puzzled for a minute 'Oh, you mean the Sceptics Soc! No, I got dragged into that by my flatmate. She's a new postgrad as well so we were wandering about together.' She stopped.

'Er . . . what's she in?' Monk said, too quickly.

'Botany,' she said, and she rolled her eyes upwards as if the subject was synonymous with dung.

'Yeh? Far out,' Monk assured her. 'Got a few mates in botany.' He was trying to be really laid back, right, because he was *definitely* interested, and so far he hadn't gotten any of the usual stupid flaming maths-type cracks about the way he liked people to

47

say his name, like with Euclidean norms and normal vectors and orthonormal projections and all that cock, so he added, 'Er . . . listen, er, who is your supervisor?'

Oh *shit*, you're rushing this, he thought. There you go into the job again. God, you'd talk shop *on* the bloody job. Slow *dowwwn*, Norm. Show her how *cooool* you are.

'Kane,' she said. 'Doctor Kane.' And then she slapped her hand to her mouth. 'Oh hell, I'm supposed to go to a seminar this morning. He's giving this seminar about . . .'

'I know,' Monk put in. 'I'm going too. No hurry. We've got another few minutes yet.' Bloody thing was too early anyway, at sodding nine o'clock. Norm wasn't really a morning person. She'd just said something like 'Oh' when he'd said he was going her way, and that made Monk feel funny somehow so he decided to shut his mouth for a while and regain his super cool. So he looked into his coffee cup and tilted it a little to make the remaining drops in the bottom run around the base. He could feel her watching him.

Elaine Sweet kept on sipping, stealing glances.

Not exactly Robert Redford was he, but there was scope. His longish straw hair might be nice if he washed it more often, and it was wonderful how eyebrows that met in the middle were improved by a little plucking. Blackheads needn't be a problem either given the correct soap and thorough rinsing, and those finger nails probably came from messing about with some old banger of a car. She knew lots of boys who messed around with cars. And long noses were distinctive.

Norman Monk hoisted his long nose up at an angle and blinked his pale blue eyes.

'You'll like Steve Kane,' he said casually. 'He's not bad. Absolutely bloody brilliant in his area. I guess you're in quantum theory if you're with Steve.'

She dipped her head vigorously. 'Is that your subject?'

'Right,' Monk told her. 'Steve Kane is my supervisor too.'

'Really!' she exclaimed, and there it was again, that same feeling as before. This time it was the way she said 'really' as if it was too interested and kind of forced or something. Norman Monk squirmed inside. She knew he was keen already, or did she? Of course she did, and she was coming on, pretending to suck up. Getting ready to make a fool out of him.

Or was she?

It wouldn't be a good idea on her part if she was.

NINE

Jack Lamarre thudded along Lavender Hill, heading east, with a pain under the right side of his ribs and a searing rawness in his gullet. He had begun to ignore the stitch in his side but that burning annoyed the hell out of him. It seemed unfair, because he'd set out already wary of burning his throat but despite a lot of breathing through the nose and repeated lubrication by swallowing it had happened anyway.

Still, don't bitch. You wanted a blow-out, and running six miles into work is a blow-out. One foot in front of the other, that's all it takes; just keep thinking of the good it's doing you, rah, rah, rah . . .

Jack steamed on until Wandsworth Road began to swing up into South Lambeth and then he stopped. Not for a rest, for a paper. He always used the same shop, whether in car or track suit and he had for months, which was a quirk of history in a way because there were other newsagents much nearer his flat. It had happened because this particular man opened earlier than any of the others on the way in and Jack often came in early, so this was the one it had become.

Lamarre usually took the *Sun* and the *Telegraph*, a fact which many bodies of the Yard had simply learned to accept, but which a few of them, like Al Prendergast for example, knew him well enough to understand. Some people are either/or in their habits, but Lamarre wasn't.

The newsagent peered through his bifocals and took Jack in from feet up to head and then down again. Striped trainers (lightweight), baggy green tracksuit trousers tucked into white socks, tracksuit top patched dark with sweat (yellow sweatshirt peeping out from collar), glistening neck, dripping face (with gasping mouth), glazed eyes focused afar off, and hair tangled beyond the norm through bobbing up and down one hundred and fifty times a minute.

'Running in, Inspector?' he said, on the ball as ever.

'Aye,' wheezed Lamarre, incapable of more, and fell upon the counter. He thought fleetingly about throwing up.

'Bad business that,' the newsagent said, tapping the pile of papers under Jack's sweltering brow. 'You in on that, are yer?'

Jack dragged the top copy across in front of his face.

HOGAN SLAIN the *Sun* was yelling, two inches high, above a photo of the late departed star, and below which was the line: *talkshow host found on golfcourse.*

Below that, in decreasingly bold print, came the text, which took up the one tenth that was left of the front page and a column and a half of page two.

Chatshow King Nelson Hogan was found dead yesterday morning on the golfcourse outside his home. A police spokesman stated that he was poisoned and that the case was definitely one of murder. Scotland Yard have been involved. The news has stunned the entertainment world and . . .

Most kind, Lamarre conceded, straight into the background stuff. They hadn't even had a go at him for all that polite piss he'd thrown out about not prejudicing lines of inquiry when he didn't want to answer their questions. Well, *they* hadn't anyway; what about the others?

The *Telegraph* managed to share out its front page between this and a few world events. Hogan had to slum it with a civil war in Africa and the biggest fire in living history in Oregon, and all three of them ran second headlinewise to Mrs Thatcher's latest barb vis-à-vis Cabinet wets who risked emasculation by revolting over a mini-budget. The actual prattle itself was much akin to the *Sun's*, basically restrained and quickly into the padding.

It was the same with the others, as far as Lamarre could make out from what he saw. Which was a relief, at least.

Jack breathed out and went back to page three of the *Sun*. Hot shit, he thought, straining, she's built. He had the impression he'd seen her before, *Men Only* possibly, January seventy-nine probably, volume six, number three at a guess, not that it mattered.

The newsagent's question was obviously not meant to be answered, which was why Jack hadn't bothered to think of anything to say. Now a queer little silence reigned, with the detective propped on the counter leaning on his forearms and the newsagent squatting on his stool, one looking at the other, both blinking slowly and periodically like a pair of reptiles in a tank.

'Want yer bloody 'ead seeing to,' the newsagent opined.

'Doesn't do a blind bit of good, yer know. Kill yerself, you will.'

'Got any throat pastilles?' Jack said.

'Any what?'

'Throat pastilles. Cough drops.'

'Should 'ave,' said the newsagent, rising regally and looking in the general area of the fags. 'What for?'

Lamarre grunted. What for? What for?

'For my frigging throat, of course.'

'No, I mean is it the throat or the chest.' He did an upward motion from around his chest area with both hands clenched like a conductor requesting a crescendo. 'Are you bringing stuff up? Phlegm, like?'

'Listen,' Lamarre told him, 'I'm getting a sore throat. You got some Fisherman's Friends there, so gimme some of them.'

The newsagent tossed a packet over the counter, which Lamarre opened and popped a couple in his mouth.

'Want one?' He pushed the packet over.

'Not bloody likely. Kill you, those things.'

Give me strength, Lamarre thought to himself, guys like this are what makes the world what it is. How's that again?

He waved his two papers, now rolled together, in front of the shopkeeper's nose and turned to the door. 'See you later,' he said as he went out, though later could be just about any time. He paid his bill by the week anyway.

Jack ground himself into the three miles that lay between where he was and his office in the New Scotland Yard building in Broadway. A mile and a half to Vauxhall Cross, another half along the embankment and then a mile or so over the Lambeth Bridge and wending through Westminster via Horseferry Road and he was there.

About an hour, actual running time, he computed as he trudged up the stairs. Not Herb Elliot standard, no, but then Herb Elliot didn't have to do his rotten job either. Ten minutes to freshen up and retrieve his clothes from his office and he was at his desk just shy of nine.

And feeling OK, astonishingly.

Breakfast later, he decided, he'd wolf too much if he went down now. See what's moving first, but a coffee wouldn't kill, quite.

The incident room was crackling quietly, with about six people on line at that moment, detective constables mostly with a couple of sergeants, one of whom was not Prendergast, all poring over sheets of paper and managing to look on the verge of something or whatever although it only happened yesterday and it was only nine a.m. now for God's sake so Lamarre wasn't handing out any smartie points just yet.

A teletype was chattering softly and rhythmically, its head jabbing up and down without printing anything, its carriage stationary. Beside it a VDU, which also ran live into the big computer downstairs, displayed nothing but a single square green cursor spot in the top left hand corner of its screen.

The telephones and typewriters were silent, the white boards on the walls were blank, all save one which bore a diagram which Lamarre could not comprehend but which he surmised was obscene.

Hurr, he thought as he shoved his money into the Sankey and punched up a plastic cup full of venomous coffee, so where's who and what's what?

Jack went round a booted and few chairs, fortunately for whose occupants, certain things were in hand. They all got spoken to by their first names though; they always did on a face to face basis with Lamarre. And they all knew better than to take advantage.

A few of Hogan's golf partners had been asked to be ready to come in for a chat. That would be later on, assuming nothing came up to give him an excuse for skipping it, because he didn't see anything coming out of that, frankly. Still.

Here was something. One of the D.C.'s had bothered to chance a question on the phone to one of them about the gloves thing and it turned out Hogan mentioned he was a barehander on TV. All right, so that's how the sod knew, no mileage there.

Stockbroker? Bank manager? All contacted, but were any of them worth the time? Probably not, but he was going to have that Sergeant from Richmond up from today so he could handle some of it. Most of it. He noted again that Hogan had no surviving family — Hum.

The way Lamarre saw it at the moment, there were two possible sources of leads and one big question.

The leads, or the chances of leads, lay firstly in the capsule they'd found, which a phone call to Leech confirmed did indeed contain Aconitine and which therefore held out a hope of finding the source, and secondly in Al Prendergast's efforts with the picture. She could be left with that for the time being, he knew

52

that because he'd worked with Prendergast for some time. That would be ongoing, sure enough.

Lamarre kicked the nearest desk. Chasing poison sources are we? he demanded, starting with what? With the academic places, was the reply, like you said guv'ner. Good, Jack said.

Which left a question.

Why? Or rather; if he's a nutter, what kind of nutter? What's bugging him, pushing him, obsessing him?

Not a question that was going to be answered on Hogan's side of it, that wasn't. Not a question for agents or stockbrokers or golf mates.

Question for a shrink, that was.

TEN

Elaine and Norm came out of the coffee pit together, walked over to the Huxley (Maths plus Computing and Control) building together, waited for, entered, and rode the lift to the fifth floor together. Still together, they walked around the central well of the building and into the little lecture room where a number of others, young and old, had gathered already. Norm felt like an asshole because he'd managed about forty-four words on the way over, roughly eleven of which had not been about maths. He was boring her, he just knew it. He felt creepy.

But when they sat down, Monk deliberately left a three chair gap and a good ten feet of black bench top between himself and the girl. This could have been due to the average person's natural inclination to claim some space, or it could have been an announcement on Monk's part that he came here not to grope but to listen. It could also have been because it's easier to stare at someone from a short distance away than when you're breathing in their ear, and Norm wasn't quite through staring at this person for the time being. In any case, Monk went for this little void for reasons best known to himself and then lolled back in his chair whilst Miss Sweet rummaged about in her kitbag for an adequate supply of paper and pens. He didn't say anything, he just sprawled there with his hands clasped behind his head and watched her sideways with his eyebrows raised, blinking slowly like somebody listening to a boring speech. She would learn, of course, and quickly. These internal seminars happened on a weekly basis, attendance being largely a matter of courtesy, and if you took notes you never ever read them again. Ergo, most people didn't take notes, they merely listened and so kept open their ports into the latest ideas of whoever it was that was speaking. But she would learn.

And the speaker was here now, with his back to the lot of them, idly cleaning the board as if they were not there and he had all the time in the world. Nobody seemed to be taking any notice of him at all.

The room started to quieten down.

Steven Kane turned to face his audience for a second and then waited by the door, eyeing it for stragglers, and he began flicking a piece of chalk with the tip of his thumb.

Elaine started drinking him in. Mmmm . . .

Elaine couldn't have put words to it, any more than anybody else could have, but there was something kind of *extra* about Doctor Kane. And it was something definitely unacademic. With any of the other staff you could peel away the planet's Number One expert on cyclotomic Galois extensions or whatever and what you'd have left would be a husk. But with Steven Kane there'd be something else. Elaine had no idea what it was, but she knew it was there and she thought, guiltily and secretly, that she could maybe fancy a slice of whatever it was, because it looked good and it dressed flashy and . . .

The door closed with a bang.

'All aboard that's coming aboard?' Kane said.

He took one step away from the wall and half-sat on the corner of Elaine's bench, one foot in space, the other on the floor. Miss Sweet let her eyes wander up the charcoal clad thigh and on to the bare forearm until it met the turned up cuff of the shirt, folded back fashionably just below the elbow. His jacket, black and sporty, was on the desk up front, removed prior to erasing of board to avoid chalk staining thereof. There was a cufflink in the shirt cuff, stainless steel with a small piece of dark wood in it, very modern. He smelt of musk. Brrrr . . .

'Einstein once said that God doesn't play dice,' Kane told them, taking the whole of them in as he said it.

Norman Monk's mouth broke into a grin.

'He was talking about the statistical basis of physics,' Kane went on. 'Apparently he took a dim view of statistics — randomless, if you like — as a fundamental building block of the real world. For my money he came up with a great phrase irrespective of whether he was right or wrong. Personally I think quantum statistics is fun.'

Oh, yes, Elaine Sweet murmured, inside her head, Oh yes, I like you, I think.

Kane reached two fingers into his shirt pocket and extracted a small packet of five miniature cigars, which he manipulated one-handed as he continued. Right now he was looking at nobody in particular.

'Of course, modern thinking doesn't go along with Einstein. Statistics — various sorts for the use of — enjoys a strong position in theoretical physics doesn't it? Most of you will know as well as I do that current ideas demand that the fundamental particles of matter should obey very rigidly-defined systems of statistical axioms, one of which for reasons I find *totally* mysterious is named in honour of Einstein.' He smiled and looked straight into Elaine's face, catching her gaping. 'Needless to say, our new postgrads, hot from finals, could tell us all about it.'

Bose-Einstein stats, Elaine thought quickly, the other one is Fermi-Dirac and, God, he's not going to ask bloody questions is he? They don't do that in seminars, do they? Not with staff present?

No, of course they don't.

Kane was on his way to the board, still talking, and that was when Elaine remembered the title of the seminar, right then; 'Intermediate Quantum Statistics is Fun.'

Elaine wrote it down.

And then the shit smote the fan.

Kane threw it at them in spadefuls. First, by the way of an appetiser, he gave them a lightning review of the recent efforts of Vasimovich towards an elucidation of the field, using projective geometrical analogies. Crap, he told them succinctly, his cat could have done better, not that he kept one. No, the approach to this kind of thing was via generating functions — pause for effect — that was the only way to put a hole into intermediate quantum stats, that and no other. Surely they'd heard of generating functions?

Elaine thought she loved generating functions. No really . . .

Kane gave them half a dozen boards full of generating functions, pausing here and there to clarify a point or dismiss a comment. Occasionally, Norm knifed in with a remark that sounded damned impressive although Elaine wondered a couple of times if he was doing it just for that reason.

He was, although Kane didn't mind.

It was over in half an hour.

Elaine Sweet flicked through the little pile of notes she had made. Patchy and scratchy, with errors and omissions where she'd gotten confused or misheard or just not kept up, they looked depressing already. She just *knew* she'd be unable to read them in a year or so. Or maybe in a day or so. Everybody was trooping out.

She and Monk started to leave but Kane held up his hand. He didn't look at them, he just held up his hand at them and went on talking to Professor Koenig, who had sat stone still at the back of the room for the whole of the talk but had now decided to let go on his way out. Koenig was waving his arms about like a gibbon, pointing at the board and pulling his chin down like a prizefighter. Kane just grinned right into his face as if humouring an idiot.

'What's he want?' Miss Sweet said.

Monk shrugged. On him it looked like a nervous tic writ large. His battered combat jacket jumped up and down like the top of a tent.

Kane finally got rid of the professor.

'Er, was that OK?' he asked as he walked over. His hand was up and his thumb was pointing back over his shoulder to the board.

'Well . . .' Elaine Sweet blushed a bit, but not much. 'I got a bit muddled actually. Towards the end.'

'Muddled? By what?'

The eyes drilled into her face for a few seconds, inquisitive brown pools, searching her mouth, her forehead, her cheeks. Then he swung around and the light brown hair bounced as his head turned. It was fine hair, shining; clearly groomed fastidiously, and it hung just on the collar.

'Something in that bit?' he said softly, because what was on the board was obviously the last bit, the bit towards the end. Elaine knew she should have come clean. He looked at her again.

'Well quite a lot of it actually,' she said, trying to gush somewhat. God, she hated saying 'actually' all the time. She'd tried so hard to break the habit, actually.

'Never mind,' Kane murmured, and this time the eyes mocked her, quite distinctly, before they rolled away to Monk who was leering like an ape at a window. Steven Kane went over to the desk, wiping the chalk from his fingertips with his handkerchief before picking up his coat. He had twisted the single page of notes he had brought into a tight little pole and now he was flattening it and bending it over from one end into a hard knob of paper.

'I wondered if you'd like to drop in to my abode for a drink,' he said airily as he came back towards her. 'It's a good way to get on a first name basis, don't you think?'

'Love to,' said Elaine, wiggling inside.

'Fine. What about tonight then? Bit short notice, I know, but I'm having a crowd of other people along too. Don't hesitate to bring a few guests of your own.'

'Yes, fine.'

'OK.' He glanced at Monk. 'You'll come as well Norm? You can bring Elaine along with you.'

'Yeah, right.'

'Norm's got this amazing car,' Kane told her as his arm came slowly up and started coiling back for the throw. 'Bentley is it, Norm?'

'Wolseley.'

'Anyway. There's so many holes in the floor he wears those long underpants to keep his lower half warm when he's driving the damn thing.'

The arm snapped forward and the chunk of paper clanged against the side of the waste bin in the corner.

'Rubbish,' Monk said.

'Have you got some long woolly undies,' Kane asked her, brown eyes glinting madly.

Elaine blushed. Again. These two were definitely tight.

Somewhere way down deep at the bottom of her mind a distant little voice peeped a note of warning and wondered mutely about what she might be getting into, but she wasn't listening really. Not really.

After they had all gone, Steven Kane remained leaning against a bench in the lecture room, just thinking, for what you would have called a long time. Then he walked slowly out and over to the computer room, which was just a terminal room really, two floors below, containing a couple of VDUs and a printer, enough to work with without having to go all the way down to the machine itself.

All things considered, Kane preferred to avoid using computers, but it was in the nature of his field that a certain amount of contact with them was unavoidable. Most of his students ended up on the machines at some time or another, though it remained his candid view that those who went in for quantum stats *only* via programming themselves round the

58

difficult problems (and a few departments had gone that road) were barking up the wrong tree, frankly dearie.

Still, it was a useful skill, because most of those kids weren't going to get a job in *this* game, and some of them were wizards at cybernetics, if nothing else.

Must look that word up soon, Kane thought.

Both of the programs he had run overnight had finished normally, as they nearly always did when he used them, but they were excrutiatingly slow. On his way up the stairs he wondered vaguely if he should put some effort into assembler-coding the most time-consuming segments, bearing in mind that the computer time saved as a result of doing it had to be balanced against the cost in his time of getting it done. Maybe he should hang that on a student. Elaine Sweet perhaps, and that was his final thought on the subject before filing it at the back of his head and turning to algebra, because another bloody week had gone by, hadn't it? God, what a *bore*.

The scripts were waiting for him.

Each week, the first year undergraduates in the Honours Maths course at Imperial received three lectures on Algebra plus lectures on various other branches such as analysis, mechanics, statistics etc. In addition, they were required to attend one tutorial per week in each subject and for this purpose were divided into tutorial groups of about six individuals apiece. Each group had a tutor in a specific subject. The member of staff giving lectures would set problems to the students each week on his or her course, and the solutions had to be handed in by a certain day to the relevant tutor who, after solving them himself, would mark their efforts and pass the corrected scripts back to their owners at the next tutorial.

Much of this tutoring was done by postgraduates eager for beer money, but some of it was also done by staff. Kane was staff, although as Research Fellow he had no lecturing load, and he didn't need pin money, but he had agreed to take on a group to help out. Which was a move he now regretted every week, when the scripts appeared on his desk.

The tutorial was at three, so the festering things had to be marked by then, and as usual he hadn't even looked at the problems himself yet. Sometimes he would just go around to Douglas Budd, whose course it was and whose bent mind had dreamed the problems up, and just demand the solutions, but

Douglas would always give him a tut-tut or this-won't-do which invariably made Kane want to spit in his face and walk out.

Anyway, today he felt good. Imaginative almost.

Taking the problem sheet out of his desk he sat down and read it through. It was linear algebra at the moment, abstract, but nothing too woolly. From the questions it would seem that Douglas had reached dual spaces although hell's bells, five questions on that was nothing short of hammering it to death. The first one he recognised as a textbook result which they'd all get right because with six kids searching through all the worked examples in print at least one of them was bound to find it, and then he'd tell the others. The next two were obvious anyway, which left just four and five possibly needing a modicum of thought.

Doctor Kane took up pen and paper and applied himself to the last two problems, keeping the ideas simple on account of the limited armoury available to the tutees, within bounds of which Douglas would have made them soluble. Or so you'd think, but then Douglas could be such a prick.

Half an hour later, seething slightly, he got them out. Then he picked up the first of the six wads of answers and started to plaster it with red. Being a perfect little shit, this crud got nothing right apart from his name, so he didn't take long at all. Kane merrily moved onto the others.

Ignorant scum, all of them.

In his frequent evil moments, Kane often toyed with the notion of taking some of the important theorems and constructing 'alternative' proofs which were 'shorter and neater' than the standard proofs and which were therefore 'useful in exams'. He would then seed these proofs with subtle fallacies, visible only to curious examiners, and wouldn't that screw the little vermin up? Oh my, yes.

But of course, he couldn't swing that one without serious repercussions to himself so it remained nothing more than an amusing fancy to bring on a smile when irritation and boredom soared to critical levels. Kane had lots of amusing fancies like that.

Elaine Sweet was almost one of them, of late.

Attractive enough for a table-ender, as a pal at Unilever used to say, but never worthy of his full attention, no more than any other female on the planet. He could stomach a helping of her

60

heaving flesh though, given an opening. Might well do in fact, though not to tread on toes; that was to be avoided. And Norm looked fairly keen just now.

Steven Kane was very hand in glove with Norman Monk in more ways than one. They drank together, sported together; their work in q-stats was inextricably bound up together. They were friends, or at least friends in so far as either of them needed or valued or even understood the concept, anyway. And whatever else you could say, their relationship certainly wasn't overly affected by the differences between them, which consisted of nothing more than a five-year age gap and a Ph.D. and Monk was closing in on the latter one right now.

No, Kane decided, he would leave Elaine for Norm as things stood. Later maybe, if Norm got bored and she was still warm. A taste of her creamy thighs before she split for good in three years' time? Oh yes, very likely.

In the meantime, Kane had a regular bolthole in Soho, which was all he'd ever needed anyway, ever since he felt the urge at all.

That might not be a bad idea soon.

ELEVEN

Prendergast outlined the tactical problem. You had to give her credit for guessing there'd be one.

'My assumption is, Jack,' she said, 'that you don't want this Reaper thing spread about. I mean the picture. The way I see it, we may have to let out a lot more in the way of detail before this is finished, but the actual picture, i.e. the book and the page and that note thing. All that stays under wraps. Am I correct?'

'Correct,' Lamarre confirmed. He felt weird after clubbing the DC's. If he didn't fancy her, and she wasn't so good, he'd be thinking she was too familiar. Or would he?

'Because otherwise we get nuts sending us copies by the ton,' Prendergast spelled it out.

'We get nuts anyway, as soon as any hint of grim Reapers gets out at all,' Lamarre emphasised, 'but yes, we don't want those details released.'

'Because if we do get flagged again, we want to be sure it's the killer,' Prendergast studiously reiterated.

'I think we've both got the point,' Lamarre said, inserting a Fisherman's Friend into his mouth and tossing the packet on the desk in front of Al Prendergast. A couple of the little brown lozenges spilled out onto the blotter. Prendergast eyed them suspiciously. 'The problem being?' prompted Lamarre.

'The problem being, (a) finding out where all the copies of the book are, and (b) finding out which of them has that particular page missing *without* letting somebody know *exactly* what we found stuck to that body.'

'Libraries should be easy,' Lamarre challenged. 'You can nail the library copies down no sweat.'

Judging this to be the moment, Al produced the list of all libraries in the Metropolitan area holding copies of *Bruegel the Elder — Later Works* and laid it out before Lamarre's lop-sided glare.

'They have computers too,' she said, 'and what's there is part

62

of their database.' Good word that, she thought. She'd looked it up, and eventually fathomed out what it meant. 'They gave me that list over the blower.'

He didn't ask who 'they' were. City Hall, maybe, or whoever it was that ran the damn libraries. Jack wasn't an expert on the subject, not being a big reader himself, like.

Lamarre chewed his Friend. His throat was clearing up.

'That's just the start of the job, though,' he pointed out. 'How you going to check them?'

'That's what I want your say-so on, Jack,' she told him. 'Either we visit each one and look for ourselves, and there's a lot of them — ' she waved an elegant, braceleted forearm over the list, which Lamarre had already estimated contained the locations of maybe fifty libraries, branch and main, sprayed over an area twenty-seven miles across and damned near twenty miles deep, ' — or we ring them up and ask the librarians to check for us. And that's a lot of librarians who know what we don't want known.'

'Noting any that're out on loan,' Lamarre commented irrelevantly, definitely not rising to the challenge.

'Would be a lot quicker,' Al said.

'Bloody right,' Jack agreed. He gave it some impromptu consideration. No way round it, short of dragging in a lot of effort, buzzing beat cops and sending them into libraries, boots first, that kind of thing. Nah.

'Ring 'em up,' he decided. 'But try and impress it on 'em we want it kept hush. Think of a threat or something. Treason, official secrets, any sodding thing.'

Prendergast nodded, very sexy for the time of day, but made no move to leave the office. One of them was going to have to say it, might as well be her.

'Didn't have to use a library?' she said. 'Could have bought a copy from a bookshop?'

Lamarre smirked mirthlessly, like a condemned man contemplating the swordsman's blade, a gesture forced out of desperation.

'Didn't even have to do that?' he replied, 'Could have just walked into a bookshop and torn out the page. Why buy one? Why leave a face with somebody?'

'I could start with the publishers? To get a list of shops.'

'Could have been a secondhand shop,' Jack said quickly, slotting it in like a dart. 'Big secondhand turnover in art books, I believe.'

Long silence, exchanging of wry smiles for the use of.

'Do you know how many bookshops there are in London?' she started to say.

'Great job, this,' Jack beamed.

'It's the most bookish city on earth.'

'Go to it, Al,' Jack said.

Prendergast reeled out, mentally beating her splendid breast.

Jack Lamarre watched her go, feeling just as sorry for himself as he did for her. She had other hands to help of course, but he knew the form because he had worked with killers who left little in the way of traces before, albeit never a psycho like this one seemed to be. You generally had something to move on but, as in this case, it often looked so fruitless and grinding, even before you started, that you went at it half-cocked. You just went through motions, hoping for something to come up and get you off the ground, and sometimes it never came. And in the meantime you had to find motions for people to do that didn't send them into a torpor or a fit because coppers were human; they didn't enjoy phoning libraries and bookshops any more than the yahoos at Dagenham enjoyed spraying car bodies. A job was a job, but sometimes it broke your arse.

'Ahem,' somebody said.

Jack Lamarre looked round and thought, 'Oh, piss, shit and fuck.'

Taylor was crouching outside the door as if fearful of entering lest, doing so, his presumption should result in an embarrassing and unseemly ejection. All of a rush, Jack recalled his earlier conversations in Richmond with this man, who, according to his local Chief, was up and coming. Jack remembered he was slightly insolent, which he regarded as a good thing, and on the bad side, he had this jock accent. Jack had a faint thing about jock accents.

'Well topple in,' Jack said dully.

Taylor bowled in and sat down without being asked, muttering some aside or other.

Lamarre let him breathe a couple of times and then said 'Who's first, then?'

'What?'

'Who's first, I said. You going to tell me what you have or haven't picked up in the locality first, or am I going to tell you what we've dug up at this end first? Before I tell you what's next.

64

For you, that is.'

'Next?' Taylor wasn't used to Jack's style.

'Bloke called Sherman's next for you. Victim's ex-agent. Don't like him. Bit of gentle probing for you next.' Jack bared his teeth and added, 'But give me the the the non-news first.'

Taylor gave him the non-news from Richmond, which basically ran to nothing. No potential Hogan killers in the pub, none in the rotary club, none in the golf club, none under the stairs . . . Jack cut him off before he finished and started to tell him about poisons. He also showed the sergeant the very famous note.

Taylor looked scared by the poison thing and curiously neutral about the note. Gawkish at times, like a ring-tailed lemur.

'Currently we've got this bugger down for a technician of some sort,' Jack told him rounding off. 'That's putting it broadly, right? Could be a doctor, could be a student, but somebody that knows how to handle poisons, see. Because this stuff takes some handling, or so I'm told.'

'Whoever it is has some weird ideas on how to communicate, too,' Taylor put in, very quickly.

'Like the note, yes?'

'And the picture. I mean, what's the message we're meant to get?'

Lamarre shrugged. 'The picture I don't know. The note looks like a tease to me, but the crossword-clue style of it seems odd. I've got a date with a tame psychologist sometime, so I can thrash all of that out with him. Should be able to say more tomorrow.'

There was a faint thudding noise looming up from outside, like that you'd get from an elephant doing close order drill. Tickle always loomed up like that.

'On your bike, then,' Jack rudely informed Sergeant Taylor, shoving a thin wallet at him across the desk. 'The line on Sherman's in there.'

'What you going to be doing?' Taylor inquired casually, as he stood up.

How's that, Lamarre thought, count ten.

'Me?' he said, temporarily rigid. 'Well, like I said, I'm going to see a bloke at Middlesex Hospital.' Then, feeling suddenly belligerent, he gaffed on, 'Before that I might take in a strip show somewhere, unless you can suggest something better.'

Taylor smirked and cleared off quick, biting off his lower lip as he went with Lamarre adding 'Keep your mouth shut' at his back. He nearly kneed Superintendent Tickle in the crotch on his way out.

'That one of your draftees?' Tickle said.

'Yeah,' Jack said, still gaping. 'Funny one, he is, sir. They told me he was good.'

'Lot of good ones about Jack,' Tickle said, planting the piece of paper in front of Lamarre's scruffy shirt front. 'Lot of them are funny sods as well.' He was giving Jack a meaningful look then, full of hidden depth, like 'know what I mean, Jack. Very funny sods a lot of them are. Cheeky with it.'

But of course Lamarre had read it by now, at least twice. It was typed, like the other, and laid out the same way. What it said was:

> 2 down
> Cut to the fifteenth after the fifth
>   Reaper

Bad time, Jack thought, mouth drying up, forehead tightening, neck rising, I'm in for a bad time.

TWELVE

Elaine Sweet was having a bad time already with a professor.

It had been the same old line. Koenig always came out with it at the start of his Galois theory course, and some new, fresh, unsuspecting postgrad always fell for it. Every year it was the same; some sucker caught it in the teeth.

First of all he'd stalk back and forth across the room, giving them the spiel. 'This is a difficult topic, I make no bones about it,' he'd tell them. 'The ideas go deep and' — pointed but succinct pause — 'the Main Theorem, when we get to it, is profound.'

'It will take some time to get there,' he would warn them, 'and I do *not* want to discover later that you haven't been following a word of what I've been saying.' He usually took off his rimless specs at that point and gave them a series of meaningful nods. His spiky hair, which radiated from the top of his skull like the Statue of Liberty, would shudder ominously. 'You will have been wasting *my time*, which is infinitely more valuable than yours.'

A gracious trust-me type smile usually appeared then, followed by replacement of glasses.

'So I want you to *stop* me, understand? The moment you become confused. If you want me to go over anything again I shall do so. And again if necessary, and again. Do *not* sit there hoping it will become clear because it won't. This is a postgraduate course. I hope that's perfectly clear to all of you.'

Then he'd start.

And this year it was Miss Sweet.

After about twenty minutes, in fact. That was when her hand went up and she said 'Excuse me.'

'Well?' Koenig gave a small sigh.

'What's little g of h?'

'I beg your pardon?' Koenig glowered gently.

'Right at the bottom.' She was pointing at the line in question. 'Little g of h equals H over big G of h. What's little g of h?'

67

'What do you mean — "what is it?" ' Koenig started buzzing like some device going into an explode sequence.

Elaine went 'Eh?'

'You mean you don't *know*?' the professor said, his voice rising on 'know'. He looked at it, at her, at it, at her, and everytime he came back to her he looked madder and madder.

Elaine Sweet felt herself flushing. 'Well, I don't understand where it's come from. It's not defined — is it?'

'Look here,' Koenig snarled. 'My budgerigar could understand that.' Somebody laughed but they shut up damn fast when Koenig gave them the eye. 'That is the quotient group, of course, what on earth did you imagine it was?'

'Well, er . . . ah.'

'That's third year stuff, child. You shouldn't have to ask that. You've been through an exam on that, have you not; how in God's name am I to get through this lecture course if you cannot be expected to recognise a quotient group?'

'Sorry,' Elaine murmured, wishing she could dematerialise or something.

Koenig shoved his face back into his notes, inwardly lamenting the demise of the medieval system he'd enjoyed at Heidelberg, where a scholar got whipped off the precincts for hebetudes like that. Soldier on, he advised himself painfully, it is but once a week.

The others kept glancing at Elaine in sympathy because she was about two shades beyond violet and wet-eyed to boot. She was breathing heavily too, her lavish bosom rising and falling like an Atlantic swell.

'Child?' she thought, fulminating, 'child?'

She'd give him child. She'd show *him*.

Naturally enough, Elaine and the other members of the class followed the rest of the lecture perfectly so no further questions were necessary, were they? With just the occasional suspicious glare backwards Professor Koenig clawed his way to the group of automorphisms of a field over a fixed subfield and then he called it a day and swirled out.

'I'll get you,' Elaine told him, trying to send a bad vibe on behind him, although she didn't know what she meant just yet.

Elaine's flat wasn't more than a quarter mile from the department, in one of the flashy white fronts across Queen's Gate. Very pricey, and it needed her old man to help her out with it, but by and large she reckoned she'd landed on her feet when it came up.

Daph was already home. She was laid out on her bed wearing a towel wrap and a fag and a frown.

'Going anywhere tonight?' Elaine breezed, saving it.

'Seeing Brian,' Daph coughed. 'Probably go to a pub, or something absolutely fab like that.' Big pout and careless puff.

'Fancy a party?' Elaine said, thinking, my, you're in a stinker.

Now Daph was interested. She knelt on the bed, revealing all. The change was dramatic, almost.

'Oooh yes. Where is it?'

'Don't know. I'm going with another postgrad from Maths. His name's Norman.' They both cackled a while at Monk's expense. 'I only met him today,' Elaine added. 'Anyway, it's at a postdoc's place, he's my supervisor.'

'Staff?' Daph said, waxing bilious again.

'No, he's dishy. And it'll be full of postgrads I should think. You could bring Brian.'

Daph didn't say anything then, as if she was stuck for something sufficiently barbed, but Elaine wasn't ready for a fight just yet, so she said, 'What's the matter? Had a row with Brian?'

'What?' Daph said, like she was distracted from a thought. 'Oh no.' Pause again, there. 'No, I was just getting a bit, well . . .'

'Bored?' Elaine didn't know why she should say bored.

'Kind of, yes,' Daph said. 'Sort of maudlin. You know.'

She brightened up then, with some effort, and Elaine got the sudden impression there was this unfinished line of thought in the air that Daph had been working on when she came in, only now Daph had decided to shelve it for the moment and kind of come back on the air.

'Look, I am sorry Elaine. I'd love to come to this party. Just what I need. I'll ring Brian, shall I?'

'Tell him to come here,' Elaine called after her as she went out, to the phone in the hall. 'We'll all go with Norman.'

Norm wouldn't mind. Much.

Elaine didn't feel like eating so she decided to have a bath and change into something else before thinking about food. Something sexy was what she had in mind for Steve Kane and Norm and anybody else who was going to be there, although not too sexy because she didn't want them to think she was a harlot, did she, just a sort of vamp.

She finally decided on a change of jeans and a velvet shirt that stuck tight and dipped very low at the front. It tied up under the nect with a string that went through the collar, leaving a circle of exposed flesh on her chest from which her cleavage peeped out like a little mountain valley, with rich pastures further down. Good enough for them.

Brian arrived while Elaine was dressing, and it was shortly after that, while Daph was shoving cheese in Brian that Norm turned up.

Monk surprised her.

In his grey slacks and his loose hanging black raincoat he looked approximately human. In fact, he looked downright natty. In fact, he almost made *her* feel underdressed in her rotten bloody jeans. Elaine could hardly manage the intros, so it was 'flatmate Daph — Norm, Norm — Daph, Brian — Norm, Norm — Brian', and she was eyeing him up the whole time.

'Hey, Norm. You look great.'

Monk nearly flowed out of the chair.

'Uh,' he growled. 'You mean this old thing. It's just something I threw on.'

Combed his hair too. No — he's *washed* it. Oooooh!

'You don't always dress up like that for Steve Kane, do you? Come on.'

Monk wriggled again. Well, hang it, what's he meant to say? He could either say yes, which wasn't true, or he could say no and admit that the whole thing was for her benefit, which he didn't want to do. But then, Monk never worried about saying things that weren't true, and he didn't know that women dress up for men all the time.

'Yeh, keeps him sweet,' he muttered.

Elaine said 'oh', but she was still impressed. Maybe she should meet Norm somewhere more conducive, as it were, she thought, like a disco maybe. Damned if she was going to do the asking though. Never threw herself at anybody.

'Steve's place isn't far,' Monk said. 'It's in Fulham, only a couple of miles. I thought we could stop for a drink on the way. That OK with you lot?'

'Right,' they all chorused.

'Where?' Elaine said.

'Anywhere,' Monk said.

That was OK. Elaine had taken a drink with many a boy

before. She wondered, amused almost, what Monk had in mind. Well, one surprise could mean another, right?

His drink was a surprise for a start. Southern Comfort, he told her when she asked, American whisky, and she found that was something she hadn't expected. Wasn't it expensive? Yes. Did he drink it all the time? Yes. Not beer? No, not beer, didn't like beer.

'Used to,' Monk said, 'but I just went off it. Can't take that volume of liquid these days.' He flicked the whisky glass so it pinged at him. 'I could drink this stuff all day, though. Want to try it?'

She took a sip. 'Gosh, it's strong, isn't it? Lovely smell though. Phew!'

She ain't used to the hard stuff, Monk concluded.

'Don't you drink ordinary whisky? I mean, Scotch and Irish?' Not that she did herself.

'Sure,' Monk said, rolling his head around. 'But I prefer this.' He threw it down his throat and added, 'Steve introduced me to it as a matter of fact.'

Get away, Elaine thought. Steve again, eh? There was that funky postdoc again, hoooo . . .

'That's a liqueur whisky, innit?' Brian said.

'A what?' Norm asked him.

'A liqueur whisky. Unless I'm mistaken.'

Norman Monk gave it another look, sideways on, as if the answer to this inquiry was coded mysteriously in the colour, and visible against the light.

'Dunno,' he admitted. 'I just drink it.'

'Right,' Brian said.

Monk looked at Brian for a second, wondering what he should talk about. The two girls seemed to be intent on pulling Elaine's velvet shirt into a point somewhere on the forearm.

'Forensic science, was it?' Monk said finally, 'That's what Elaine said, wasn't it?'

'That's it,' Brian said. 'Been at it about four months now, just under. Graduated from I.C. before that.'

'Yeh, so she said.'

'Right.'

Another little look.

'Listen,' Monk said. 'You're not in on that murder of that TV bloke are you? Nelson Hogan I mean.'

71

'Yes, I am actually. Didn't Elaine say. I mentioned it to her and Daphne.'

Monk thought, 'Daphne?' and said, 'No, no she didn't. What're you doing then? Fiddling with that poison? Analysing it, like?'

'Nah,' Brian waved a hand. 'Nah, I'm not a chemist, I'm a physicist. Anyway, poisons in bodies comes under Pathology. My boss is a pathologist, but I'm on the physics.'

'What physics?' Monk wanted to know. 'Where does physics come in?'

Brian did a coy little thing with his head, and put on a demure grin as well to go with it, but he didn't say anything else. Or at least, he didn't seem to want to.

Monk let it go for now. He didn't go much on this Brian bloke to tell the truth. What the hell was a liqueur whisky anyway?

Monk bought a bottle of wine at the bar and they all bowled on to the Dawes Road, off which Kane had his lair. On the way they discussed domiciles in general. Steve's place was a maisonette type of joint, Monk said, with an upstairs and a downstairs and a back entrance with a kitchen and a bedroom and a bog and other civilised trappings like that, not a rathole like what he lived in, though anything was better than hall he reckoned, by which he meant randier, and didn't Elaine think so too, to all of which she just said yeh, right, and whereabouts was his place anyway?

Hammersmith, he said, further west.

As it turned out, there *were* a few others. Kane had perhaps another half dozen postgrads there besides them and what looked like a few younger members of staff. It was a real bachelor pad, and he had this big living room which he'd more or less cleared so they could spread out and screw around on the floor or whatever. There was just a table for the booze and a few big cushions on the carpet and the stereo in the corner. Very informal, just as Elaine had been subconsciously hoping. Everybody was very hung out. She wasn't underdressed. Monk looked a bit toffed up, as it happened.

'Hi,' Kane said, *very* pally, though his eyes had the same sharpness in them, 'What did you think of the Monkwagon?' Kane nodded at Brian and Daph as he spoke, and motioned them all over to a table full of bottles.

'Didn't notice,' Elaine said, taking the wine glass he was

pushing at her, and that was true. Just another student heap, wasn't it?

'Beat that, Norm,' Kane guffawed.

'Balls,' Monk said. 'She noticed. She's just dead cool.'

Doctor Kane was indicating the bottles. 'The glasses are all the same, but there's all kinds of liquids. Name one.'

Miss Sweet perused the selection. 'Let me see. I'll have aaaaa . . . Southern Comfort!'

Monk had the bottle in his hand, of course. Now he stopped dead and stared at her, astonished. Never! She couldn't be able to handle this stuff, surely? She'd lie down like a whore, wouldn't she? You could hope, anyway.

'All yours,' he said. 'Hold out your hand, gal!'

Sometimes, pondered Elaine, I'm just stupid, but she was going to down this if it killed her. Impulse drinking not to be recommended in company of strange men, mother said, but anyway.

'I don't suppose you know this lot,' Kane was saying, 'I won't take you around though. Damn silly, that kind of thing. Stick with Norm, he'll introduce you to people.' He winked at her as she sipped her whisky and tried not to pucker up noticeably. 'Not that any of them are worth knowing,' he added offishly.

Won't be so bad if I drink it quickly, madly decided Miss Sweet. She handed Kane her grand ultimate in demure smiles. I could stick with you, she tried to make it say, but Kane was looking at somebody else by that time. Later then.

Monk hauled them over to a knot of kids who were arguing about the music. Basically, there were two competing points of view flying about, the first saying that pop music represented the shape of things to come for the next four centuries and the second to the effect that it was irrelevant crap. Neither argument had a chance in hell of being demonstrably correct but both of them had backers who seemed zealous to the point of mania. Elaine Sweet and Norman Monk listened to it for a few minutes without trying to get in at all. Daph and Brian tried to look interested.

'What makes you think you can judge, anyway?' snapped a youthful graduate with a Zapata moustache. His target was a conformer in tweeds with a parting down the middle of his head that could have been made with a hatchet. Both had beer, but Zapata had his thumb knocked over the top of his glass in the manner of a seasoned pro.

'Didn't claim to be a judge,' retorted conformer. 'I'm stating the obvious. You telling me I need qualifications to state the obvious?'

'Obvious, my arse!'

'What's obvious?' Elaine asked.

The tweeds turned to her, since it was his point that was in dispute.

'What's obvious,' he said earnestly, 'is that the overall standard of musicianship among serious musical artists is definitely higher than it is among so called pop artists. I'm talking about their sheer ability to play instruments, see. I'm talking about people who write real music instead of churning it out with a spade or something. It's a thing that only comes after years of study and work. Tell me what popstars know about study and work. Go on, tell me.'

'That's technique!' ground Zapata. 'That's just technique.'

'So it's technique. I'm telling you it's better, and it's *obviously* better, and anybody who says it's not must be a bloody idiot.'

Zapata put his fists up on either side of his head, one gripping the beer glass, and clenched them until they shuddered, and the little bit of beer in the glass went frothy. He gnashed out his reply through clenched teeth, with his eyes popping, and a tortured grimace on his hairy mouth. 'There's more to it than technique. Can't you grasp that?' He rounded on Elaine in desperation. 'We've been here before. He thinks playing the flute boils down to blowing down the end and running your fingers up and down the outside. He thinks music doesn't count unless . . .'

'Look, listen, I . . .' Tweeds started into Elaine again.

Zapata had his hand out on Tweed's chest.

'Unless it's got this *melody*.'

He said 'melody' as if it signified something unutterably simple minded, a thing that higher forms of life would eschew as childish. Tweeds was glaring.

'That's right, that's damn well right. Just 'cause you don't like melody.'

'I didn't say I don't like melodies.'

'That's what came over. You think melodies are stupid. Got to be heavy metal for you. Got to be a bunch of screaming yobs holding guitars up in front of them like phalluses. You can't play a guitar at all in that position, did you know that? Let alone play it well.'

'Phalluses?' Elaine giggled. 'Yummee, phalluses!'

'Do you like Stockhausen?' said Monk to the man in tweeds.

They all stopped for a split second, as if none of them had realised he was there, although some of them must have seen him come over. But he somehow got the statement in during a silence so that, even though his voice was low and soft and toneless, the question cut in and hung there as if shouted.

'Who, me?' Tweeds said.

'If you like.'

'Well, I can't say . . .'

'Bit low on conventional melody, isn't it?'

'Yes, all right, but . . .'

'Not exactly pop music, is it?'

'Agreed.' Tweeds, the conformer looked uneasy. Zapata was grinning and waiting.

'Are you familiar with Stockhausen at all?' Monk said, quickly.

Brian started smiling at that exact and precise moment, and Daph did as well.

'Not much,' Tweeds admitted.

'Can you name a single piece?'

'No. No, I can't but that's got nothing to do with . . .'

'Webern?' Monk said, 'Heard of Webern?'

'Who?'

'Berg? Messiaen? A man of your classic leanings must have heard of Messiaen.'

The boy in tweeds was finding this unpleasant now, not hugely unpleasant like actual pain, but disconcerting and hurtful, and Monk was enjoying it, as if it was a game. He acted like a cat that has just crippled a mouse and then watches it. His eyes stayed locked on to those of the other man as if he didn't want to miss any of the writhing and contorting that his attack was causing.

'Henze?' he went on, 'Bowles? Cage? Berkeley?'

'What are you on about?' the kid in tweeds blurted. 'What's all this got to do with what we were talking about?'

Monk eased off, as if he had decided the game was over for the time being.

'Just a few serious musicians,' he shrugged. 'Thought you might have at least heard of them, considering your feelings about serious music, like. I mean, none of them write anything very melodic, do they?'

'I have no idea,' Tweeds said stiffly.

'Oh yeah, I forgot,' Monk swallowed some liquor and Zapata hooted like a chimp.

Norman Monk kept on watching his man over the rim of his glass with a cheerful but wicked gaze even though the tweeds boy had resumed his contest with the moustached one. And Elaine kept on watching Monk right up to the time he realised it and turned to her and smirked.

It was then she glanced away and noticed Kane. He was filling a glass for somebody else, and when she caught him staring at her, he winked. Or *was* it her he had been staring at, or was it Monk, or was it the argument?

Confused at being confused, she went back to Norman Monk and said suddenly, 'I hate Professor Koenig.'

'Really?' Monk said. 'Can't have that, can we?'

Daph and Brian had joined in the other group by now, but Elaine had this sticky feeling that Kane was still watching her, not that she wanted to look again.

Much later that night, very much later, when all innocent folks were asleep and the bad things were out on the prowl, Reaper sat by the glow of a table lamp and looked at two of the cuttings. There were others, but these two were sort of linked, vocation-wise, if that was the word.

The pop star was on the left, with his group behind him (Samson Delilah, strong and sexy) and the photo had him in an onstage pose with this intense look on his face, all sweaty and tighteyed and his legs all blurred as he rendered his lyric. It was a handsome face, sort of craggy it said in the *Melody Maker* where the clipping came from, and Reaper had decided it would be nice to smash it in with a hammer.

Either that or the DJ's face, though there was another treat in store for him.

The DJ was on the right, snapped in front of his covered-in swimming pool outside his swanky house in Hampstead, where Reaper was pleased to have learned he lived alone, whoring apart. He'd worked his pricey car into the photo too, a sleek Ferrari, peeping out behind his stupid grinning person.

Reaper picked up the lance head and looked along its three-foot length to the tapering, razor-edged, needle tip. Medium mild steel

76

it was, all Reaper's own work, and the shaft for it was in the cupboard, in three four-foot lengths that fitted together like tent poles. It was deadly all right, you could have harpooned a shark, if you had one swim by.

Smiling gently, Reaper reached for the hammer and hefted it, enjoying the tactile appeal that brand new tools seem to have. Actually Reaper had found the buying of the hammer quite an education, because who would have thought that a hammer wasn't just a hammer? Who would have imagined there were so many sizes and weights of head and such a range of prices, no doubt pertaining to the hardness of the steel, to say nothing of the wood of the shaft, of which Hickory seemed the best for the job, according to the nice man in the shop anyway, who was very helpful and pleasant, fortunately.

Reaper liked shopkeepers anyway, in fact.

Come on then, Reaper tried to decide, who gets the hammer and who gets the spike? The question had to be answered because they'd have the note by now and they might just figure it out so the move had to be made soon. That was always the strategy wasn't it? Don't give them *too* much time.

Reaper left it to pot luck in the end, waggling the lance head from one photo to the other, left right, left right, eeny, meeny, miny, mo . . .

PART TWO

Some one came knocking
At my wee, small door;
Some one came knocking . . .

Walter De la Mare

THIRTEEN

Next morning, Lamarre finally got over to the shrink. The Middlesex was just an excuse. Well, more or less.

Lamarre could have spoken to a psychiatrist — or was it psychologist? — at any number of hospitals. Guy's and St George's were more common choices in fact, because they had the big forensic departments (Leech had a post at Guy's) and their shrinks just got involved more than the others. The trouble with them was they weren't on the edge of Soho, and the Middlesex was.

The thing was, what with one thing and another, Lamarre never did get much breakfast so that by midmorning onwards he was rabid for some rotten food, so when he had to go out somewhere he sometimes made an event out of it and went to a restaurant. Other cops could come that macho bit with cold pies and coffee pissed into paper cups by machines if that was what they thought solved crimes, but Lamarre could never see it.

He was going to Soho, to eat Chinese, because that was his favourite (Szechuan, even, actually) and *then* he was going to see a shrink.

Jack Lamarre was, by any Western standards, an expert on Chinese food. Not that a decade in the Crown Colony necessarily made you an expert on Chinese food, or on Chinese anything for that matter, but Jack had a fondness for food and something different and new in the comestible line was certain to attract his interest. That was what had got him into it when he first went to Hong Kong, his interest, and if it had not been for his interest, he naturally wouldn't have become an expert.

It had been the same with the language, although you could never have called him an expert in that. But there again, interest had carried him forward and he could at least converse. Not fluently, no, but passably, which meant that he used the appropriate phrases and tailored his language and manner of voice to the person he was talking with, which is the way with the

81

Chinese and the standard by which they judge the handling of their language by others.

After a short time in London he had used his knowledge of Chinese food and talk to seek out the best restaurants, although they naturally came and went with the passing of time. Right now he had three regulars, all within the furlong of each other in the Shaftesbury Avenue-Oxford Street-Charing Cross Road pocket that was Soho at its most Soho-esque. They were all well established, run by men with their fathers, and all of them knew Lamarre well. He had conversed long and fruitfully with the owners, staff and patrons of these restaurants, gradually acquiring confidences and giving them in turn. And, truth to tell, there *were* things he had learned that had been of value to the police, although he had never betrayed a trust, and never would.

There was something floating in the air these last few days, in fact, in the very house in which he now sat. He had sensed it first a week ago. Triads perhaps, arming someone for protection? Jack had never gone into the Secret Societies so beloved of the Chinese, though the Hong Kong force had a whole department for them. But he knew that in London it was drugs, and not protection, that was their main activity. Still, it wanted probing, whatever it was, and later he would probe, very gently. Not now, because he had another problem now and the floating thing needed time and a velvet touch, but later.

You'd never have imagined that Jack Lamarre could have a velvet touch but some people knew it for a fact. Al Prendergast had almost guessed it.

Lamarre was halfway through his almond chicken when the old man drifted up. For a suitable period, neither spoke; the detective simply carried on shoving bean sprouts and cubes of brown meat into his mouth and the old proprietor just sat opposite and admired his style with the chopsticks.

It was one of Jack's favourite meals. All he had to say was 'chicken' and they knew what he wanted. They would even do the bean sprouts instead of the rice without him having to say.

'You have returned quickly since your last visit to us,' the old man said, speaking slowly for the sake of Lamarre's Chinese. 'If I may say so.'

Jack knew that there was an implied complement in the old man's use of his own language, rather than English. It was a kind of invitation. It had to be accepted, without question. Lamarre

82

marshalled the sounds together, sought the tone carefully before replying.

'With the greatest deference, I have business in the locality. Naturally, I could consider no other place in which to find this dish.'

'Thank you,' smiled the proprietor, whose name was Sheng Dao Lee, 'we are unworthy of your patronage.' Jack bowed quickly with his head at the precisely required moment. 'But tell me. This business? It does not concern our community, I trust?'

There it is, Lamarre thought. Something's floating. But leave it, don't probe now. It's another problem.

'No,' he said, still eating, since protocol did not require him to stop, or even to avoid speaking with his mouth full. 'I'm on my way to Middlesex Hospital. I seek the opinion of an expert on a matter concerning the recent murder of the celebrity, Nelson Hogan. It's a matter of the greatest delicacy, though you of course are my confidant, Sheng Lee.'

'You prostrate me, meritless as I am,' said Sheng, extracting another jerk from Lamarre's head.

'Not at all,' Lamarre said.

Sheng Dao Lee passed his hands, knifelike, in front of his chest. Small, curious movements that Lamarre knew belonged to the Tai Chi. In his mind's eye he saw the old man practising it, his trancelike movements perfected by half a century and more of repetition. It could control thoughts.

'You hunt the man responsible,' he said, in a voice so totally and utterly neutral that it was indescribable as anything. Not a statement, not a question, not a challenge, nothing. They had tones like that, to go with all the others, like a gearbox had a neutral. Lamarre had never mastered it, not even nearly.

'Man?' the policeman asked, realising he had another question for the shrink.

'Person then.' Another fanning of the hands.

Jack took in the smile. A small reproach.

'Yes,' he admitted. 'We had thought of the murderer as a man, so far. I apologise for my vulgar response to your observation.'

'Please think nothing of it,' the aged Chinese assured him. 'But tell me. Are you confident in your inquiries?'

Dear God, but you're sharp, Lamarre thought. Once again he marvelled, as he had had cause to do before, at this man's uncanny ability to penetrate another's mind. What in the name of heaven was it? It wasn't that he himself was the kind of man that thought out loud, wearing his feelings all over his mug, so *what*, for God's sake? Could his knowledge of people be so vast and ancient that he could literally read faces? Eyes?

Lamarre had never lied to the old proprietor of his favourite restaurant. He had never even tried to put one over on him in any way, through nuance or omission or anything else. It wouldn't have worked; it would have just lost him a priceless link to the whole Chinese thing here in Soho.

Still, nuances apart, there had to be a flashy way of answering that one, without just saying no, or no, not really. Or no, not in the least.

Lamarre lifted his voice, slightly, and stroked his hand, chopsticks and all, across the space between them, as if beckoning to the sky.

'Indignant destiny stalks a murderer,' he said. 'There is no avenue of escape. The hand of fate is relentless.'

Sheng Lee nodded his approval and let the tousle-haired Englishman go back to chewing his meal. He waited for perhaps another half dozen mouthfuls before he decided to say it, and then he let go just as another choice brown chunk was on its way in.

'You fear this person will kill again?' he ventured softly, eyes glittering like jewels, and Lamarre damn near took off the ends of the ivory sticks between his teeth.

How was it possible? How? The policeman felt like jumping up and screaming the question to the whole bloody place in case *somebody* knew how. He hadn't mentioned the possibility to anybody, he hadn't even let the fear gnaw its way into his own mind, not so it was hurting him anyway. All he had was this feeling, this glimmer, and the old man had reached right in and touched it.

'Yes, perhaps,' was all he said, because he couldn't find anything poetic then, not to save his life.

FOURTEEN

'Why?' Parker said. 'Why do you feel that?'

Lamarre chanced a shrug. The man was so undoubtedly friendly, his manner so incredibly sincere that you almost didn't want to offend him by not being able to answer. Was that part and parcel of a psychiatrist's job? Lamarre wondered. Expert with the kid gloves, like? If it was he did it damn well.

Lamarre thought that was a dumb question, frankly, unless he was overlooking something subtle. He felt the Reaper was going to hit again because he'd bloody said so, like he did the first time. Hadn't he?

Well hadn't he?

Professor D.J Parker, Consultant Psychiatrist, did not press the policeman. He just said quietly, 'Feelings interest me,' as if he was addressing nobody in particular and then he looked at the photograph again. He leaned forward over his desk with his arms folded and stared at it close up as it lay before him.

'The second note could just be a tease to upset you further,' he said, absently, staring harder.

'I didn't think so,' Lamarre insisted nicely.

Parker looked up, eyebrows moving.

'A police officer's sixth sense,' he stated flatly, leaning back again.

'I just feel this killer's in for an innings,' Lamarre said with a slight defensive note in his voice.

'I'm not ridiculing it,' Parker told him. 'In fact, from what you've told me about the victim's circumstances, I wouldn't necessarily disagree with this feeling of yours. I was merely stating an alternative possibility.'

'How do you mean?'

'By what?'

'About the victim's circumstances?'

'Well,' Parker said, 'you say that the indications are that Mr Hogan was whiter than white. In other words, this is not a

85

criminal murder, by which I mean a professional murder.'

'That's the way it's looking.'

'Just so. And he was not married, had no family at all, no particularly close relatives even, so we forget murder for profit in the first instance.'

'He didn't even have a will,' Lamarre said.

'Quite. And then of course there's the picture. This, ah, this signature, you called it?'

'Just a thought,' Lamarre said.

'And of course the two notes.'

'Correct,' Lamarre said.

'Yes. What I was about to say was that, in my opinion, such things would be uncharacteristic in a straight case of murder by a sane professional, or an amateur driven by motive of gain. Correct me if I'm wrong.'

'Seen a lot of pro's,' Lamarre said, 'and a lot of amateurs, but I've never seen anything like that.'

Parker nodded, very hard and slowly. Then he said: 'Very well. So you suspect that you find yourself left with something like a maniac. Yes? I'm afraid I think you're right about that.'

'Yes. Whatever maniac means. You'll have to tell me.'

'It's not a very precise term,' Parker told him. 'We tend not to use it. What you have here is a psychopath.' He tapped the picture of the Reaper on 'here' with the tip of his index finger.

Jack Lamarre turned the word over in his mind a few times. Psychopath. It had a sinister feel to it, technical but frightening. It wasn't like nutter, or fruit, or lunatic, it was more scary than those. It implied destruction and savagery. There was something inhuman about it, something . . . vehement? He needed a word . . .

Psychopath. Psychopath. God . . .

'I don't know what a psychopath is,' Jack admitted, 'but I need to know if you're telling me I'm stuck with one. Do you mind?'

'Certainly not,' Parker said mildly. 'Shall I tell you what kinds of traits you're looking for?'

'Tell me what one is,' Lamarre said, after a little delay.

Parker thought this slightly unkempt officer was no fool. He brought his hands together into a prayer shape, and let the tips of his fingers brush against his lips. Across the wide expanse of desk, Lamarre noted his perfect white cuffs and his solid gold cufflinks, as well as the cut of his expensive pinstriped suit.

Bet you're on a fair screw, he thought swiftly, almost unconsciously.

'For a long time,' Parker started, 'we held the view that the psychological make-up of human beings was a function of two sliding scales. One scale measured the sociability of a person, with the extrovert at one extreme and the introvert at the other, whilst the other scale measured intrinsic stability. Its extremes had a calm trait at one end and a moody trait at the other.

'A given individual existed, we thought, at some point on both scales more or less independently. For example, an individual might be extroverted but also unstable or he might be extroverted and stable. In the first case, dominant personality traits would be aggressiveness or excitability, whilst in the second case he would simply be lively or responsive. Similarly, an unstable introvert would appear anxious or pessimistic whereas a stable introvert would seem thoughtful and controlled. These traits that I describe occur in regular combinations — thoughtful and controlled, excitable and aggressive, and so on, and all of these characteristic combinations are quite normal. You follow that?'

'Sure,' Lamarre said.

Parker said, 'OK. What is *not* normal are *extremes*, such as extreme introversion say, or groupings of traits which do *not* correspond to the common groupings I mentioned just now — for example, an easygoing pessimist. Such abnormalities are called syndromes, and need not be identified with mental illnesses. You understand that, it's important? So far I'm talking psychology, not psychiatry.'

'Fine,' Lamarre said, but of course if Parker had suddenly jumped up and snapped, 'Right, Lamarre, define the difference between psychiatry and psychology,' he would still have been stumped.

The psychiatrist gave him a sympathetic look.

'That picture is now known to be incomplete,' he went on. 'We now realise that there is a third dimension, as it were, in addition to those of sociability and stability. It measures the extent to which an individual is, for want of a better phrase "tough-minded" — or indeed, is not. At one extreme of this third scale are the traits of extreme cruelty and total lack of human-itarian feeling, whilst at the other is the person who reacts tearfully almost to the sight of injured birds. Once again, we all have our point on this scale, along with our points on the other

87

two, and again there are common norms and the norms in turn define abnormalities. And again I stress, that the abnormality need not be equated with illness.'

Coming to it, Jack decided. He sensed it when the cruelty was mentioned.

'So what's a psychopath?' he wanted to know.

'A psychopath is an individual that scores highly on the toughness scale, that's all,' Parker replied. 'Whilst at the same time exhibiting traits characteristic of the other scales as well.

'An extreme case, in which the other scales cease to have any significant effect at all, so that the individual has no other characteristics but those high on this third scale might well be considered a case of mental illness. That condition is generally known as psychotic.'

'A psychopath isn't a psychotic, then?' Lamarre tried, to check.

'Let's not get confused over terms, Inspector,' Parker said patiently. 'A psychotic sticks out like a sore thumb. He is troublesome, vicious, totally selfish, and so on, but most importantly, is unable to modify his behaviour and so disguise it in any way. He is rare. The psychopath, on the other hand, displays all of these characteristics to a varying extent, but *also* has the other traits I mentioned earlier. In other words, he can also be sociable, or controlled, or outgoing, or pessimistic and so on.'

'So he's not obvious,' Lamarre said.

'No, frequently not. Nor need he be insane in the clinical sense. His condition is usually termed a character disorder. He may not be dangerous, or he may successfully channel his high third-order traits into his job, say, by becoming a ruthless businessman for example.'

'Or a top copper,' Lamarre laughed, wondering why the fucking hell he had to go and say that.

'If you say so,' chuckled the psychiatrist. 'On that point I bow to you.'

Lamarre said, 'When is he dangerous?'

Parker shrugged with his mouth. 'When these traits take over. When they get control. When they start to determine the things he *does*. Then he becomes . . . well, the common word is predatory.'

Predatory, Lamarre thought, that's the word.

'There are common traits, very common,' Parker went on. 'They add up to the almost classic clinical picture of the psychopath.'

'Yes?' Lamarre prompted, when he stopped.

'He may have a superficial charm and a genuinely high intelligence,' Parker continued. 'He does not suffer from delusions, is not nervous, and is capable of lying and deceitfulness in a perfectly casual manner. He does not suffer from guilt or remorse and frequently fails to learn from experience.' The consultant paused, as if pitying the creature he was describing. 'He may behave in an antisocial manner without motivation, or with only a slight excuse. He is frequently iconoclastic, attacking cherished and traditional beliefs simply to be destructive. He is egocentric. He may indulge in unusual hobbies or interests and may jump from one such diversion to another at whim. He will present conflicting points of view on the same issue as if both were his genuine opinion, often with great skill and persuasion, and frequently he will tailor his argument deliberately to oppose another individual simply to hurt their feelings or humiliate them. He is incapable, very often, of genuine affection, so his sex life is usually impersonal.' Another silence, and then, 'Found anybody like that, Inspector?'

'Hellfire,' Jack thought.

'I repeat, though,' the psychiatrist went on, without waiting for a reply, 'that these rather fearsome traits may be accompanied by others of a perfectly normal type, mingled with them, veiled by them, if you like.'

'Why did you guess that our killer is a psychopath and not the other one?' Jack said.

'A psychotic, you mean? Well, as you say, it's a guess. The psychotic is emotionally disturbed, badly so. He'd be likely to tell someone what he'd done, or even threaten it in advance. Certainly he wouldn't be capable of the kind of planning and stalking that seems to have gone into this. An attack in the street, perhaps, but not this kind of thing. This was planned. Psychotics don't plan, but psychopaths do.'

Lamarre hung off for a tick there, trying to get his thoughts in line. OK, right, fine.

'What I want to know really,' he said eventually, 'is why, in your opinion, this person , whoever it is, man or woman we don't know, did this thing.'

'That brings us back to the picture, in my view,' the psychiatrist answered. 'You see, I don't agree with you that it's a signature. I don't think this person is referring to himself with this image. I think the original symbolism is much nearer to what he's getting at.'

'Not with you.' Jack peered over the desk.

'Death respects nothing and nobody,' Parker said, holding out a hand. 'The victim had the world by the hair didn't he? Successful, beautiful, envied, admired, etc., etc., apparently untouchable. Except by death.'

'You don't think it's specifically Hogan he went for, more the fact that he was out of reach on his pedestal, like?' the cop burbled.

'That is my feeling,' Parker said. 'And I do agree with you, that we could just have a woman here. It's possible.'

'Right,' Lamarre honked. 'In any case, do you or don't you think he might be coming around to kick over somebody else's pile of bricks?'

'That was your feeling,' Parker said.

He was still smiling.

Taylor was in with that Sherman klutz longer than he had expected, so when he rolled out on to the platform he spied Harold Higginbotham right off. The reporter was waiting right at the end, close to the tunnel mouth. Taylor hoped he was feeling miffed at being kept hanging about, the little twat.

The Detective Sergeant punched out some chocolate from the machine on the wall as if he had all night, before he slid up alongside. Then he studied the ten-foot long suspender clad thighs in the stocking ad across the tracks.

'I presume,' Higginbotham said, 'that since you've hauled me all the way up here, you are graciously inclined towards any suggestion.' He eyed Taylor's crunchy bar thoughtfully.

'What I'm graciously inclined to do is give you more grief than you'd think possible,' Taylor said. 'But as it is I'm short on ready.'

'I told you,' the curly little runt told him, 'I have sources of money. You won't retire on it, but you could call it a fair supplement. Case of a sympathetic editor, yes?'

'You mean later, right?'

'Got to see the goods first. You give a little, I give a little.'

'Suppose I've only got a little right now?'

'Like I said, Sergeant. It's an ongoing thing.'

90

Taylor screwed up his choc wrapper and flicked it onto his instep, kicking it towards the live rail between the tracks. There was a rushing noise building up as a train approached, pushing the air down the tube ahead of it.

'OK,' the detective said. 'This is the way it's going to be, no argument.'

'I'm listening.'

'OK. I give you what I've got as I get it, but only what I decide. You pay what I want and it won't break your back because I'm not risking anything for you, right?'

'Agreed.'

'If it gets big, then we rethink the whole thing, right?'

'Have you done this before?'

'*Right*?'

'Right. Agreed.'

'You cover your end the way I tell you when my pals come bending your ear, right?'

'Agreed.'

'OK,' Taylor said, looking huffed.

The train crashed out of the hole then, drowning the conversation, but all Higginbotham said was, 'Let's hear some goodies then?' and Taylor said, 'Let's see some green,' or something like that.

FIFTEEN

'You first,' Al Prendergast said. She was saving her bit, though it was evens that Lamarre knew she had *something*, otherwise she wouldn't have chased him down, would she?

Lamarre pushed his finger against the bottom of his glass until it slid down and found the table top. The tall glass with 'Carlsberg' etched on the side of it moved an inch or so on the polished surface causing the golden liquid inside to wobble slightly. Lamarre watched the froth of the head settle again on the inside.

'Psychopath,' he said without looking at her. 'That's the buzz-word. A predatory psychopath. Shrink reckons he's got a down on success. Wants to spoil it. Wants to tell us all not to be too cocky.' He kept looking at the glass. 'Something like that anyway.'

'We await alike the inevitable hour,' Al almost quoted.

'What?'

'Poetry. Gray's Elegy. "All the pomp of heraldry".'

'Yeh, right,' Lamarre said, cottoning on. 'Well this son of a bitch reckons he's the time keeper.'

'Didn't have it in for Hogan then? Specifically at any rate?'

'Oh yes,' Jack said. 'But Hogan and who else? That's what bothers me.'

'You reckon?'

'Can't shake it.' He finally met her eyes. 'That second note.'

Al said, 'What did the man say?'

'He didn't want to agree.' Lamarre made his voice a lot more sarcastic there than was really called for, but he was feeling lousy about it because he knew now that he had expected too much of the psychiatrist. It came from not dealing with maniacs before, he realised suddenly. If you didn't have that kind of experience then you hadn't dealt much with shrinks. So when they were all you had all of a sudden you expected more than you'd a right to.

Come to think of it, why didn't they find somebody who *had* chased a psycho before? They dived in too fast, that was why, before they knew what was going on. Yeah, that was why. They should have let the district people hold it till it became clear that the picture and the note was all, told all, meant all. Then they'd have known who to send down from the Yard.

Aw, shit.

'He can't disagree I suppose,' Al said. 'In case you're right. I mean he can't risk that, can he?'

Lamarre gave her a look that warned against detective sergeants trying to patronise inspectors and then went back to his ale. I should have been a trick-cyclist, he ruminated morosely.

'We've found the book,' Al said.

Lamarre's face didn't change, mouth-wise or eyebrow-wise, and his head remained at the same angle, like the whole set of his body, motionless but for the finger stroking the glass, but his eyes snapped up and became hard. It was like a lizard, stoning it on a rock, noting the arrival of a fly.

'Where?'

'Library in the Old Brompton Road.'

'Where's that?'

'South Kensington,' Al said. 'They said it was out at first but then they rang back. It was on the wrong shelf, right at the back among the large prints. That's where you'd sneak off to rip the page out, yes?'

'Right,' Lamarre was coming back on the air. He realised now that there had to be that delay, because if the thing wasn't on the shelf, the right shelf, then it was theoretically out. But they wouldn't know, (would they?) *who* had it out without searching through *all* the members' tickets because they associated books with names in a lending library, and not names with books. Was that right? Maybe it wasn't, maybe they were just sloppy in the first instance and then got a conscience. Still, that out/not out business needed sorting.

'Where is it now?' he asked.

'Forensic,' Al said. 'I'll ring them in a minute. See what's what. By the way, they came back to us after you went out, about the picture. It's covered in prints, naturally.'

Forensic meant the Metropolitan Police Lab. 'They' were Ron and Brian.

'Naturally,' Jack said. 'Anything on the poison?' He knew what to do about the poison, but it could wait a second.

'We've been pushing samples at Path all day, but there's more places than you'd think from what it said in the report. Leech pulled in some mates of his to spread it out.'

'Mates?'

'Chemists, he said. Analytical chemists. Said he's got a lot of mates who could help out with the samples. Well *I* didn't know any, Jack.'

'OK,' Lamarre smiled. 'But it's *Doctor* Leech, Al.'

'All right, Jack.' Very softly, and then, coming back to normal; 'Anyway, I suggested he concentrates on places near where we got the book.'

Oh yes, Lamarre thought, oh yes, you'll do. That was the move.

'Which are?'

'Three of them so far. Two hospitals plus Imperial College which is part of the University.' Jack grinned again. 'That's fine, Al. That's fine. Was that what you wanted to tell me?'

'That's it.'

'Fine,' he said again. 'I'll go and see Leech now.' He stopped while she flustered over the no-Doctor and then added, 'We'll have a meeting at the Yard tonight. Me, you, and the big noise from Winetka. What's he at, anyway?'

'Who? Taylor? He's been out all day.'

'Not giving you any stick is he?'

'No?' Prendergast looked confused. 'Should he?'

'Never mind,' Jack said, 'I just got an impression. If that's it we'll go. Chase 'em up on that book, Al. Make sure.'

'Right.'

Lamarre started to get up, pouring the last of his lager down his throat as he did so. Prendergast stood up too, and she waited until he got through smacking his lips and opening his mouth in that disgusting ritual men had with beer, and then she said:

'Jack? Er, my parents are coming up to town soon. I'll need an evening. Dinner date OK? If it's a bind I could . . .'

'OK. No, that's OK. Just leave a number for us. When's it going to be?'

'Oh, sometime in the next few days. Listen, Jack . . .?' Lamarre stopped, having started to move. 'I wondered if you'd like to come along. If you think it's, well . . . well, proper.'

He almost asked her why, of all things, as if ten years with the Chinese hadn't taught him anything at all about manners, but he didn't because there was an obvious reason why. Jack had known it for a while. They worried about her being a cop, and she worried that they worried.

'Why, I'd be very pleased, Al. We'll both leave a number, right?'

'Thanks, Jack,' she said as if she knew what he was thinking. And then the nose went into its routine and the smile came on, and Lamarre reeled.

''Bout six,' he said, 'or later.' And then he was gone.

Sergeant Prendergast went over to the phone which was on the wall between the entrance to the loos and dialled Ron and Brian.

She asked a part of a question and then stopped and listened. Whatever remained of the smile vanished from her face as if she had been slapped.

After a few more seconds she dropped the phone and ran across the pub and out into the street, looking around this way and that among the crowds, but Lamarre had gone.

SIXTEEN

Henry J. Parratt, PhD, was going visibly crimson.

He wasn't all that upset yet, because Kane had barely started on him, but fast colouring was one of his many problems (halitosis being another) and he responded with a flush to even the beginning of an argument. You could see it moving up his neck and cheeks as if he was filling up on the inside with some pink liquid.

'Pardon,' he said, glowering at Steven Kane suspiciously, although Kane seemed harmless enough for the moment.

'I said that University Computer Science departments, as they call themselves, are next to useless.'

Kane was draped over the chair in the Maths department coffee room, watching Parratt from the other side of a long white melamine table. One arm was hanging over the back of the chair, dangling in space and occasionally drifting up to twist a strand of hair at his collar.

There were others around the table, mostly staff, but with a sprinkling of postgrads. Elaine Sweet was there, and Professor Koenig. In fact, Elaine Sweet had been hanging around Koenig most of the afternoon, though he didn't know it.

Now they were all ears, waiting to see what Parratt would say. He'd have to rise to it, surely, was the common unspoken hope.

The reason they all expected a reaction from Henry J to Kane's little barb stemmed from the fact that Henry was a lecturer in computing and computer science, and had been ever since his doctorate five years earlier. Henry had never been out of universities, unlike Kane, and did no research, also unlike Kane. Instead he taught and devoted himself to examination matters, and the subject he taught and examined had always been the same; computers and computer science.

Henry gave courses on integrated circuitry, peripheral storage devices, operating systems, high level languages, assemblers, compilers, artificial intelligence and anything else he imagined was fashionable. He considered himself an authority on the subject in general and he considered his courses second to none and right now he considered himself slightly *en prise* because this was the first time anybody had presumed to suggest otherwise.

Albeit indirectly of course, at least so far.

'I'm sure I don't know what you mean, Steven,' Parratt said, not challenging yet.

'Of course you don't,' Kane said smoothly, a languid and manicured hand rising to his neck. 'Part of the reason you people *are* so useless is because you don't even realise how useless you are.'

'Perhaps you'd be good enough to explain that.'

'All right,' Kane said nicely, a wicked little leer coming over his face. 'Take operating systems. You give a so-called course on operating systems. It's rubbish, isn't it?'

'Certainly not.'

'What does it teach them?'

Parratt waggled his head from side to side, weighing up the support. Koenig sat there with his filthy Meerschaum pipe dangling over his arrogant lip, and an interested look on his face. Elaine Sweet, beyond him, had half an admiring eye on Kane. The others were grinning like a pack of wolves forming a semi-circle round a trapped animal somewhere on the edge of some cliff.

'Well, it teaches them about operating systems of course,' he claimed, trying to get at Kane with a sarcastic note in his voice, but Kane ignored that.

'*What* about operating systems. How to write one? Does it teach them how to write one?'

'In principle, yes.'

Kane leaned back.

'The OS/360 operating system took two hundred and fifty man-years to write. How could you teach them to do that, even in principle?'

'Don't be preposterous!'

'Why is that question preposterous?'

'You've chosen the biggest operating system ever written,' snorted Parratt.

'I chose a real one,' Kane pointed out. 'Let's face it Henry, reality isn't your strong point. The principles you're so fond of are just things you get in textbooks. That's all you do, read stuff in textbooks and heave it out in lectures.'

'I *beg* your pardon?' The others were starting to laugh. Henry didn't like that at all.

'It's all you've got,' Kane went on. 'Because you don't actually *do* any computing or computer science — because it can't be done in universities. It's too expensive, too commercial. It's all done outside, in industry.'

Henry was halfway to magenta now. 'That is not fair,' he attempted to say.

'It's all true though, Henry. From the making of the computers to the applications. All industry, no academies.'

'Processors are made in university departments,' Parratt almost shouted. By his side, Koenig squirted out some smelly fumes and nodded equitably, not that he knew or cared if they were made on Mars.

'Toys,' Kane snarled. 'They buy a few chips and make a few toys and that's how they pretend to do research. How can that compare with the developments at IBM, or CDC, or Burroughs, or DEC, or Prime, or the hundreds of other firms out there in the real world. They spend millions, they employ thousands. That's the way the game is played.'

'There are applications I teach,' Parratt clung on, vaguely.

'Like what? Communications? That's one of the biggest. You don't teach it. I dare say you don't even know the state of the art. Real-time programming? The basis of nine out of ten applications is it not? You don't have a course on it. Distributed processing? Becoming more and more important, but you only have one processor at your disposal, and that's a mainframe.'

'Distributed processing?' Koenig said, 'What is that?'

'A lot of computers sharing a workload between them,' Kane said. 'It involves computers talking to each other.'

'Splendid,' Koenig said, jamming the pipe back between his fangs.

Henry Parratt had just gone as red as his available blood supply could manage and now he was starting to sweat. Up to that last broadside, Kane could have been using 'you' to mean computer science lecturers in general, but that lot was aimed right at him, Henry J. What was also bad was that Koenig asked his question of Kane and not him, which might have seemed insignificant, but Henry was accustomed to being held in awe around this table as the tame but deadly man of the machines. He hadn't realised Kane knew so much, and now he was frightened he could be swamped with more.

He felt chastened. Hurt even. And it showed.

'I consider your views somewhat extreme,' he said, but defensively now.

'You're just bridesmaids in this computing scene,' Kane said vindictively. 'All so called lecturers in computing are.' He sniffed out a word. 'Parasites really.'

Parratt stumbled to his feet as the phone rang over by the cups. He was pulling out of this, he had decided, because for some reason Kane was just being vicious, and that he found distasteful, not to say intimidating. Throughout the whole exchange, Kane had not moved or changed his posture. Now he just watched and waited for Henry to come back for more.

Well he wasn't. That was it. On the way out he answered the phone.

'It's for you, Werner,' he told Koenig, and with a final glance at Steven Kane, he walked out, silently creaking at the seams.

'Me?' Koenig said to all of them, as if a phone call at coffee was a wonderous thing, marvellous to the mind.

Kane pushed his gaze over to Elaine. She was looking at him, an almost-smile on her lips, chin on palm.

'Doing anything?' he said.

What does he mean, wondered Elaine. Doing what? Stats? Work?

'Going home,' she said.

'Later?'

Elaine flew through some contortions. She *was* doing something later, dammit, she was seeing Norm. Not that she was mad to see Norm but she'd agreed to after allowing him a mild grope in his car, so she couldn't drop it, so she had to say yes. And when she said yes she was busy he wouldn't ask her out for a drink or a meal or show or a screw or sail or sauna or whatever and she wouldn't be able to say another time.

'How d'you mean,' she finally tried, looking for it.

'Doesn't matter,' Kane said.

Oh hell, pined Miss Sweet, oh hell, oh hell, oh hell.

Which was when Koenig exploded.

'Whaaaaaaat?' he howled at the phone. 'You did what? With what authority?' He listened for a moment. 'I most certainly did not! Pardon? Pardon? Yes . . . Well it's quite clear to me it was a prank on the part of some person . . . I have no idea, I assure you.'

Everybody was all ears now. Nobody at the table was speaking.

'Please allow me to talk to the manager,' Koenig railed to whoever it was. 'I see. When will he be back? Yes,' he looked at his watch, 'yes, if you would. I shall be on this number for a further half hour. Then I shall come to you. What did you say your name was. Adelphi is that?'

Kane and the other staff exchanged mystified stares. Whatever it was it looked good.

Koenig banged it down and rounded on them.

'Does anyone know where the Adelphi Garage is situated?' he said in a sinister tone.

'Isn't it along the Cromwell Road?' somebody said, 'yeah, it's down the Cromwell Road.'

'Got a problem, Werner?' Kane asked. Koenig had a big car didn't he, one of those six seater Peugeot ocean-going jobs with four funnels and a mast.

Koenig took a breath: 'Some *clown*,' he started slowly, 'some *lunatic* has had my car towed away for an MOT test. From *this* car park, *without* my knowledge.' The faces were splitting into smirks already. '*That*,' he said, jabbing his meaty fist at the phone, 'was the garage, telling me it's *ready*, if you please!'

There was the smallest possible silence then, just enough for emphasis as Kane very quietly and very seriously posed an enquiry.

'Did it pass, Werner?'

The guffaws crashed out.

'If I catch the imbecile resp . . .' was all anybody heard Koenig say before he was drowned out in the peals of mirth.

Even Henry would have laughed, if he hadn't gone.

Elaine did, definitely. She got a special satisfaction out of it, too, because she owed Koenig one and now she'd given it to him. Norm had done the phoning up to the garage for her, because she couldn't have pretended to be Koenig and a girl's voice would have been a giveaway anyway. But it was her idea, and she'd been waiting to see the result for hours. She laughed, along with the others, but you'd have had to watch her eyes to see a difference.

SEVENTEEN

In his room, after the meeting, at his desk, alone, Lamarre started to sweat inside his soul. He didn't look worried, with his feet on the desk top and his hands cupped behind his head and a low, tuneless whistle (more of a hooting hiss, actually) coming from his mouth, and his chair rocking gently on its rear legs, and his eyes blinking rhythmically.

But he was.

Where are you? he thought, looking at the cluster of coloured pins in the map on the wall. Who are you? What are you?

Leech had given him a very promising start to the evening, considered in isolation. Lamarre had gone straight to the man after leaving Al Prendergast and Leech had had some good things to say about poison i.e. *the* poison. It turned out that there were not three, but four places in the Royal Borough of Kensington and Chelsea that held samples of the notorious Aconitine; The Royal Hospital, the Western Fever Hospital, Mary Abbots' Hospital and the Botany department of the Imperial College of Science and Technology. Leech and his boys had dropped all others in favour of these four, taking them in that order, and naturally it had turned out to be the last. Even then they nearly missed it because Mary Abbots' contribution had been close to the stuff in the capsule as well, so it had needed checking. Leech had gone on and on and on about weird tests involving spike-shaped traces on the screens of oscilloscopes and the colours that things gave off in flames, none of which Lamarre could imagine himself ever having heard before. Not that he cared, because right now he wasn't mad about understanding the thing — it wasn't as if he was getting to *charge* anybody for God's sake — he just wanted something to move on.

And Leech gave him Imperial College.

Not a hundred per cent definite, the scientist had warbled, but close enough.

'How close is close?' Lamarre had demanded, with a sideways

glance at the oscilloscope. 'Sixty per cent? Seventy per cent?'

'Ninety per cent,' Leech had said. 'If you like numbers. Personally I'm not a numbers man.'

Lamarre had grinned and had begun to take his leave, usual polite thanks to the accompaniment of, naturally, but that was when Prendergast came through on the phone, and that was what started his lousy rotten sodding nightmare which he was enduring now.

Just when he was starting to hope he was wrong.

About the feeling that was, about the second note.

But it was the wrong book.

That was all Prendergast had said first off. 'Wrong book, Jack.'

Lamarre hadn't got it immediately, so he had said 'What?'

'Wrong book. I mean wrong *copy* of the book. The picture pinned on Hogan — the *page* pinned on Hogan — it wasn't torn from the copy we found in the library.'

'But that copy has the page missing. You said so, Al.'

He had realised by then what she was saying, and he thought, 'Fuck! You're slow because this is what you were afraid of,' but Al was going on, spelling it out.

'The torn edges don't match, on the Hogan page and on what's left in the book. It was torn from some other copy, but somebody also tore that page from this one . . .'

'Somebody?' Lamarre had snapped in. '*Somebody?*'

'Could be just a missing page, Jack. It doesn't . . .'

'Follow,' he had snapped again, snarling now. 'I know it doesn't follow. You want to make a bet now?'

'No, sir.' Al had said softly, her voice even quieter from the other end of the line, 'no, I don't. Sorry.'

Lamarre had looked over his shoulder at Leech, who had not moved since he went to the phone and was just standing there, watching, looking disinterested, not self-conscious in the least, half amused even.

Lamarre had said, 'Yes. Yes, it's all right, Al,' and then he had started to knead the bridge of his nose and screw up his eyes. 'Er . . . listen, Al. You've got to get back on to all the libraries in the South Kensington area, and all the bookshops as well. You'd better take in the neighbouring districts as well, and when I say districts I mean police districts. Tell Sergeant Taylor to buzz 'em for you and get 'em to give you some arm. Every library, every bookshop, now, tonight. After hours or not, closed or not.

Understand.'

'Understood, sir,' Al had said.

Then she had hung up. Not him, her.

Not a great conversation, that, he reminded himself now as he stared at the pins.

So far, the count was seven. Lamarre had a coloured pin for each of them, plus one for Imperial, and that pin was white. From where he sat they formed a tight bunch, left of centre on his wall map of the inner metropolis.

Three bookshops had been found to have *that* book on their shelves, with *that* page missing from it, and they were in Gloucester Road, Thurloe Street, and Exhibition Road, the last one virtually on the very doorstep of Imperial College. Of libraries it was four up to now, the one in the Old Brompton Road that Al found first, but now joined by the Central, over in Pellimore Road, plus two more further east, in South Audley Street and Buckingham Palace Road.

The South Audley Street branch was where the Hogan print came from. That was definite now. Not much, but definite.

Seven copies of *Bruegel the Elder — Later Works* and seven identical missing pages showing the detail of the grim Reaper.

All in a cluster, not much more than a mile across.

Couldn't be a coincidence, could it? No chance.

Lamarre suddenly found himself thinking about Taylor.

'Personally I reckon it *is* a signature,' he had opined, chewing the stem of his specs.

'What?' Lamarre had said, looking irritable.

'The picture. Happen he actually thinks he *is* death. So a picture of death is a sort of signature, right?' Taylor rehung his glasses and added, 'Superintendent reckoned it was a thought.'

'So what?' Lamarre had wanted to know, looking even more dangerous. He was trying to imagine Taylor and Tickle together. In a corridor was it? Or a cubicle in the gents?

'Nothing,' Taylor had said, 'just thought I'd point it out as a possibility, that's all.'

'Right. Now you've pointed it out,' Lamarre had said, for the sake of having the last petulant word.

Why didn't he like that bugger? To hell with that.

Hanging one hunch on top of another, Lamarre reckoned there wouldn't be any more. Now this hunch was based on a kind of logic but only a very tenuous variety that could easily have been pulled apart — in fact you could have put a truck through it — but which was only half formed in the policeman's mind anyway, which was why it materialised as a hunch. Basically, Lamarre took it as a starting point that this fragrant little rat whose person he sought did indeed inhabit or at least frequent the environs of South Kensington, and had taken the poison for the first murder and the calling cards for what Lamarre now feared would be further murders from sources within this area. All Lamarre was assuming there was that this wasn't some cute pixie from Pinner, or somewhere else miles away like Edgware, or Dagenham or Surbiton, who had just tried to make it *look* as if he came from South Ken by taking his goodies from there. There were two reasons for thinking this: (a) having opened the score in Richmond you wouldn't necessarily expect the police to find his sources of pictures in Kensington as quickly as they had and (b) the same applied to the poison which was located largely through it's own peculiar ageing characteristic, and which probably could not have been got in the first place except by somebody who didn't know or know of the botany department at I.C. — and that of course was a line of inquiry all on its own, oh my, yes.

Having decided that this was a South Ken denizen, Lamarre could go on to say he was fussy about using the area as a source of the picture. Guessing, Lamarre reckoned he had exhausted all the libraries up to and slightly beyond its borders but then, rather than go further out, had come back deep inside Kensington and raided three bookshops to get some more. In other words, the killer had elected to stay in South Ken, even if it meant going from libraries to bookshops, where watching eyes watched you closer.

That was the way Lamarre saw it, anyway, and what it spelled to him was that if there were no more in South Ken, then there were no more. and, so far, there were no more and Al must be running out of bookshops in the area by now.

Not that another half dozen killings was good news. You wouldn't want to think that. That was bad news indeed.

There was no ducking it. That was the way it was shaping up, even Taylor's interviews confirmed it now, as expected. There was nothing and nobody connected to Nelson Hogan that could conceivably lead to a murder. There were no debts (absolutely the opposite), no shady friends, no nasty habits, no secrets. There was no wife or relatives to make it personal. There weren't even any resemblances between the man and anybody who was kill-worthy, to make it a possible wrong target. There was only what they had thought already; a random killing by a psychopathic slayer for a motive unknown that could only be guessed at by a psychiatrist.

A killer who was preparing to strike again, using the same calling card. A killer who had obtained as many calling cards as he thought he would need before setting out to use them because he was clever enough to allow for good luck. The kind of good luck that would have the police waiting in the libraries if he took them as he went along.

God, but it looked bad from the police-image point of view, when you *knew* what was going to happen, even some of the details of it, and you couldn't do a damned thing to stop it. It just . . . looked . . . bad.

Of course, Lamarre knew how to cover himself, at least to some extent. What you did in a situation like this was to scream loud and hard, but in the right direction, which in Lamarre's case meant a person to person to the right one of *them*. Them being the brass. The trick was to get something on record, that you could point to later if you had to.

'What's your move when it does happen, Jack?' the famous Detective Chief Superintendent Tickle had enquired. 'Assuming it does happen.'

'It will happen, sir,' Jack had insisted, without sounding anything but level. 'I thought I'd need a brief from you, sir, on that.'

'You'll get a brief, Jack. But I want your feelings first.'

Not so much a murder hunt, more a sodding game, Lamarre had thought, but he had kept his voice very professional and smooth and like that.

'I'd want to bring in the media, sir,' he had said, without much hesitation because that really was what he wanted. 'No messing about. Get 'em in hard. Tell them what's going on. Give the . . . give him some exposure.'

'With you there, Jack. What kind of exposure.'

'Maximum exposure,' Lamarre had said, feinting left.

'Maximum means everything doesn't it, Jack? Wouldn't want to give them everything. I mean you couldn't give them the notes and have them publishing the pictures and plastering the book and page number all over the place. Next thing you'd have thousands of the things coming in. More crossword clues than the

'I wasn't thinking of going that far,' Lamarre had said, thinking there'd be hundreds maybe but never thousands. Would there? 'Wouldn't give them the number of possible killings yet to come either,' he added, illustrating a mind at work.

'Still want to be in on that, Jack!' Chief Superintendent Tickle had said, before Lamarre let him go. You're hooked, Lamarre had thought. You'll remember that conversation.

He had thought of pulling Prendergast and Taylor back in but then he had decided to go out into the incident room and give it to the lot of them. The warning, that was; Steel yourselves for it, it being some more murders and a possible shitstorm from press and public combined. In the end, he had said, it's for the good of us all.

Yes, it was a nightmare at the moment, in essence, and if it hadn't been a nightmare, numbing his mind, Lamarre might have sat back even further and asked himself just *why* the killer (to be) was working South Kensington to death for pictures rather than catch a bus up to a library in Brent. Or Woolwich. Or Croydon. Or whatever.

It would have been a good question.

Reaper kept on beavering away with a little black winding knob, round and round it was going, with the counter on the top clicking up one more count for each turn of wire added to the coil, so there was no need to keep a tally.

The number of turns of wire is a primary design factor in the making of a transformer, though the actual construction is a maze of practical complexities involving eddy currents, insulation breakdowns (both to be avoided) and flux compressions (to be encouraged). Reaper had settled for an interlocking 'E-I' plate design, sawing and shaping the plates personally, and borrowing the coil winder from the Physics lab at the college. It had to be back before morning; hence the marathon session with it now. It was a matter of playing safe and getting what you want really, because of course you can buy the rotten things, but buying things leaves a face to be remembered and Reaper wanted to minimise that, plus of course the majority of transformers on the market are step down types whereas Reaper wanted to step the voltage up for Miriam.

Way up.

As for the perfume spray, that was no problem at all, any chemist's shop anywhere for that, (no face danger for such a little thing, they sell thousands) but the four mm pipe to match the drill bit, that took some finding what with it having to be fairly rigid, but Reaper found one in the end. Sleeve of a choke cable actually; one would never have thought of it.

Miriam was none other than Miriam of Miriam Fashions known to ladies everywhere and she was on the wall as well by now, photo by Annabel complete with article all concerning what a terrific hit she was turning out to be in the States, though Reaper frankly never imagined the Americans to be half as gullible as the British when it came to fashion. Still, she wouldn't be conning anybody for much longer with her garbage, the narcissistic little whore, not for a thousand quid a go like it said nor for anything else because when the electrons started to ride that field she wouldn't know what the hell was going on, not even in the millisecond she was going to get to think about it . . .

Velvet heat for thinking who it was going to be, Reaper always thought so clearly then, yes, yes, very clearly. Stay ahead, Reaper thought, they have the capsule you left them by now, so they'll know where the venom came from and that was fine, but stay ahead, get the explosive now, don't wait, don't stop, just say goodbye to Miriam . . .

EIGHTEEN

Madge shambled up the laurel-lined drive of the house, her boots crunching on the gravel, muttering to herself as usual all the way to the door.

'Stay in bed all day f'rall I care,' she nagged her distant husband (Ern, currently unengaged). 'Lazy, bone idle louse.'

Madge fiddled for her key, which she kept on a separate ring all by itself and which always ended up at the bottom of her massive handbag, underneath the many tissues and betting slips that she hoarded there.

'Dirty pig,' she mumbled, a final comment upon Ern before casting him from her mind for the morning.

She slammed the door behind her with a foot and proceeded through the hall and right back into the kitchen. She always had a cup of tea and a sherry before starting the cleaning. Mr Mayo didn't mind so she had given up rotating the bottles on a daily basis and topping up with water after she'd taken a belt. In fact, he'd recently *told* her to help herself to a drink whenever she wanted to, hadn't he? 'Oh thank you, sir,' Madge had said, fluttering her eyelashes demurely, 'p'raps I will.' Still, he had more money than sense, it had to be said, even though he was generous with his sherry. You only had to look at some of the stuff he put in this place to see that: paintings you couldn't tell one way up from the other, horrible big mirrors with writing all over them, and stuff like that, all over. Not tasteful, Madge reckoned, and Madge prided herself on her taste, especially her taste in sherry.

This kitchen was nice, though. Gorgeous, it was. Split level grill, microwave oven, all them freezer things all built into the wall, and one of them big copper chimney things over the hob. Madge thoroughly approved of Mr Mayo's kitchen. Had somebody here last night by the look of it. There were two glasses on the work surface by the side of the sink, both with a finger or so of something in the bottom. Madge rinsed them out while the kettle was warming and then lit a fag and waited until it started to sing. Then she made her pot of tea and went back into the hall to put on her carpet slippers.

She was just back in the kitchen when the phone rang.

Fussing slightly, because she liked her tea *very* hot with her sherry, she waddled into the lounge, where she noticed immediately that the curtain that usually went across the French window was drawn back. The whole room was flooded with sunlight, still angling in low from over the pool.

''Ello,' which was a typical Madge effort on the phone.

'It's eight thirty, darling,' said a husky female voice.

'What?' Madge said.

'Who's that?' said the voice, considerably changed. 'Is that Mr Mayo's residence?'

'Yer,' Madge said, the fag drooping from her mouth, and the smoke stinging her eyes. 'I'm his housekeeper. Who's that?'

'Could I speak to Nick, please dear? This is the BBC.'

'He's not 'ere,' Madge said. ' 'E's never 'ere at this time, when I get 'ere.'

There was a kind of tutting noise from the other end of the line as if the girl, whoever it was, had grown suddenly tired of this stupid conversation with this stupid woman scrubber-up. During the pause, Madge noticed the Ferrari parked just beyond the patio outside the window and thought, 'funny . . .'

'Well, are you *sure*,' the girl said. 'His show goes out at nine and he's usually here well before eight thirty. Look, he's not in bed is he?'

The husky female voice thought it damn likely he might still be in bed because he'd tried very hard to get *her* into bed the night before and he'd drunk a hell of a lot of liquor in the process. That was why she'd put on the sexy tone to start with in fact, because on consideration, she wasn't averse to a second round.

'Could be,' Madge said, thoughtfully almost. 'I just seen 'is car outside. It's not usually there. 'Ang on.'

Madge dropped the phone on the onyx table with a certain crack and humped off up the winding wrought iron staircase. It was a sort of imitation Rococo, like in all the worst Hollywood homes and Nick Mayo had had it installed following a trip he made to do an in-depth interview with Tom Jones in California, at the star's mansion. Madge didn't care for it much, too bloody fancy.

The bedroom was at the end of the landing.

Madge knocked first, very lightly, and when that got her no-where she increased her rapping both in frequency and force. Then she shouted, 'Mr Mayo. You in there?' but there was still nothing. Finally she put out her hand to the elegant brass knob, withdrew it, put it over her mouth, and then put it on the knob again and twisted. Very slowly, she opened the door and peered inside.

The bed was empty, and so was the room.

Suppressing a now admitted fear of finding she didn't quite know what, Madge took a few deep breaths and went back down the stairs into the lounge.

'Not 'ere,' she said.

'Well where the hell is he?' said the silken tones of the beeb.

'Well, I don't know I'm sure,' Madge grizzled. 'I only clean 'is 'ouse for him, dun' I?'

It was then, at that precise moment that Madge noticed, out of the corner of her eye, the slightest, smallest, little movement from outside. It was a flutter; something fluttered. Looking hard, she saw it.

It was a piece of paper, jumping in the breeze and it seemed to be on the top end of a piece of cane or bamboo or something that was poking up out of the swimming pool. And as she watched, the pole drifted sideways, very slowly, as if it was a flag attached to a buoy, or a raft, or an airbed, or a . . .

'You say his car's there?' the girl from the BBC was asking. 'His Ferrari?'

Madge was watching the pole.

'Hello? Are you there?'

'Yer,' Madge said, vacantly. What the bloody 'ell *was* that thing? Bit of paper on a pole?

'He's definitely not at home? He's left?'

'No,' Madge said, absorbing one question at a time, and then: 'Yeh, 'e's left.'

'Well thanks anyway,' said the girl, who was actually an assistant producer, and who had suddenly realised what had happened to Nick Mayo. 'He obviously couldn't start the car and he's on his way by taxi. Bye.'

'Tata,' Madge said.

Ought to get a better car, she thought, walking towards the

French windows and the patio and the back drive and the lawn and the *pool*. Like a Rolls Royce. Madge preferred a Rolls to a Ferrari any day.

Looks like bamboo, Madge thought. Looks like a picture, as she approached the edge.

The first thing that struck her was that the water was pink, which seemed odd, though pink — odd was as far as she got because she was at the edge by then, looking in, and that was when she let out the first of her long breathless wails.

NINETEEN

'That's in Nevada,' Elaine cut in.

'No,' Monk said, wagging his head and twisting his face as if seized by a cramp. 'Noooooo! Reno was the man's name. Major Marcus Reno, Seventh Cavalry. Look.'

Monk drew an arrow upwards from the bottom of the diagram along the Little Big Horn River towards the clutch of Little A's that formed his picture of the Sioux-Cheyenne-Arapaho village on that fateful day long ago. June 27th, 1876, he had told Elaine, quick as a flash.

'Reno came up from the South, attacking the bottom edge of the village. Villages were always strung out along rivers. He'd have run into the lodges of the Hunkpapa Sioux first, because they always camped on the end of the line. That's what their name means.'

'Really,' droned Elaine, blinking slowly, once.

'Yes,' Monk said. 'Now the village could have been five miles long, and Indian witnesses say Custer was maybe ten miles north of it when Reno hit from the south. So they could have been fifteen miles apart when the attack started, and Custer a good twenty-five or twenty minutes away.' He paused for breath. 'I reckon that's what made the difference.'

'Do you,' Elaine said. 'Do you really.'

'Yes. I do. Are you *listening*.'

Elaine had just seen Steven Kane barge through the swing doors of the common room and head for the coffee dispenser. Black, no sugar, was what he'd punch out, she knew that by now.

'Yes, sorry. Yes, Norm?'

Monk eyed her sideways for a second. Hmmm.

'What I reckon is, the Indians didn't *know* about Custer, so they all went for Reno instead of splitting up like they were meant to and panicking. They poured out all along the village and those that couldn't take him on head on . . .' he drew an arrow down the side of the village, 'came charging down the side

112

and caught his rear. In military jargon they turned his flank.'

'Turned his flank,' said Elaine with her eyebrows up.

'Yeah, right. And he had to retreat into the nearest tree line.'

'Right,' said Elaine. She was watching Kane once more. He was standing with a steaming white cup in his hand, looking about him.

'But it was the *speed* of it,' Monk emphasised, with his fore-finger and thumb together like a chef, 'the speed of it was what left Custer out in the cold because by the time he came trundling up they were mounted and ready.' Another arrow on the map, showing Long Hair coming down from the north.

Kane had seen them now. He was on his way over.

'And that was the end of Custer was it?' Elaine asked, with a sudden renewed interest.

'Not half. They wiped out his whole command in the first rush,' he nodded as Kane sat down, acknowledged a long slurping noise. 'Two hundred and sixty-six officers and men. Custer had seven troops of cavalry. Or was it five?'

'Better check that,' Elaine said.

She looked at Kane as she put that in and she had a distinct, though faint smirk on her face as if she was seeking approval for the sarcasm. But it vanished when Kane ignored it and instead leaned forward towards Norm with an expression most earnest and intent.

'Tell me, Norm,' he said, 'was General Custer scalped as far as we know?'

'We don't know for sure,' Monk told him. 'Tatanka Yotanka —'

'That's Sitting Bull,' Kane said quickly.

'— Bull Sitting Down, yes. He is *said* to have said that Custer wasn't scalped or mutilated like practically all the others. But the dispatches of Generals Crook and Terry, or those of Colonel Gibbon whose men may have found the bodies, don't say one way or the other as far as I recall. I'll check, Steve.' He considered it for a while. 'Yes, it's significant if they didn't.'

'Respect for the enemy, as it were,' Kane nodded. 'Yes, that's what I was getting at.'

'The relationship the Indians felt for Custer you mean,' Monk said. 'Hmmm, yes.'

'Quite,' Kane said.

What the hell is this, Elaine thought, frontier tales?

But they had both stopped. And they were both looking at her.

113

Why?

'Well then,' Kane finally said, slapping his hands on to his knees. 'How's Elaine then?'

'Fine,' cooed Elaine, chancing a purr, though not too much for Norm. Norm wasn't bad with his hands on present form. 'Ought to be thinking about work I suppose.'

'Work?' Kane said. 'Work? What's work? Not even lunch time yet. Don't work before lunch, do we Norm?'

'You bloody don't,' Monk said.

Kane gave Miss Sweet one of his winks and tried to picture her configured like the whore he had been with in Duke Street last night. That is; manacled to the bed by the wrists, in leathers, head down, rump up awaiting the lash. She had suggested it. Said she thought he was ready for it, the stupid, simple cow.

Would Elaine ever suggest such a thing? To Norm? To himself? To anybody?

'Seen Werner today?' he asked Monk, thinking of anybody.

'No,' Norman Monk told him, and then he chuckled, 'but I've seen his car.'

'You heard about that, then?'

'Yeah. Good, eh?'

'He didn't think so,' Kane said. 'Reckons he's going to castrate whoever did it.'

Is that a warning, Elaine thought. Is it? Does he know?

'Never find out, will he?' Monk said dismissively.

Kane picked up his coffee again.

'Probably not. Definitely not.' He took a drink, winced, put it down again. 'Anyway, Norm. Everything all right? Going smoothly is it? According to plan?' Thesis, he meant.

'Perfectly,' Monk said, quietly. 'Got a lot done last night.'

Elaine Sweet said nothing, but they were both looking at her again.

Al Prendergast sorted this one out before anybody else, though it looked obvious in hindsight, just like a lot of things.

'Fifteenth letter of the alphabet is O,' she told Tickle, Taylor and Jack. 'May is the fifth month, so it's the fifteenth after the fifth, get it? May-o.'

They looked like three drips, standing there gaping at her.

'The cut is the first name, right. Nick? Cut? Yes?'

'Shit,' Tickle hissed, almost inaudibly. 'I don't believe it.'

'Try harder,' Lamarre said.

TWENTY

Wonder how I'll look on TV, Lamarre thought.

He was standing there in the incident room, facing the assembled horde of media men, watching the one with the camera on his shoulder. There were press people as well, more of them than the radio and TV types obviously, though Lamarre didn't think of press as media — press were press. By and large Lamarre didn't mind the press at all, but he had a grand disdain of the media.

Right now Detective Chief Superintendent Tickle was on his feet too, chiding the last questioner over a point of principle as he called it, not that these jokers lost any sleep over points of principle, nor Tickle for that matter either.

The Chief finally sat down, sniffed loudly and pointed to the next question. He looked like he was in for a bout of 'flu'.

'Collard. *Evening Standard*.' The reporter spoke with the confidence of a man with a big circulation behind him. 'Inspector, you say that you have conclusive evidence that these murders were committed by the same individual?'

'Yes.' Don't expand on it yet, Jack told himself.

'What evidence?'

'He left a calling card of sorts. When I say "he" of course I'm using a figure of speech.'

'You think the murderer may be a woman?'

'I didn't say that, did I?'

'What sort of calling card?' somebody else wanted to know.

Jack took a good chestful of smoky air before going on.

'I would prefer not to elaborate on that if you don't mind. As I'm sure you gentlemen can appreciate, we have certain lines of enquiry in progress and we must balance our willingness to co-operate with you against our need to safeguard those enquiries.'

And safeguards there were, too. The library folks had been menaced into silence. Whoever it was that fell over Nelson Hogan on the green had been cajoled, and the screaming Mrs Mopp never got a good look at it.

Did he sound too patronising though? he worried slightly. You didn't want to make out you were just tossing them scraps. They didn't like that. They could get mean about that.

On either side of him, behind the line of tables they'd rigged against one end of the huge room sat various senior detectives from the Yard and from the two districts directly involved, together with secretarial section personnel such as secretaries and press relations specialists who had come because they thought they ought. Without exception, the whole row of them displayed a superbly practised air of utter nonchalance at Lamarre's attempts to deal smoothly with the lions of Fleet Street.

'I see,' said the Collard bloke after some consideration, during which Lamarre thought it was pretty good, none of them wanting to butt in, like, until Tickle gave them the nod. How did he *do* that?

'Perhaps,' the *Evening Standard* man went on, 'perhaps you would elaborate on the methods used in the murders. I gather the first case involved poison of some kind?'

'Yes, it did.' Safe ground this, Lamarre thought. 'The poison is called Aconitine. It's an alkaloid. Extremely toxic.'

'How was it administered?'

'No comment. Sorry.'

A couple of them snarled a bit, but Lamarre flinched not at all.

'And the second murder, Inspector? That of Mr Nick Mayo?'

Lamarre had that fresh in his mind. Ought to have, considering he'd come here hot foot from the path lab, where Leech had given him the whole gory bit, bible and verse, complete with pokes and prods upon the unprotesting cadaver of the DJ. A rather wet and slimy Nick Mayo was face down on the slab at the time with his face peering over the far end, resting on his chin, and a piece of dowelling rod sticking horribly up from the hole in the centre of his back. Apparently, as it transpired, Leech was measuring the entry angle, which he had estimated at about thirty degrees below horizontal, indicating the killer struck from behind the direction in which Mayo was swimming (or facing) so odds were that he never knew it was coming. The long steel tip had gone clean through, emerging just below the root of the neck. Leech had waved the glistening, tapering, honed and bloody point of the thing under his nose. Nasty, he had said. Aye, nasty, Lamarre had agreed.

'This isn't very pleasant,' he warned. 'Mr Mayo was killed by

116

a single thrust from what appears to be a home-made lance.' Most of them stopped scribbling and looked up at him. One at the front muttered a kind of prayer. 'The weapon passed through his upper body from back to front, rupturing the pulmonary artery, which would have led to rapid and unavoidable death.'

'Did it happen in his house?'

Lamarre glanced at Tickle, who nodded imperceptibly, signalling his agreement to go ahead. Fine with Lamarre that, because this was all good juicy stuff to keep them off the main issue, or at least allow him to slide it over them without a fuss.

The psycho bit, that was.

'No,' Jack said. 'He was killed whilst swimming in his pool.'

And he was. Some water in the lungs, Leech said. He died in the pool, not somewhere else.

The Detective Chief Superintendent decided this hound had got enough air time so he waggled his claw above his head and said, 'Next question please. Ah yes, Mr Rickers.'

A lot of senior cops in the Met knew Rickers. A tough newshawk for the *Telegraph*, he had been around a long time and he could handle the police, most of whom had a clear respect for his paper and himself. Neither was to be trifled with. Lamarre knew it as well as any of them.

'At the risk of completely annihilating all your lines of enquiry, Inspector, have you noted any connection between Nelson Hogan and Nick Mayo which could bear upon their murders?'

'Both in showbiz,' Lamarre said quickly. 'But no other connection. Certainly nothing we could point to.'

'Nothing in their past, perhaps?'

'No. Not so far.'

'Was robbery involved?'

Lamarre steadied himself by breathing again.

'I believe we've been over that one. It appears that robbery was *not* a motive. In fact, neither house was entered. We're pretty certain of that.'

'I see.'

'I should add —' Lamarre started to say and then he stopped but then decided to go on, '—I should add that it's early days with Mr Mayo. We're looking into his background at the moment, but the incident only occurred this morning, remember.'

'Then there *could* be a connection.'

'Well, I . . . It's possible, I suppose.'

The Chief was in then. 'I think we could have another question, please.'

'One moment please, if I may,' Rickers said. The rest of them started smirking, here and there. 'You did call this press conference, did you not?' He was tacitly menacing Tickle with the whole lot of them combined there. Lamarre almost blanched.

'To present you with facts, yes,' the burly superintendent replied hotly. 'Not to indulge in speculation or to discuss confidential areas of investigation.'

'Indulge me for a moment, Superintendent,' Rickers lunged on, apparently having acquired the bit, so to speak, 'what about a Secret Society of some kind? Have you considered that?'

'Hell, no,' Sergeant Taylor muttered, juuuust loudly enough for Lamarre to catch it. 'Not a bad idea though,' he was whispering to the person on his left, speaking out of the side of his mouth like a pimp.

You're dead, Lamarre thought, bloody Russian front for you.

The Chief glared straight at the *Telegraph* reporter without saying anything, but he was met by a blend of innocence and insolence.

'I don't think so,' Tickle finally succeeded in saying, with his voice middling level. 'We'll bear it in mind. Now the next question please. Yes, sir.'

'Harold Higginbotham, *Hounslow and Richmond Gazette.*'

Jack Lamarre's eyes locked on him. Harold who? Hounslow what?

Tickle *almost* stopped with his backside hovering over his chair.

Practically every other media person in the room started grinning widely.

'Inspector. You've said there was, or is, no connection between these killings.'

'Correct,' Lamarre said. 'Killings,' he repeated mentally. He had a feeling about this chap already.

'So you could not have known that Mr Mayo was in any danger.' A statement, not a question. He was leading to something.

'No. Of course. Naturally we would have protected him.'

'Naturally. In fact, you didn't know that anybody *specifically* was in danger.'

What do I say, Lamarre thought. No? Yes?

'No.'

Harold Higginbotham, *Hounslow* etc., curly little runt in tweed jacket with leather elbow patches, paused.

'But you called this press conference with remarkable speed. Clearly you intended to call it before Mr Mayo's unfortunate demise.'

'Did we?' Lamarre said, sickly.

'Didn't you?'

'Well . . .'

'Am I right in saying that you anticipated a second murder, Inspector?'

The Detective Chief Superintendent was rising to his feet.

Harold H went on: 'And that this anticipation was not based, as you have said yourself, upon any links between the two victims, but on what we must surmise is your assessment of the person responsible?'

You talk a lot, Jack thought crazily.

'Just a moment . . .' Tickle started to say.

'Are we dealing with . . .'

'One moment please . . .'

'. . . homicidal maniac?'

Shit, Lamarre thought. Not from fucking Harold Higginbotham, for the love of God.

The whole room started to heave at the seams then. A lot of newsmen jumped to their feet. A couple, to the horror of the secretarial section people, fled the room, clearly in search of public telephones. Some of the cops began to show signs of stress by closing their eyes in silent agony or chewing the corners of their mouths.

Lamarre sat down, with his head revolving slowly on his shoulders, round and round and round, picking his nose with his thumb as it went by.

Tickle was quietening them down, pushing his flat hands out into the air as if he was trying to topple an invisible wall.

'We, hrrumm. We were coming to this,' he announced gruffly.

'Come to it then,' somebody shouted.

'All right, gentlemen, all right,' Tickle inhaled very hard through his nose. 'What we were about to mention before Mr, ah, Mr . . . was that there is a possibility that the murderer is deranged.'

'By deranged,' Mr ah, Mr went on, being still on his pins, but now looking ultrasmug, 'you mean he's a . . .'

'I mean that is the clinical opinion of an expert that the officer in charge of this case has consulted,' almost screeched Tickle wildly.

'Based on what?' came back Higginbotham. 'This calling card you referred to?'

You're wasted in Hounslow Jack conceded ruefully.

'Yes,' the Detective Chief Superintendent gasped.

'Surely you can tell us a litte more Superintendent. About this card? Is it a message? A sign of some kind?'

'We just can't tell you that, d — .' Lamarre almost said 'dammit' but looked right into the fat lens of a TV camera before he checked himself. 'If we were to be specific, there would be imitators. We would be swamped with hoaxes of every kind. It would confuse the investigation. Can't you see that?'

'Certainly Inspector. We merely . . .'

'He thinks he's death,' the Chief suddenly said, 'he thinks he's the grim Reaper.'

Again, the whole crowd stopped and stared.

That's not right, Jack thought, glad I didn't say it. Brilliant move though. If they won't let go, give 'em any old thing. Smart police work that. Training tells, see.

The whole room seemed frozen. It was strange, and strongly fascinating. Jack closed his eyes and waited for one of them to say it and sure enough, one of them did.

'He thinks he's *what*?'

But Jack wasn't listening any more. He kept his eyes tight shut, for what difference it made, because he could hear the place breaking up all around him.

TWENTY-ONE

For what remained of the working day, Lamarre just kind of sat back and watched it ballooning before his eyes. Oh, he had to take a hand in it of course, or at least appear to. He had to brief the medium ranked dicks who came in squads to join in, so they could brief the battalions coming in their wake. He had to vet the statements they were drafting for the radio and the TV slots that he, thank God, didn't have to do, where somebody would describe the possible/probable/hopefully somewhere near the mark characteristics of the kind of ravening homicidal lunatic the press would be advertising by then, and then invite the public at large to mention it if they thought the neighbour next door fitted the bill, or maybe they had an uncle, wife, brother, niece, father or husband, daughter or son who looked likely, all they had to do was ring this number — pause, display, read over for the short sighted — and they would be treated with strictest confidence. Men with handfuls of phones had moved in within the hour, because as soon as the statement went out, the switchboard would start buzzing. It always did; there were always axes to grind out there, the public always responded with overkill.

Jack Lamarre felt oddly separate from it, like a person at the dentist feels separate from his mouth after the injection of his gums. His voice was talking, his fingers were pointing, his eyes were seeing, but he was somewhere above it all, floating disembodied.

The only positive thoughts that seemed to come from his real conscious self were unrepeatable things concerning the prospects in the afterlife of Harold Higginbotham, ace stringer of the *Hounslow and Richmond Gazette*. Jack wished a pox on him, among many other items, him and all his line.

He stuck it out until the evening editions appeared, having decided he would avoid the TV coverage by just not watching it, but these he'd get stuck in his face no matter what, so best to get it over with and then put them aside.

'Police withhold details of sinister calling cards . . .' Harold Higginbotham goaded from his column, 'Inspector J. Lamarre, the Scotland Yard officer heading the operation, refused . . .'

The rotten little prick, Jack seethed.

HOGAN KILLER STRIKES AGAIN, yelled the *Evening Standard*, followed underneath by *PSYCHO MURDERER KILLS DISC JOCKEY* in half headline size.

Lamarre thought, dear God help us, and then read far enough into it to find the inevitable 'grim Reaper' paragraph before biting the corner off the page and starting to chew it. Then he forced himself to finish it.

And then, without another second's hesitation, he stood up and walked out. Passing Al Prendergast he just said, 'Take the night off, Sergeant. You'll need it,' and then he didn't look at her again, though he knew she wouldn't need telling twice.

Al had been out earlier. Out but working.

Fuck them all for now. Let the mad son of a bitch kill half the fucking city if he wanted. Who cared?

Jack knew where he was going, and it wasn't anywhere near a TV set or a radio or some clown standing on a pavement next to the hoarding and bawling the whole thing in your ear. 'Read all ab . . .'

Half an hour later he was there.

Somewhere outside was Gerrard Street, dead centre of the rush; busy, honking, stinking, swarming and seething. It was all no more than yards away, but here, *here*, in this cool, white, small room it was sooooo quiet. Jack savoured it for a moment longer, breathing long and slowly, as deeply as he possibly could. He was standing with his feet wide apart and his knees bent, facing the wall. His fists were tucked into his armpits, raising his shoulders back and dropping his lungs, giving them room to ventilate to their maximum. He would need this air that he was getting now because his opponent was better than he was; younger, fitter and better. All he could claim was the greater strength, should the chance come to use it, though that was unlikely.

He turned slowly and found his man ready, waiting respectfully along with the referee. They would have waited much longer, had that been his whim.

Kung Fu is not administered like the Japanese things, full of bullying and put-up-with-it-out-of-courtesy type pushing about,

with come here and stand there and bow and break and breathe now
and fight now and stop and start and God alone knows what else. It's
far less regimental than that. Kind of more personal, in
a bout it's just man against man, once it starts, until it finishes.
The referee judges, but does not interfere or conduct.

He waved them together, a slight little gesture with the forefingers of both hands and then stepped back to the wall. Through
the glass, from the lounge bar in the clubroom beyond, spectators
leaned forward. Most of them were Chinese, all were from Soho.
One of them was Sheng Dao Lee, respected here as elsewhere,
but especially here as a master of the Tai Chi Chuan, which is
the epitome of all physical art, as every oriental knows.

The young man started to circle, left to right, his open hands
moving rhythmically in front of him. Lamarre watched him without moving, gazing at his round moon face, and its flat
expressionless eyes, hardly flickering under their slit lids.

I bet you're fast, Jack thought, I bet you're fast as hell. He had
never seen or fought this one before, though he knew that the
young Chinese was an exponent of the Pak Hua, or monkey style.
That meant speed of reaction and a lot of ground covered in a
split second. It meant he could fly.

Lamarre had tried the monkey style and had found himself too
solid and squat for it but he had stuck out for something. You
had to have something in Hong Kong, besides the damn gun,
because half the time you couldn't use it, even if you wanted to,
though Jack hated the rotten things anyway. And a lot of the time
it was just big kids or junkies gone spare, or some woman who'd
flipped over something or other (Chinese women got very frayed
about things) and hell's bells, you couldn't blow people like that
away, you had to do better than that. So Jack had learned what he
could, as well as he could, about the thing they called Kung Fu, and
dammit if he hadn't got keen on it. Which was funny because he'd
have been the first to hoot and haw when Enter the Dragon stuff
came on. He'd have been right up there jeering, if he didn't know
better now.

His style was Wing Chun, the Tiger, which suited him best
because of its emphasis on strength and power rather than any
acrobatics. The Wing Chun fighter chose his moment well,
engineered it even, rather than relying on an opportunity and
placing his trust in the lightning speed needed to turn opportunity into accomplishment. Not that the young man circling Jack

was wearing pads out of fear of his power, no more than Jack was wearing them for any similar awe of the lashing feet of the monkey man. The pads were an agreed thing; they had both elected to fight hard this time, to immerse themselves in it. Jack because he wanted a mental break from his life, the other for reasons of his own.

The pads were of foam, shaped for wrists, ankles, insteps, throats and bound on with sleeves of elastic bandage. It was the pads that had drawn the audience to the glass.

The circling continued. He had been right round once now. He would not complete another circuit; he would close before that. There would be a moment, just one, when he was *about* to come. That was when he would be vulnerable, right then. Right now.

Jack charged.

The monkey man dropped sideways as Lamarre steamed in, planting his left hand on the floor and whipping his right arm back as a counterweight for the right foot that arced up to the policeman's throat. Lamarre checked and smashed it away, bent his knee as he ducked for the ribs, his hand coming down like a cleaver towards the black suited torso, but then he buckled. Folding his leg was the error. Unlocked, it had no strength; his opponent had simply flicked his leg away with a light blow behind the knee. *Goddamn* but that was bad. He shouldn't have bent his leg like that. A monkey man bent his limbs, not a Tiger man. He should have stayed tight, all the way.

They had rolled away from each other, stood up, recommenced the stalking. This time the young Chinese struck quickly, sensing Lamarre's anger and self-disgust, but to be dead honest, Jack didn't have much chance by then.

The first pass was a feint, to throw him off balance. The second one sent a foot sailing into his collar, followed by another — no, the *same* one, dammit — sinking into his side. Gasping, he slashed deep and wide, catching what could have been a wrist before a third kick took him in the small of the back. Then he went down, smiling, and the referee judged it to be finished.

My fault, Jack thought, rolling over to admire the new strip lighting, I should have had him right off. God that would have been nice, it really would.

He felt infinitely more relaxed now. He was composed again. All it would cost him were the aches in his body.

After a while he went off to shower and then came back into the clubroom. Sheng Dao Lee was seated alone.

'Do you await another, Sheng Lee?' Jack inquired.

'No,' said Sheng, his seamed old face crinkling up like a piece of tissue, 'please sit.'

Jack set his drink down on the little round table with its picture top covered by a glass sheet, and waited deferentially for the elder man to initiate the conversation. He got a surprise when it happened.

'I have read of the second murder by the person you seek,' he said with a slight inclination of the head. 'Please excuse my mentioning it, if it is improper.'

Mindreading again, Jack thought. Uh-uh.

'Not at all, Sheng Lee,' he said. 'Only I would have surmised that such a sordid affair was beneath your attention.'

'It troubles me that you are troubled,' the old Chinese said kindly.

'Am I troubled?'

Sheng Dao Lee tolerated this minor lapse of courtesy for the sake of circumstance. He decided to pretend he had not noticed it.

'You feared another murder after the first crime. What is different now?'

'Nothing,' Lamarre said, and then he added. 'I'm troubled.'

'Your fear now is for something worse,' Sheng said. 'That the killings will go on.'

That's obvious, Jack thought, no Chan Canasta trick there.

'Yes,' he admitted. 'It bears hard upon me, Sheng Lee.'

'Then you must catch this person.'

'Begging your pardon, Sheng Lee, but that is easier said than done. The killer has great cunning. That much is becoming clear to us.'

'So does the monkey man,' Sheng said, with his eyes twinkling like topaz in his brown, shiny face. 'But you almost caught him, did you not? And in the end, a monkey was able to trap a tiger.'

Trap? Jack thought, Trap?

'I failed miserably,' he said. 'A most lamentable display. I am ready to vomit at the thought of it.'

'No,' Sheng said firmly. 'You read him clearly. Your judgement was correct. Only the execution was flawed.'

Lamarre stopped trying to think of the next flowery line. He didn't want to talk about this. He didn't even want to think about it. He wanted some other thing in his mind.

'Sheng Lee?' he said softly, asking but not necessarily expecting an answer. 'Is someone threatening you? Triads? Do they want protection money?'

Sheng Dao Lee shrugged and looked at his watch.

'I have no problems,' he said. 'Other than life. If you will kindly excuse my atrocious manners I must attend to my restaurant, which will be opening soon. May I expect you later?'

'Yes, thank you, Sheng Lee. But much later possibly. I would like to think for a while first.'

'I will be honoured by your company. A guest perhaps?'

'No. I'll come alone. But later.'

Sheng Lee bowed and Jack was careful to return a deeper one, though it was unnecessary to rise. He watched the lithe old figure walk gracefully out of the lounge and then went back inside himself, pondering. A couple of young men were playing Pai Kau on an adjacent table, the dominoes moving like lightning between them. Jack looked at them without watching.

Cocked that up, didn't you?

But the old guy could do with some help. Maybe.

He was still contemplating it when they brought him the phone and then Tickle bulged up in Jack's ear like a boil.

'You listening,' came his familiar grate. 'We got this ten minutes ago. As far as the PO can tell it was posted somewhere between High Street Kensington and the Cromwell Road, between Marloes Road and Stanford Road. That's Mary Abbots area, right?'

Jack froze. Oh no.

'Jack?'

'Yeah,' Jack blinked. 'Yeh, go on Chief.'

'*Three down*,' Tickle said, and then he said it very slowly, like he was a reporter requesting copy. '*After endless mud, I am not quite palindromic Mary.*'

Jack blinked again. Harder.

'Got that, Jack.'

'Yeah,' Jack said, thinking 'after what?'

'It's signed by Reaper again,' Tickle muttered. 'So far nobody's got a fucking clue who it's about. Better stand by for something nasty though, Jack. Looks like this bugger moves fast.'

'Yeah,' Jack said.

TWENTY-TWO

Miriam finally whizzed into the Mews somewhere between midnight and twelve thirty a.m. She jumped out of her powder blue TR7, kicked the door shut and almost strode to the entrance to her petite little cottage before she remembered that a car had been stolen from the Mews recently and the police had warned residents about elementary precautions, such as locking the wretched things. She didn't actually *care*, on any profound level, whether the vehicle was taken or not. It was insured, she could afford a dozen anyway, but the whole thing would have been such a frightful *bore*, darling . . .

She went back and locked it. Then she went inside.

Miriam had had a hard day, what with one thing and another. The whole winter collection had to be reviewed by the end of the *week*, for God's sake, and some of those stupid girls didn't know how to wear a smile, let alone the contemptuous sneer that she wanted for her stuff, far less the articles themselves. Honestly, dear, she'd been at bloody fever pitch since lunch time, burning St Moritz like joss sticks and downing Noilly Prat by the pint. Didn't *anybody* understand her requirements? *Why* oh *why* were they all so damnably stupid.

Miriam leaned against the inside of the door with her back to it, shoved her fingers through her wild spikey coiffure and breathed deeply, through her elegant nose.

Tomorrow, she decided, things would get done, and she meant done.

In the meantime, it was a good night's sleep, *alone* thank you darling, for once.

Had it not been for the pressures of the winter collection, and the rank stupidity of the rest of the fashion fraternity, Miriam might well have gone home to one of her splendid houses on the fringe instead of her mews cottage in Chelsea. She also might have dragged some willing lover back with her; one of the dozen or so she kept in her stables for when mood made its demands. In either case, the black figure that watched her arrival, totally motionless from the shadows opposite, would simply have melted away, to return on another night. The figure knew she would come, though, almost certainly, because the ground had been prepared with great patience and great cunning — pause to reflect. Patience and cunning. How often had the two been paired, but how few were those that could truly claim to have cultivated both?

The figure knew there was some little time longer to wait. It leaned back to the wall and eased the weight of its feet.

Inside, Miriam kicked off her clothes and stood in her lounge naked, wondering whether another belt of Noilly Prat could possibly make any difference. Deciding she didn't know but cared less, she half-filled a glass and took it upstairs, flicking the downstairs light out as she went.

It was a very small cottage (though you wouldn't have thought so from the price); just two rooms upstairs, one at the front which Miriam used as a bedroom and office. That was where she created her creations: it was from there that the marvels of her imagining were showered upon a breathless world, from Knightsbridge to Fifth Avenue. Well almost to Fifth Avenue, anyway. There was no guest room, since all guests slept between Miriam's legs or somewhere thereabouts.

Miriam took her robe from the cupboard and draped it over the duvet so she'd have it in the morning, swallowed the last of the drink and turned out the light. To hell with make-up, to hell with shower, to hell with teeth, to hell with everything. Very quickly she became drowsy and started to drift. The bed felt cool against her body. She slid her legs from side to side, relishing it. Involuntarily she moaned with comfort. Subconsciously she wished she'd brought somebody back with her after all. Larry possibly, he knew what to do when she was tired, he was . . . so . . . mmm . . .

Her breathing became deeper, louder, reg-u-lar.

Outside the five mm wood bit started to turn, gently and slowly, with only the slightest pressure. The hand-drill made no noise, being freshly thickened with grease. The bit was new, very sharp and it bit easily into the soft wood of the door . . .

The figure flicked the pentorch over it periodically as it went through, checking the depth and the angle, making certain it would emerge inside at precisely the right spot, just below the top catch. The hole was running upwards at about fifty degrees to the horizontal. About right.

When it was done, it repeated the drilling at an identical point below the bottom catch. Then the drill went noiselessly into the bag on the ground and gloved hands took out the perfume spray with its ever-so-difficult to get bit of pipe on the end.

A bit of practice at home had sufficed for the spraying. The pipe would emerge inside at an upward angle in front of the catch. The hole for the oil was in the side of the pipe so the spray would come out horizontally almost, wetting the catch thoroughly without having to rely on gravity and viscosity to spread it around. It worked nicely. A couple of squeezes on the rubber bulb outside was ample.

The figure gave it a couple of squeezes for both catches. Now they were both covered with a film of oil on the inside, but it was colourless and odourless and the holes would be concealed underneath the catches so nobody would know they were there without actually touching them. It put the spray away in the bag, took out the transformer and the crocodile clips and the leads and the thin steel pins and placed them on the ground. Then it bent to the fuse box that was attached to the wall, about six feet to the side of the door. It was not locked, of course, because the meter man had to read the dials inside from time to time. The figure had looked inside it before, naturally, so there was no delay in locating the power circuit . . .

This better be good, Miriam thought, when it became clear to her that what had wakened her up really was the door bell, and what was more, it was still chiming. For a good length of time, she lay on her back blinking up into the dark before she yawned, threw back the quilt and lay there some more. The bell kept of dinging.

Oh, all right, she said, to herself, meanly, as she swung up and sat on the edge of the bed. Squinting at her luminous radio-alarm she saw it was almost one thirty a.m., so she said 'Oh, for pity's sake, darling,' and stood up. Slipping on the robe, she stumbled down the stairs.

She *might* have leaned out of the window or something, of course, it was a possibility. The figure could not discount it, not having been inside to see whether or not the bedroom window ever got used, but had she done so, there was something prepared to get her to the door. It would have been a case of pretending to be a copper, which all things considered seemed rather good, and then there was some line about her office up in town getting burned down so she'd have been all flustered and wouldn't have remembered the voice even if she'd survived what was about to happen, though it was an unremarkable voice anyway.

And she wasn't going to, was she?

The bell was still going when Miriam came out of the stairwell and went to the door. She was barefoot, and still tying the tassle round her waist as she switched on the light that lit up the path outside and saw the black clad figure through the frosted glass of the door standing there with its hand up on the bellpush, so that for the last few instants of the conscious life she actually *did* think it was a cop, before she reached out with both hands and gripped the two catches, top and bottom, to open it and something slammed up her arm and across her chest, blanking out all thought, locking limbs, jamming open eyes and mouth . . .

The figure waited until it saw her fall backwards and be still, watched the motionless form lying there on the hall floor and smiled. Time would tell if it had been a success was all it thought as it ripped the clips away and took the pins out of the catches and dropped everything into the bag, and the thing to do now was go. Without help, she had little chance, even if she still had a spark of life, and there was another job to do before morning.

Entirely defunct, and cooling at the rate of about one and a half degrees per hour, Miriam lay on her parquet floor until the milkman arrived. He nearly missed her, but when he realised the porch light was on — a thing which struck him as peculiar now that it was light — he stuck his face against the translucent glass and squinted inside. Seeing what he saw, he charged out of the Mews and up and down the road until he found a constable leaning against a wall with his thumb in the top pocket of his jacket, idly watching a street cleaning lorry working its way along the gutter. The constable raced him back, had a squint of his own, and broke in through a front downstairs window while the milkman looked on, filled with awe and excitement because, unlike the constable, this was the first time anything like this had ever happened to him. The policeman was about to open the front door when he realised there was something oozing down the frame in a long colourless thread with a droplet on the end, and he stopped. It didn't take him long to find the holes under the catches, and that was when he started to get suspicious, because only a constable he might be, but he wasn't an idiot.

'Dead,' he said to the milkman, through the window, 'you'd better hang about.' Then he started squawking into his handset.

That was about seven thirty.

Leech and his acolytes got there about eight. Lamarre got dragged in half an hour after that, just after a bloke calling himself Larry turned up, temporarily all smiles. He was sobbing in the lounge, just now.

'When'd it happen?' Jack said to Dr Leech, as he stood over the late Miriam, with his hands jutting out of his raincoat pockets. He let his look linger on her crotch, which had been exposed in the fall, and he felt slightly ashamed, but only for a second.

'Call it between twelve and three this morning,' Leech said, 'I'll know better when I've had her in the lab.'

Life and soul, Lamarre thought, as Leech started to hum *Stars and Stripes forever* without taking his eyes off the corpse.

'Any idea what killed her?'

'Not yet,' Leech lied, because he didn't want to say right at this precise instant, though of course he would say very soon. You didn't withhold ideas from the police, it wasn't done. 'What do you make of those holes, Inspector?'

Jack Lamarre stepped over Miriam's legs and bent forward to examine the holes. Obviously he noticed what looked like some clear slime creeping down off the catches, but he didn't fathom it right off.

'Doesn't look like a means of entry,' he muttered, 'though it could be. New one on me if it is.'

Leech wasn't looking at him when he glanced up. Instead he was half grinning at one of the forensic kids. Brian, in fact, who was squatting outside the door. Then he looked at Lamarre, but said nothing more.

Lamarre went into the lounge, still hoping. So far it wasn't anything for his plate. So far it was a probable murder, sure, near Kensington, sure, but nothing more. Enough to get him here, but that was all. In the other room, he ignored the man curled in the chair and ambled over to the bookshelf. Almost immediately he saw a big softback with the word, 'Miriam' down the spine, which

131

he took off the shelf and started to riffle through. It was a trade booklet of some kind, full of big glossy colour photos of girls in incredible gear. There were gold and silver lamé suits, pink and yellow tights, striped lengthways, which reminded Lamarre of medieval jesters, and all manner of outrages. One of them even had a pair of wings on her back. Another had what could have been rows of studded dog collars up her thighs. Dear oh dear.

'This her stuff, is it?' he asked the shuddering Larry.

'Yes,' sniffed the young man in the armchair. He sat up and put his head in his hands, so his big teddy boy quiff hung down over his thick crepe soled shoes.

'Bit way out if you ask me,' Lamarre opined.

Larry lifted up his blotchy face and held out his hand.

'It was *crap*, sweetie,' he said, verging on hysteria. 'We all *know* that. But it made a lot of bread. Is that a reason to kill her.'

'Jumping to it a bit aren't you, lad?' Jack said, putting the book back. 'Who said she was killed by anybody? She could have had a stroke.'

'Somebody broke in, didn't they?' gargled Larry. 'I'm not completely thick you know.' His voice broke on 'thick'.

Lamarre realised that the man was out on his own for the time being, thinking crazily. What he needed was sedating, not questioning. He was useless.

Leaving Larry staring across the room, he went back into the hall. This time Leech and Brian were conferring, and when Lamarre reappeared, Leech came straight to him.

'Come over here, Inspector.'

He pulled Jack down onto one knee and showed him Miriam's left hand. On the outer edge on the index finger, and the flat of the thumb, were two faint brown stains.

'Burns,' he said quietly. 'If I'm not mistaken. But no ordinary burns. There's no blistering, see? This browning is actual charring of the skin surface. If you want my bet, that's an electrical burn.'

'She was electrocuted?'

'I think she probably was. And that stuff,' he pointed to the oily slicks below the latches, 'is what, Brian?'

'Just some kind of high conductance oil,' Brian said. 'Could be one of a number. Soon find out.' They were both giving him their all so he went on. 'I reckon he shoved some kind of spray or hose or something up the holes, so's he could get the stuff all

132

over the door catches.'

'He wired the locks,' Leech explained. 'In all probability anyway. He knew she'd have to grab one or both of them, in fact both I'd say. So she'd get the shock when she opened the door. It looks like he was worried about skin resistance foiling his little trick, though. The skin's got a big resistance, see Inspector. If your hands are wet, then the resistance is less, because water's a conductor. Only this oil goes one better if it's what we think it is, because it's a much better conductor than water.' Leech shut up for a moment.

Lamarre followed that. God Almighty, this looked like a frigging pro.

'How'd he wire the locks?' Which didn't get an answer because he was rising as he said it, and going outside.

'What's in there?' pointing at the box.

'Fuses, meters,' Brian said.

'Have you looked?'

'Not yet.'

Lamarre bent down and put he eyes right up to the little knob on the outside of the box. So far, it was the only possibility for a print, so don't touch. Opening his pocket knife so he could slip open the box without using the knob, he was suddenly stopped by young Brian who jerked across him to point at the drainpipe beside it.

'New scratch there, sir.'

Leech came out and looked, so all three of them ended up gaping at an inch-long, half-inch-wide mark on the pipe where the paint had been scraped off, exposing bare metal.

'What the hell's that?' Lamarre said.

'That's his earth,' Brian told them confidently. 'One of the catches would have been live, the other earthed, so when she put one hand on each she'd have got it right through the chest.'

'Fatal, is that?' Jack stupidly inquired.

'Massive muscle contraction in the chest usually,' Leech said. 'Causes severe respiratory failure, or could even crash the heart. Fatal in either case.'

Leech and Brian stood up as Lamarre started to open the fuse box. They carried on discussing the technical side of electrical homicide like a couple of ghouls while the policeman eased back the little white door and peeped inside.

'Wonder if he used a transformer to get a bigger current?'

Brian conjectured.

'Assuming he got his source from in there?' spake Leech with an erudite sniff. 'Could have done. It's difficult to estimate the current, but those burns indicate something bigger than mains to me.'

The Reaper was grinning out at Lamarre, who was turning sick as a parrot and thinking Dear God help us.

'Right,' Brian said, 'see anything, Inspector?'

TWENTY-THREE

Considering what she was about, Elaine damn near jumped out of her jeans when Daph clamped clammy hands around her eyes. She jerked so hard she almost had the VDU on the floor, which would have meant four hundred and ninety quid of somebody's money. Daph was laughing.

'What *are* you doing?' she asked, looking at the screen, though computing wasn't her bag so it was just meaningless to her. 'Bit early for work, isn't it?'

'Just messing about,' Elaine said, flicking a few more keys and causing the contents of the screen to roll off, before Daph had a chance to read it. 'Got to get the hang of the system. Messing about's the best way.'

Daph just nodded.

'Come for a chat?' Elaine said, lightly, though it was a hike from Botany to Maths, so odds on Daph was on her way in. But no, wrong again.

'Yeah,' Daph said, and then she added, 'guess what? We had a robbery last night.'

'A robbery.' Elaine tried to imagine somebody pinching plants. But she knew better than that.

'Well, more of a theft,' Daph said. 'There's some cable missing.'

'Cable? What, like electric cable?'

'Right,' Daph said. 'There's a lot of it in our stores 'cause we run lots of incubators and things for plants and so on. Anyway, some of it's gone. Technician's accusing all the postgrads, daft old fool.'

Elaine just wondered.

'Why should anybody pinch a piece of cable?'

'Dunno,' Daph said. 'Lots of reasons I suppose. Anyway it's not all if you ask me, because they've got the police here and they're interviewing everybody in the department. It's swarming with them.'

'What?' Elaine seemed, ah, keen.

Daph just let it soak in.

'Have they had a go at you?' Elaine said.

'Right,' Daph told her proudly, 'first thing. But they weren't just on about the cable. They were on about more than that.'

Elaine went 'Oooh' and smote her cheek, so Daph leaned forward with relish, like.

'They wanted to know about the poisons in the labs and like whether I knew how to handle them and if I ever did handle them and all that.'

'Poisons?'

'Oh we've got lots of plant poisons. Horrible they are. Anyway, they were asking me where I'd been for the past few weeks.'

'Weeks?' Elaine gasped.

'Right. Every night and every morning, but especially the last few mornings.' (Elaine was smirking.) 'Well I mean, it's embarrassing isn't it? I had to say, didn't I?'

Elaine was still smirking.

Lamarre got back to the Yard at about eleven. He was tired, thirsty, pissed off and irritable.

Prendergast was waiting in the corridor. She mentioned it right off, though Jack reckoned he had most of it by now.

'Mire without the E, right, Al? That's endless mud. Then there's "I am" to make Miriam which almost reads the same backwards so it's not quite palindromic.' He was stabbing it out as he walked. 'What I want to know is, what kind of half cocked bloody Oscar sodding Wilde is handing us this shit, and where the hell does Mary come into it?'

'Miriam's an old form of Mary,' Al told him nervously. 'I checked.' She was half expecting a backhander, the way he seemed to be.

Lamarre flung his coat onto a filing cabinet and grinned hysterically. 'Right Al,' he said. 'Let's get to it. Got to pull this Reaper. But lemme get some tea first.'

'Sir.'

'Trolley anywhere in sight?' He'd arranged for a trolley to come round three times a day, with food on it to save people trickling off to canteens. 'I could use a ham roll.'

'Sir.' She wasn't grinning. She wasn't anything.

'What?' Oh no, not another. 'What's up?'

She was pushing a picture across the desk.

'I was just about to get that over to forensic. It's another one, sir.'

Up, Jack, he thought frantically. What could possibly be up?

'Who?'

'Sir?'

'Who?' he yelled. 'Who's fucking dead now, Al?'

'Nobody, yet,' she said, apparently firming up, to counter his imminent collapse into neurasthenia. 'This time it's just the picture that's turned up. You'd better go to the interrogation room. Sergeant Taylor's dealing with it.'

'Yeah, right.'

She came with him down the corridor. On the way, he asked about the Miriam picture. Bookshop, Gloucester Road, she told him. On the list.

Taylor was sitting across a bare table from a swarthy man with dried mud on his clothes. On his feet were wellington boots, turned down at the top, and these were encrusted with more of the hard yellow crud. The man looked nervous, his ruddy, burly face was drawn and hung, and he kept running his hands around the rim of his flat cap.

Lamarre leaned down to whisper to Taylor.

'Well?'

'He's a quarryman,' Taylor hissed. 'And he's missing some dynamite from his quarry, isn't he? That's what he found instead.'

'That' was the picture.

Lamarre muttered. 'Why the hell did you bring him in here? This room frightens people.'

'Uh?' Taylor looked surprised and slightly on guard. 'I didn't want to talk about it in front of everybody,' he said, and then he added, 'sir.'

'You could have used my office, you twat.'

'Yes, sir. I'll remember in future.'

Taylor slithered out, leaving Jack Lamarre looking at the quarryman. The man coughed and nodded at him and said hello, but still he kept his hands off the table, as if he was afraid of a truncheon suddenly descending across his knuckles without warning.

'What's missing, mate?' Lamarre said, studying Reaper à la Bruegel, number four. 'From your quarry, I mean. Where is it, by the way?'

'Up above the North Circular,' the quarryman said. 'Welsh 'arp reservoir.'

'What were you doing there today? That early, I mean. Bit of double time, like?'

'Me? No. I just went in to keep an eye on it like. I get paid for doing that.'

'I'm with yer,' Jack said. He had avoided asking the man's name, not wishing to appear unduly interested in *him* so much as *it*. 'What's happening there then?'

'They're pushing out the Sailing Club,' he said. 'Want a bigger marina like.'

'I see,' Lamarre said. 'Got to move a lot of earth then, eh?'

'Earth's easy,' the quarryman said. 'It's the rock that needs blasting.' Then he clammed up, conscious of having mentioned the reason he was here.

He's scared stiff we'll accuse him of not keeping enough security over it, Jack realised then. Bound to be.

'What's missing then?' he asked again, with a nice friendly, pally, sincere, trust-me type smile.

'Twelve sticks of medium strength dynamite,' the quarryman told him after thinking about it. 'Plus two blasting caps and a firing box.'

'The whole kit eh?' Jack observed.

'Yeah.'

'I presume a blasting cap is a detonator, the thing you shove in the dynamite to set it off?'

'Yeah.'

'And the firing box? That's the thing you wire to the detonator and sort of wind up and press a plunger and off it goes?'

'Yeah,' said the quarryman. 'Only there's no plunger. It's just a button.'

'I see,' Jack said. 'Tell me. How big is a stick exactly?'

'Eight ounces,' the man said.

'And how big a bang is twelve sticks?'

'Medium strength?' sniffed the quarryman with an authoritative air. 'Shift a good few tons of rock, that would, no danger.'

'OK,' Lamarre said, trying to hold the nonchalant expression on his face. 'And you found this picture here where exactly?'

'Inside the bunker, where the dynamite'd been nicked from. What is it?'

138

He didn't know, Jack thought. Not a man for current events then. You meet one occasionally, wouldn't know about another ice age 'til their teeth froze together.

'Just something we're very concerned about,' he said. 'And you'll have to be very quiet about, I'm afraid. If you'd like to go and have a cup of tea with that nice pretty girl that came in with me a minute ago, she'll tell you all about it.'

'Oh, yeah. All right,' said the filthy quarryman, cheering up no end. 'Yeah, right.'

'By the way,' Jack added. 'How was the bunker secured?'

The man was waiting for that, clearly.

'Listen chum. It was bloody tight. Padlocks top and bottom of the door. They must have been sawing for bloody hours to get the buggers . . .'

'Sure,' Jack said. 'We'll take a look. It's all right. Nobody's having a go at you.'

The man went out, huffing and puffing, but mollified. Al would settle him down.

How did he know where to go? he asked himself, for what difference it made. Well, it's easy really. Just drive around, keep your eyes open, watch the men at work. You could spot a bunker, anybody could, it was the law on keeping the stuff on sites that needed tightening up, though that wasn't the point either.

What mattered was that he was going to blow somebody up. God, Lamarre thought, he's actually going to blow somebody to hell and he's telling us in advance. And there's nothing you can do about it. Nothing at all.

TWENTY-FOUR

Parratt began to flip, but only slowly, as his beady eyes went through it a second time. As a rule, Henry went red, but this time he was going white.

It began thus: *To all undergraduates, Maths Department,* then a space of two lines and then an introductory paragraph which commenced: *All questions for the 2nd y. mid-session exams, and Part I finals in mathematics are kept inside the 1906A computer filestore, in a high security file . . .*

It was at that point, on the first reading, that Henry had first begun to feel funny, because he sensed a certain businesslike, no-nonsense air about it by then.

It proceeded thus: *To access the relevant file, log in to George III on any of the 6A's VDUs (ask a comp-option person how to do this) and then do* precisely *the following . . .*

It was all there, the whole rotten lot. The filename, the subfile, the password, the attach, list, spool, and all the other commands and procedures. A child could follow it. Anybody, but anybody, who read this could dump out the whole set of exam questions for the coming year's exams in about ten minutes, if that. Aaaargh . . .

Parratt let out a strangled bellow and tore the sheet of neatly typed paper off the notice board. It was at that moment that he realised it was xeroxed, so he wailed again and started racing to the first alternative notice board he could think of. Halfway down the stairs he came to his senses and it dawned on him trying to chase all the copies of this heinous note was unrealistic. Better to check to see if the damned file *had* been read, and then either erase it or cover it with a new password. He dashed for the machine room.

Henry prostrated himself over a VDU and called up George. George was the operating system of the ICL1906A computer upon which this horrible event had transpired. A soulless snob, George conversed via a subsystem called Jean, answering questions pertaining to the management of information streams kept on the computer's discs and tapes, known in the jargon as files.

Henry identified the exam question file and demanded to know how often it had been accessed in the last twenty-four hours. He couldn't ask how often it had been spooled out to a line printer or to a teletype because that kind of information wasn't retained by George, unless you programmed it into the file, which Henry hadn't, so when George/Jean primly informed him that there had been six accesses, he realised that he had no way of telling what *kind* of accesses they'd been. It could have been lecturers shoving in more questions for their courses, as he'd personally bullied them all into doing, or it could be somebody doing, doing . . . *this.*

Frantic by now, he screwed the sheet up and all but shoved it in his mouth. Then, unable to think of anything else, he ordered George to erase the whole file.

Somebody would die for this.

Still colourless, he hauled himself away to tell the departmental head.

'My dear Henry,' Koenig said, knocking out his pipe on the side of the waste bin, 'if there's a problem with my questions, you'll have to take it up with Dorothy. She handles that kind of thing for me.'

It was well known that Koenig would have nothing to do with computers, and though he had agreed to putting the exam questions in the machine, he had steadfastly refused to put his own questions in himself. His secretary, Dorothy, on the other hand, enjoyed playing with the pretty keyboard displays, which made a change from typewriters.

'It's not *your* questions, Werner,' Parratt said, as the pipe went on clanging deafeningly, 'it's everybody's. Somebody has got at the file.'

'What!' Koenig said, suddenly clearly angry. 'What!' He stood up, knuckles down on the desk like a gorilla. 'If you are telling me that somebody has destroyed that information after all the work my secretary and all the members of staff have invested in building it up . . .'

'Not destroyed, Werner! . . .'

'. . . we might just as well have stuck to the old method. Nothing wrong with pen and paper I have always said . . .'

'Werner!'

'Pardon?'

'Werner, please listen. It's *not* been destroyed. It's been leaked.'

'Leaked?' Koenig looked like a man to keep a distance from, which Henry Parratt did. 'What do you mean by that, Henry?'

Parratt straightened out the ball of paper in his hand and laid it on the desk between the Professor's fists.

'I found that on a notice board in this department, on this floor. I don't know how many others there are, or how long they've been up.'

Koenig started reading.

When he looked up again, he too had changed colour. Together they made a handsome pair, the one blanche white, the other a fetching shade of puce.

Next door, in Dorothy's office, Elaine had to work hard to keep her face straight when Koenig let rip. The sheer excruciating agony of Parratt's situation more than made up for her not actually being in the room to witness it.

The Prof was bawling about identifying the typewriter she'd used now. Well that was alright because it was right here; it was Dorothy's typewriter and that was as far as they were going to get there.

Steve Kane had been right to cut Henry Parratt down to size, she thought pitilessly. He really was a nothing person. It had been quite easy to find out the filename, terribly easy in fact. She had just listed out the filestore library and then asked the system for a runoff of any title it had, stopping it when it tried to oblige, because the only ones she was interested in were those for which it wouldn't. It was the one that threw up the demand for a password that she was after. Of course, any undergraduate doing comp-options could have probably got that far, but the password would have stopped them there.

But not her.

Henry would have to learn to shut his office door.

Catching her victim at the notice board and following him around to watch him being pegged out to dry had made Elaine late for her meeting with Norm, so she had run, splay-legged down the ramp towards the common room. He had been waiting, as usual.

It wasn't that she was fed up with Norm, or that she really

thought she had a chance with tasty Steve, it was just that, well, if you were going to get balled you wanted to optimise the ball boy, so to speak. But then, to give him his due, Norman Monk could try when he wanted to; just lately he'd been dressing even better than before, as if he was working up to something.

Going to try to get me in bed, Elaine thought, looking at him. Well, he just might.

Norm was explaining the hair-raising customs of a savage Dravidian tribe known as the Khonds, who flourished in Bengal in the nineteenth century before the British Army decided to wipe them out. Cannibalism was his latest fad, or so it seemed. This shower had an engaging habit of lassooing their victims on to revolving wooden elephants and hacking lumps off them as they went spinning round.

Hilarious, Elaine thought. You'd find it hard to believe, but Norm was actually capable of drawing pictures to go with this stuff, if he was encouraged. Miss Sweet concentrated on the TV up on the wall, because it was news time and a crowd was gathering underneath the set. Should shut him up with luck.

The newscaster gave out Miriam as the first item. A few students watching made noises; one of them whistled, another said something about a hat trick. Then the scene switched to the Mews where the man-on-the-spot shoved his face in front of the goings-on and made it clear the whole thing was a recording. 'The question on everyone's lips now is,' he assured the nation, 'when will the grim Reaper strike again? This is — ' The newscaster came back on then, admitted that the report was made earlier and then repeated the police request to the public for assistance. Once again the number of Lamarre's incident room came on the screen. Ring it, they said, any time, for any reason, however silly, please, do it. Or failing that, rub up a constable.

Elaine reckoned she knew that wretched number by heart now, and then she suddenly perceived that she had another built-in dig here, for some deserving sod. Parratt perhaps? How would he react to having the police drop in and harangue him about his whereabouts? Or Koenig maybe? No, she had plans for him yet, more plans.

Somebody else then.

She was beginning to enjoy this.

Meanwhile, chez Lamarre . . .

Sergeant Taylor had been fielding most of the fruits that had cropped up since the Reaper hit the headlines, but this one was special. This one he sent on to Jack Lamarre.

The whole incident room had seized up when he was led in and through to Lamarre's office. Even now he was inside they kept passing the glass partition to have a look at him. Jack was beginning to get riled. Any minute now he'd go out and box a few bloody ears.

Jack was sitting behind his desk with his head resting sideways on his palm, trying very hard to be patient. On the other side of the desk, against the far wall, stood a tall figure clad from head to foot in a long crimson robe that draped onto the floor. At the top of it was a deep hood that all but concealed the man's face, though if you looked hard enough you could make out some horn-rimmed glasses in there. Over his shoulder the figure bore an enormous scythe with a blade fully five feet in length, which would have caused some alarm had it not been obviously fashioned from a piece of four-ply, painted silver.

'What did you say your name was?' sighed Jack.

'I am the Red Death,' the figure replied.

'Oh aye, that's right. Red Death.'

'Yes.'

Jack blinked, wondering how to play this.

'Now, er, why did you kill these people exactly? Let's take Mr Hogan for starters, shall we?'

'They are a vexation to the spirit,' proclaimed the Red Death.

Jack went, 'Oh right.'

The figure spread his arms out sideways, so his scythe was revealed as virtually weightless.

'Ten thousand more shall die at my passing,' he announced.

'Get away,' Jack said calmly. 'Listen, you don't read Edgar Allan Poe, do you?'

'I beg your pardon?' said the Red Death in a perfectly conversational tone.

'Poe, Edgar Allan?' Jack said.

'How did you know?'

'Intuition,' Jack said.

'The man saw with vision,' Red Death said pottily, reverting to role.

'Not half,' Jack said. 'Now me, I like *The Pit and the Pendulum* best. Did you see the film?'

The Red Death was obviously totally flummoxed. He coughed in a most unsinister manner.

'I, ahem, did see it, yes.'

'Why don't you sit down?'

Hesitating slightly, the red robed figure came forward, hitched up his scarlet skirts and sat down. A pair of tennis shoes peeped out incongruously on the floor.

What the hell, Jack thought, Death's got to have stealth, right?

'Isn't it warm under that hood?'

The figure opposite him seemed to sag then, before throwing back the hood. Red Death was revealed as roughly middle aged, bespectacled, thin on top, and bucktoothed.

'You've spoiled everything,' he said sorrowfully.

'Sorry,' Jack told him. 'But we're very busy you know.'

'Yes, I suppose you must be.'

'You didn't hurt anybody at all, did you?'

'No,' admitted the Red Death. 'I never did.'

'Would you like a drink of something before you go home? Or maybe you'd like to take a look round. I bet you'd find it interesting.'

The man brightened up at that.

'Yes,' he said, 'I'd like that. I've never been in here before.'

'Not many people have,' Jack said as he stood up. 'You'll have something to tell your mates won't you, sir?'

Jack escorted him back out through the incident room and out into the corridor where he collared a policewoman and told her to take him round. The robe and scythe he was told to leave somewhere and pick them up on the way out.

Back inside, Lamarre stopped and looked at them all, studying their smirking faces with an expression of his own that mingled sadness and disgust, though sadness at what and disgust for whom was not clear. But one by one they stopped grinning and then one by one they stopped looking at him at all and just went on with whatever they were doing. Lamarre stayed there for a long time after that before going into his office without a word, closing the door very quietly behind him.

The policewoman dropped in with the papers about four and a half minutes later. Lamarre was seated at the desk, just looking down at the scuffed surface of it, so when she dropped the pile in front of him, he just started to read the one on top.

Which happened to be the *H & R Gazette*, with Harold H

going strong.

Jack just let it seep into his brain, but he was well into it before certain things started ringing bells. Then his eyes widened out and his mind went 'Uh?'

Bruegel? *Triumph of Death*? Cryptic bloody clues?

Jack went over it again as his annoyance rose. Then he bawled out for Taylor and immediately started going through the others to see if they had a similar quality of gen to Harold Higginbotham. They didn't.

'Look,' Jack hissed at Sergeant Taylor, 'he's even got the name of the sodding picture. He even knows about the clues we've been getting.'

'Blimey,' offered Taylor.

'Get down there,' Lamarre snarled, 'like now, see. And burn the bugger until he tells you where he got this stuff.'

'Right,' Taylor said, backing out like somebody withdrawing from the throne of a despot, quickly but not too quickly. 'Right, guvnor.'

'And don't come back till you've wrung it out of him,' Lamarre added. 'I don't want any of that protection of sources crap. This is a leak about a murder inquiry, see.'

'Got it guvnor.'

Jack just stared like a bull.

TWENTY-FIVE

Back in the common room, Steven Kane and Norman Monk had finished agreeing with each other that they could both get along with today's page three exhibit, anywhere, any time, anyhow, and then, because Elaine started huffing and blowing a bit, Norm had steered the talk around to the recent spectacular demise of Henry Parratt's ego.

'Honest, Norm,' Kane said, 'I never saw a bloke look so sick. Straight up, he looked just like he was going to throw up.'

'*Did* anybody look at the file?' Norm asked, breathless.

'Dunno. Got to assume it, yes?' Kane said. 'That means everybody's got to do their questions again. Absolutely everybody in the whole department.'

Elaine Sweet looked innocently from one to the other.

'Bet Koenig's mad as hell,' Monk hazarded.

'What do you think? He told Henry he could shove his computer up his thing (glancing at Elaine). Next time it's back to typists and filing cabinets. What I'd like to know is, who was it that put up the notices?'

'Got a nerve,' Norm said. 'More than I'd have.'

'Yeh, right,' Kane said. 'I'll swallow that Norm, but if it *was* you, mind yourself. I've got to rush.'

'It wasn't me,' Monk insisted, offended. 'It wasn't me.'

But Kane was leaving.

'OK, Norm,' he called back. 'It wasn't you. See you both.'

Monk watched him go until he was out of the swing doors, and then he turned to Elaine and said, 'He's convinced it was me, isn't he? You can see that. He's absolutely certain it was me who spiked that file. But it wasn't. I swear to God it wasn't.'

'I know,' Elaine said, showing her teeth.

'It's bloody annoying when somebody thinks you're kidding and you're not. Bloody annoying. What do you mean, you know?'

'It was me,' Elaine said, 'I did it.'

'What?'

'Come and screw me,' Elaine added.

147

'What?'

'Are you going deaf?'

'Wha . . . No. No, I'm not.'

'It's what you want to do, isn't it?'

'Well, yes. Yes.'

'So why don't we go and do it?'

'Eh?'

'Not too early for you, is it, Norm?'

'Too early?'

'It's only half past six. If you'd rather do it at midnight.'

'Oh no, no. Listen, me I'm not bothered. I mean I'm not particular. I mean . . .'

'It's what you do that counts, not when you do it.'

'That's it. That's right.'

Am I going barmy, Monk thought. This isn't what I expected. She's bloody sprawling all over me. Oh, come on, come on.

'All right?' Elaine asked, cocking her head when he'd had enough time to think whatever he was thinking.

'Sure.'

'Come on then. Your flat.'

Norman Monk drove them both to his flat in, shall we say, a daze. They clattered up the stairs, her in front, he studying her behind, and went into his room without switching on the lights.

Once inside, she bit him on the mouth and then neither of them said anything for half an hour or so during which Norman Monk had his fantasies fuelled for a decade. She bore him, she rode him, she pulled him up, pushed him down and in the end she brought him off so hard it made his back twinge and his head ring. It also left a slight ache in his coccyx, not unlike that he experienced after his finest feats of onanism.

Afterwards, after they had slept awhile that was, she lay with her head on her hand, resting on an elbow, looking down at him. He didn't realise it at first, until he sensed her breath on his cheek, and then he opened his eyes.

'What's up?'

'Nothing,' she said. But then she added. 'I've got a confession to make.'

'Oh yes, what's that? You've just given me a dose?'

'Ha Ha.' She punched him in the stomach. 'No, that's not it.'

'What's is it then?'

'I thought you were a queer. Well, I mean, I thought you might

148

have been a queer.'

Monk opened his eyes very wide then, but not angrily. He was amused. Very amused.

'Why the hell did you think that?' he asked mildly, but she didn't answer or look at him; she just ran her finger round and round on his chest.

Eventually she came around with another question, and that in fact answered his.

'What is it between you and Kane, Norm?' she asked, almost a little reverently. 'OK, I was beginning to think you were, like . . .'

'Fwends?' he said, grinning.

She giggled, 'Yes, fwends. I mean the two of you seem, I dunno, as if . . . as if there's something there all the time.'

'There's nothing there,' Norm told her. 'We're pals that's all. Drinking mates.'

'If it's none of my business, Norm . . .'

'No, listen Elaine, listen.'

Oh *fuck*, he thought. Tell her.

'It's a few things,' he began. 'Firstly it's Steve. Maybe you haven't noticed, but he's sort of out of it with the rest of the staff. He's sort of different.'

'I had noticed,' she said. 'Why is that?'

'He's got experience outside of that place and they haven't, basically, that's all. Next to him they're like big kids that never left school. He can't get on with them much, but he likes London so he sticks around. Anyway, that's why he spends more time with the postgrads than they do, that's why he comes down there into the common room a lot. It's why you see him in the union and so on.'

'So you and him became mates.'

'We had a few things in common. He likes anthropology, so do I. You knew that.'

'Yes.' Indians, Elaine thought. And cannibals.

'And then there's you,' Norm said.

'Me?'

'He fancied you as well, stupid. Didn't you know?'

Elaine Sweet reckoned she should have, damn and blast it, she sodding well should have.

'No, I didn't.'

'Well it's a gentleman's agreement at the moment. I've got the field. But the choice is yours, naturally.'

'Oh come on, Norm. You'll do.'

149

For now, she added upstairs.

'Anyway,' Norm said 'when two blokes fancy the same girl there's a sort of atmosphere, especially when she's around, I guess that's what you're picking up.'

'Lovely,' Elaine told him.

'Mad or anything?'

'Flattered. Is that it?'

'Just about. There's a lectureship he's trying to set up for me when I get my Ph.D. A bloke he knows at Sheffield might have one in Maths. He's a mate of Steve's. But you've got to keep quiet about that.'

'You make it sound like big business. It's only a job isn't it?'

'You'll learn,' Norm said sonorously. 'University appointments are a sordid matter. Honest. Knives were never sharper.'

She rolled over on her back, taking in some of the things he'd said, suppressing a mysterious feeling of guilt.

'I think I'll go now, Norm. I'm tired. Do you mind?'

'Nah, 'course not,' he said. 'There's a few things I've got to do myself.'

They weren't looking at each other, so it was just words.

Before they got up, he said, 'That thing you did to screw Parratt?'

'Yes?'

'Why didn't you bring me in on it? We did the other one together, on Koenig's car.'

'Dunno,' she said vacantly. 'Just wanted to try it on my own. Not mad are you, Norm?'

'No, 'course not,' he said, and then, in a lower voice and after a little pause, he said, 'I know another good one for Koenig though.'

'Really. What is it?'

'It's dead good,' he said, excited. 'I've been thinking it for weeks already because I never liked that bugger. Even when I was an undergrad I hated him, the foreign sod. The only trouble with it is that it might not work without money.'

'What do you mean, money?'

'It involves a lot of scientific hardware and that means dealing with firms. I can make it look good but I don't know if they'd play ball quickly enough or without some money. We could try it though.'

Elaine was more than intrigued already.

'Tell me more, Norm.'

TWENTY-SIX

Later on, around nine, it was best behaviour time, for Al's sake.

Detective Sergeant Prendergast had mentioned it to her boss again the night before, reminding him that he'd said he'd go and letting him know tonight was the night *they'd* be in town. That was after two killings and now it was after three and Jack must be up to his neck in mire, yet here he was in his beautiful never-seen-before suit and a matching tie and a crisp white shirt, shaved and combed and smelling lovely. Jack looked like an ad for Hornes and Al was chuffed as hell about it.

'Tell me, Inspector,' said Mrs Prendergast, 'this grim Reaper we're hearing about. Do the police hope to catch him soon?'

Jack glanced at Al then, inquiring. Does she know? was what the glance asked. Does this charming little mother of yours know?

'It's Jack's case, really, mother,' Al said. 'He's virtually the officer in charge of the operational side of it.'

'*Really,*' put in Mr Prendergast. 'I say, just wait till I tell them that in Cheltenham, eh dear?' He went back to Lamarre. 'Still, I don't suppose the Inspector can tell us much, eh Inspector? Everything very confidential, eh?'

'Please call me Jack,' Jack said pleasantly. 'Actually you're getting most of what there is from the press and TV. You see, it's a procedure these days. Mass publicity is used by the police all the time. The days of keeping the media in the dark are gone really.'

'Is that a fact?' Mr Prendergast said. 'Well I never. I bet there's some things though, eh?'

'Well yes,' Jack conceded demurely. 'Some things we keep quiet about. Clinchers, you could call them. Just things we'd use to make sure we've got the right chap when we pull him in.'

'Ah yes,' the older man said shrewdly. 'I've got it.'

None of this gay badinage was cutting any mustard with Mrs P though. The last thing she tuned in on was that her little girl was mixed up with a man that was chasing a man that killed people for fun.

'But are *you* involved with this Reaper affair, Alison?' she said nervously. She was fidgeting with her meal.

'Well, I'm working on the case, mother,' Al said. 'I work for Inspector Lamarre, as I told you.'

What happened to Jack, thought Jack.

'If it's danger you're concerned about, Mrs Prendergast,' Jack said, 'I assure you there's no danger. Alison's running a slight risk of flat feet but that's all.'

'But he's a murderer. And a maniac. Surely that's dangerous.'

'He's ill,' Jack told her. 'Ill in the mind.' Somewhere in his memory was the psychiatrist telling him about insanity not being the same as — what? Character disorder? He pushed the thought down again. 'Please believe me, Mrs Prendergast. The police have dealt with many people like this in the past. They're a danger to their victims, but not to the police. This isn't America, you see. Our maniacs don't have guns and suchlike. It's just a question of finding him, and then it'll all be over very quietly.'

Jack was glad she didn't actually know that he wasn't speaking from personal experience, because without that knowledge, she'd just assume that he was.

She seemed mollified now, though, judging from appearances. She was eating again anyway.

'Just how close are you to arrest, Jack?' Al's father asked, looking for a flashy phrase.

Jack decided to take that one in the outfield.

'Well, that's a phrase that gets used by everybody but the police in fact. The truth is we never know how close we are to an arrest. One day you could be stumbling about in the dark with nothing at all to go on and then suddenly, next day, you've got something like, say, a car registration number, which as you know immediately gives you a name and address and suddenly you're on the verge of closing the case. That's the truth of it.'

Jack hung up there because he didn't want to put in too many details, though he could have. He could have said that they were saturating the case in a way seldom seen before. He could have mentioned a bunch of libraries, each being taken apart by forensic teams, and a whole locality for each one of them to be house-to-housed by scores of cops, and a few hundred members for each one, all being cased out by more droves of police. He could have mentioned Imperial College being sieved by forty or so detectives for clues on Aconitine, clues on typewriters, clues on people, clues on anything. He could have talked about three victims having their histories and family trees and circles of acquaintances interviewed and probed and checked and correlated and alibied. He might have mentioned the by-now hundreds of police looking for bits of cable and transformers and odd sticks of dynamite and vendors of conducting oil, mild steel rods, bamboo and so on. And if he'd gotten fed up with all that front line stuff he could have spared a few words for the back up, the collation and the condensing and the crosslinking and the indexing and the computing and the processing and the interfacing to the press and the public and the media and the brass and the world and the flesh and the devil. Jack could have said all of that and more but he didn't. He didn't say it was all going on nonstop and that it was getting nowhere at all and that he was becoming shot away and scared shitless by it. He didn't say Reaper three, cops nil, prognosis blank.

Jack just kept it all inside, like a tight ball of string in his guts.

'So it's not a fair question, eh?'

'They're all fair, Mr Prendergast, any copper will tell you that.'

'I must say, I find it fascinating,' the old man said passionately. 'Don't you dear?' And truth to tell, Mrs Prendergast was agreeing with him.

'Well, you know, there are a great many misconceptions about police work, even today,' Lamarre said loftily, 'and of course, murder is a prime example of a crime absolutely steeped in misconception.' He was dressing it up a bit to impress them, so they'd think what a really smooth, turned-on, premier type law enforcement executive their daughter was working for.

'I should say so,' agreed Mr Prendergast.

'The most common fallacy there of course is that it's usually a question of whodunnit, whereas that simply isn't the case,' Lamarre went on. 'Usually we know perfectly well whodunnit. The problem is usually to establish proof of the fact. To complete the chain of evidence, as we say.'

He carried on like that through the whole meal. As we say, in our jargon, putting it technically, the truth is, etc., etc. He was bulling like mad and they loved every minute of it, and every so often Al would look at him as if to say thanks, Jack, thanks.

Lamarre dropped into the Yard on his way to the Vauxhall

Bridge, which was his best route home after dinner, though he wished he hadn't. Not that it would have made much difference because the phone in the restaurant started ringing just after they all left and Jack's phone at home, by his bed, would have been ringing when he arrived.

'PO sent it round as soon as they sorted it,' Taylor said, though he was thinking maybe the thing to do was keep his mouth shut.

Lamarre stared at it, trying to think. It was addressed in the same way as all the others, though the PO were accelerating the sorting of anything addressed to the police by now, and the mail section downstairs had a Reaper squad detective on them all the time. Jack could taste his meal starting to repeat on him.

Go on, open it.

Jack opened it, and read it, very very slowly, so he wouldn't have to go over the filthy thing again. *Four down*, it said, *Literally gold* and it was signed like the others, with the word *Reaper*.

'Literally gold?' Jack said softly, but not to Taylor; he just said it. 'What the hell does that mean?'

'Guv?'

Lamarre seemed to realise that Taylor was there then. The Sergeant had his usual insolent sneer on his face, which brought Jack back down to earth.

'What about this hack in bloody Richmond then? What's he got to say for himself?'

'Claims he was rung up,' Taylor said.

'Rung up? Rung *up*?'

'That's what he says.' The sergeant shrugged. 'And he won't budge. Says he was rung up by an anonymous person with a Welsh accent, claiming to be the Reaper. Gave him the stuff about the picture and the warnings and rung off. One call only, not more than twenty seconds. Claims it happened so fast he had trouble remembering what was said.'

'Man or woman?' Jack said.

'Couldn't tell. Very high-pitched voice.'

'Deliberately high-pitched, for disguise?'

'Could be, guv.'

'Like the accent, eh? Welsh one's easiest to imitate I'm told.'

'That's true, guv.'

'Probably read the *Gazette* line yesterday about us concealing details, so phoned 'em in to sow some confusion, yes?'

154

'That's what Higginbotham reckoned.'

'Oh, is it,' Jack said menacingly. 'Well it's all *balls*, right? Nothing but balls. That fucking Higginbotham's a bloody liar. He's got his bloody hooks into somebody involved with this investigation and I mean to know who it is. Are you listening to me?'

'Definitely, guv.'

Jack glared at the Sergeant for a while as he slowly simmered down, and as he stared, he began to wonder if Taylor could actually possibly really be smirking at him or was he just getting paranoid all of a sudden.

'Get Sergeant Prendergast,' he sighed, eventually.

TWENTY-SEVEN

Mickey's Moll, to be polite, was caught short.

It was a little after three a.m. when she opened her eyes and realised that it was her bladder that had woken her up, and that the call was a strong one, certainly a lot stronger that a going back to sleep one anyway.

But it was niiiiiice, here.

Mickey wouldn't have one of those continental quilts; he found that his feet stuck out from underneath it during their imaginative couplings, and you had to admit that when it got to the middle of the night like this, blankets were so comfy and warm and cosy that they took some beating, you just felt you could stay in bed for ever.

Unless you needed a pee.

Her mother didn't like blankets. Her mother liked continental quilts. Less bother, her mother said, less fuss. Mickey's Moll always agreed with her mother, though she couldn't see herself making another bed as long as she lived, not as long as she remained Mickey's Moll.

The Mickey in question, he that was surnamed Gold, and did lead the pop group Samson Delilah, was snoring on her left. She couldn't see him in the pitch dark but she could hear him and feel his bulk in the bed. Should she wake him when she got back? Would he *need* waking? She was certainly in the mood, and would definitely be ready when she'd emptied herself in the loo. They had the place to themselves tonight but brother Bobby would be round early because of tomorrow's session so Mickey would want to be up and about; he wouldn't want anything long and fancy then. Somehow this whole line of thought seemed wrong to Mickey's Moll. Wasn't it men who were meant to spend their time theorising about women's wants, and not vice versa?

You could of course be a nympho, she told herself, as she slipped out of bed and groped for the bedroom door. Without bothering to look for lights she padded out across the landing

156

towards the bathroom.

The thing that was creeping up the stairs just stopped.

In the bathroom, the girl pulled on a little light over the sink and got on with it. She had her eyes shut to keep out the light from the little fluorescent tube but her face was in the right direction so when the door made a little noise and she opened them and saw the handle move she damn near fainted. Her voice failed her at first, but then she managed to say something like '. . . that you, Mickey?'

The landing light suddenly snapped on, flooding the glass panel at the top of the bathroom door.

'Mickey?'

Across the landing the bedroom door opened soundlessly, allowing the light to slide along the wall and into the room. Mickey turned over, still asleep, to put his back to it, making a small grunting noise as he did.

A dark shape began to appear in the gap.

Finishing up in the bathroom, the girl crazily washed her hands before trying to open the door. Nothing happened. The handle refused to move. On the landing side, a short-bladed penknife was wedged in the opener slot and a leather belt was stretched from the bannister to the bathroom door handle. It would need more strength than she possessed to open it.

'Mickeeeeeey!'

Mickey Gold opened his eyes with a start and flung himself round to a half sitting position facing the bedroom door. He could not have seen the figure clearly, being half asleep still and having it against the light. He probably saw nothing more that a large black outline but in any event it wasn't seeing but surviving that was his problem because that was when the hammer took him across the eye socket, splintering it like an eggshell and sending him screaming across the bed.

In the bathroom, Mickey's girl friend heard the shriek and stopped wrestling with the door handle and covered her mouth with her hands and just stared in horror at the door. She started backing away from it, towards the basin.

Mickey caught another blow in the upper jaw as he tried to get away. His mouth was suddenly full of bits of his teeth. He was on the other side of the bed now, holding out his hands to try and ward off whoever or whatever was coming at him but when he looked through the one eye that was working he saw it

157

bouncing over the bed with its coat flying, a great batlike monstrosity leaping at him, swinging a white shafted . . .

The girl heard another nauseating screech, this time with a sob tagged on the end, like the sound of a man being butchered alive, and then no more for ten seconds or so.

Then it started.

A series of slow, methodical, splashing blows, accompanied by almost animal grunts and snarls, and broken by the sound of something being dragged about a floor.

Unable to comprehend the horror beyond the door, but equally unable to control her imagination, the girl huddled against the wall of the bathroom, crouching on the floor, with her hands crammed deep into her mouth. Spasmodically she shook her head in short vigorous bursts.

It went very quiet then.

The figure was standing in the doorway of the bedroom with the hammer dangling from its hand. The eyes burned. In the dark they would have glowed like coals. The lips housed a leer of malice and satisfaction so deep and abysmal and unspeakable that it was better for the girl not to have seen it.

She knew it was there though. She could hear it, with her senses tuned like those of a trapped beast, as it came across the landing right up to the bathroom door.

She saw the shadow in the light under the bottom.

She started to whimper, losing what tiny scrap of control she had left. Shuddering in the voicelessness of true hysteria, she started to play with her tongue. The figure leaned its face to the door.

'Shhhhhh . . .'

It was drawing the head of the hammer around the door in a series of long looping patterns. Inside, the girl's eyes followed the sound as it went up and down, side to side, and the little sound went on and on.

Shhh . . .

Lamarre had been up half the night himself, helping Taylor and his band out with the interviews and the hordes of sprouting screwballs. Plus he had particularly wanted to chat with Larry and Madge, both not back on the rails, both useless. Later on he had a mind to chat with Harold of Richmond.

Four o'clock when he toppled into bed, not long after seven

when they dragged him out again and over to St John's Wood.

Unshaven, unwashed, tired, bedraggled, tousled, sour in the mouth and *everything* else, he now stood against the wall outside the bedroom and surveyed the scene within.

Nothing was moving in there but the inevitable Dr Leech who was kneeling on one of the many pieces of paper all over the floors, doing things with his hands at the head of what Lamarre assumed to be Mickey Gold's corpse. In fact, at what Lamarre assumed to be Mickey Gold's head and you couldn't have been a hundred per cent certain of that.

The only sound in the whole place came from downstairs, and that was a wailing noise full of words like 'man' and 'God' and interspersed with the soothing voice of what was probably a cop. Who was doing the wailing, though, Lamarre hadn't ascertained yet.

Tiredly, reluctantly, his eyes took it in. Quite a bit of blood, not oceans of it, not enough to make the filthy swine actually drip as he walked out, but quite a bit. Sprinkles and smears mostly, except on the body itself and around the foot of the bed where it lay. There was a hell of a lot there. These other marks could have been where he fell against a wall, or where the hammer threw some off as it swung through the air.

Oh, yes, they knew it was a hammer. It was on the pillow for them to look at, the shape of its head almost indiscernable in the clogged mass of congealed blood, brains and hair at the end.

Lamarre looked at the bathroom door again, which he had noticed when he first came up the stairs. Those long bloody marks could be — what? A figure of eight? An S? Or just marks. He went into the bedroom, watching where he put his feet.

'We'll have to stop meeting like this,' he said to Leech.

Leech looked up at him, and when he moved his head, Jack saw that the rubber gloves on his hands were crimson up to the wrists.

'I'll stop if you will,' said the pathologist. 'It's your friend again, you know.'

'So I gather.' He tossed his head to one side. 'That's got to be the weapon, I suppose.'

'No doubt about that, Inspector. But my, didn't he use it though. I'd say he turned him over a few times to give a good thorough all round bashing. There's hardly a spot on his head that isn't . . .'

'Don't get graphic,' Jack said. 'I ain't in the mood. Just put in the brief, please.'

He left the room, wondering if a swift heave would make him feel better, and met a senior uniformed man coming up the stairs.

'Inspector Lamarre?'

'That's me.'

'I'm Inspector Davies. It's another of yours I'm afraid.'

'Right.' Jack took the paper that was being offered to him. 'Where was it?' He looked at it. Same as the others. Exactly.

'Downstairs, rolled up in a vase over the fireplace. He marked the wall over it with a few little crosses. Kisses, like!'

'Kisses?' Lamarre said softly, a look of ultimate disgust in his eyes. 'In blood, I suppose.'

'Don't think so, no. More like a black fibretip marker pen. There's one on the fireplace.'

Lamarre almost gave up trying to fathom this one for the moment. This just didn't make sense. Not this particular one, the whole thing, it just didn't scan. First he sets up the golfer with a poison most people would never have heard of, let alone be able to find, let *alone* know how to handle, and he brings it off like a professional hitman, allowing for the technique, of course. But then he goes and harpoons a bloke in his swimming pool with a lump of filed-down metal on the end of a pole, like a fucking savage lancing a fish. And then he hits the Miriam bird with a method the like of which nobody in the whole force had seen before. It must have broken his brain to figure out all that stuff with the drill holes and the oil, and then he had to wire the catches to the box, earthing one to the drain to push the charge through her chest. Leech reckoned the current that dropped her was a lot bigger than you'd have got from two fifty volts so he boosted the mains voltage somehow, transformer probably. According to forensic that meant calculations on his part to make sure he wouldn't blast out the primary fuses and spoil the whole thing. What you've got here, they'd said, is an evil genius, and Lamarre was beginning to believe that, especially when the explosives went as well, but hellfire, what's a genius doing in a place like this? Did a genius do things like this?

We've got an imitator, Jack thought. An imitator with harpoons and hammers. We've got Harold to thank for this.

But then he thought, no, wait, that's not right. Look at the timing. If there's an imitator then he's been around since the harpooning, which is three killings ago now, *pre* Harold, but they've not overlapped. An imitator could have overlapped. They're not overlapping, they're alternating. First clever, then crude, then clever, then crude. Yes, that's it, he's alternating for some reason. Why's that? To show us he's hard as well as intelligent? Probably. That's a psychopath, according to the shrink. Clever, crude, clever, crude. This one's crude, so the next one's . . .

Bombs are clever.

The next one's the bomb.

That'll have to be clever, won't it? For his own sake.

'Who's that downstairs doing the yapping?' he said.

'Dead man's brother, name of Bobby Gold. He turned up first thing and found it. There's a girl as well, in fact. She was locked in the bathroom, don't know how yet.'

'Well maybe *he* locked her in. Seems reasonable doesn't it?' Jack said sharply.

'Yes, it does. Couldn't get through to her though. She was in a sort of trance. Just couldn't talk. Didn't seem to hear anything or see anything. Stark naked too.'

'Where is she?'

'Hospital. She was in a bad way.'

Jack breathed in hard, blinked slowly.

'*Which* hospital?'

'Sorry, er, Royal Free, Hampstead.'

Jack Lamarre looked at the picture again. Which one was this then? He knew by now that the one in the quarry came from the bookshop in Thurloe Street. Still no new ones yet, which was something. Not sodding rotten bloody much, but something.

The phone was ringing in another room downstairs.

'Any point in me talking to him down there?'

'Not if you've got anything better to do,' the other Inspector said. 'I'll handle him if you want. Come back to you.'

'OK,' Lamarre said 'If you . . .' and then he stopped because one of the cops downstairs had used Jack's name on the phone. 'He's here now,' was what the cop said, 'I'll get him.' And then he started to shout up the stairs before he saw Jack coming down, so he stopped.

'Thanks,' Jack said to the Inspector in uniform, and then, 'Phone, right?' to the other.

'In there, sir.'

'OK.'

Jack picked up the receiver and put it to his face as he checked his watch.

'Lamarre,' he said, realising the rotten thing had stopped again. 'Hello?'

It started very faintly, like a rustling far away, and then it started to grow, but very slowly so Jack had to stop everything, mind, motion, breathing, everything, to try and catch up on it and identify it as it got louder, and then, all at once, as if the realisation was holding itself back until it had blossomed for a fuller impact, he knew it was laughter, lots of laughter from lots of voices, old and young, male and female, hysterical laughter, and jeering, mocking laughter which held him there with the phone against the side of his head until it just exploded full volume into his cranium and made him snatch the whole handful away.

'Hello!' he bawled into it after a helpless couple of seconds, 'who is that?' but of course the phone was buzzing by then.

Reaper smiled whimsically at the phone for a little while after breaking the connection, with the laughter still blasting away from the machine, and then, after a mysterious and unconscious frown, reached over and turned off the tape recorder, slicing the noise off like a blade, into silence.

Well, yes, perhaps it was a trifle puerile, but one needed a bit of light relief, and collecting the laughter noises had been easy, radio and TV assumed. All in all Reaper was amused by it.

Reaper's amusement took a slight step down when the comedian came back to mind. Archie Chatwin that was, photo from the *TV Times* this time, a two-page spread showing the fat lout in all his vulgar opulence, enough to make you cringe on sight.

It had always seemed to Reaper that this pig was somehow more deserving that the rest, being even less talented if that was possible. After years of smut in Northern working men's clubs, and following what could only be assumed was a temporary shortage of comedians, Archie's rise had been meteoric, as they say. They were serving him up on half a dozen channels now, in millions of homes, a star if ever there was. If Reaper hadn't put a stop to Nelson Hogan's nonsense he'd probably have been booked for that as well, so how exalted can you get?

Anyway, Reaper had decided some time ago that the world had had enough of his —pardon me — marvellous wit and superb singing voice that he was beginning to treat the people to by now, to say nothing of his beautiful mansion in Chesham and his collection of fine cars which always appeared with his pictures, together with Archie's account of how much it all cost, because that was about his style and level, with his gold bracelet and the diamond rings on both of his podgy hands, the jumped up petty little spiv.

Oh yes, Reaper felt different about Archie. Sort of cold and sick it was, not at all like the nice bloodwarm glow that came with the others, more like touching a slug. In fact, the only good thing about Archie was his general overall roundness, which seemed to auger well for a nice big splash when the time came . . .

TWENTY-EIGHT

Staff meeting, Koenig in the chair as departmental head and keen to demonstrate no loss of ribald charm despite recent outrage against his person. By way of proof he had Lilly Bankes foaming at the mouth by Agenda point two.

Doctor Lillian Bankes was in charge of admissions and had been imprudent enough to provoke Koenig in connection with point one, which was 'Committees'. Lilly said she thought there were too many of them by a half. Why, some members of staff didn't know which committees they were on, so rarely did they meet, and she knew because she'd asked around. The library committee, for example, whose function was to discuss book purchases for the departmental library, had not met in a year, but in that period a lot of books had been bought so the committee was clearly ineffective. And as for the rooms' committee, nobody seemed to know what that was for at all.

'It's for allocating rooms to functions,' somebody said. 'We have more functions than rooms so we need a rooms' committee.'

'Very funny,' Lilly said.

'Who's on it?' Koenig demanded.

Nobody spoke.

'Well, I quite agree,' Koenig said. 'This is silly. I move we abolish this rooms committee and the library committee too. Anybody who feels they have a strangling need for a certain book can just come to me about it.'

Steven Kane knew that Koenig had been hogging the book money himself, just as they all knew. He found that matter just as ludicrous and petty as all the others. This whole pantomime twice a term got him down. What was on his mind at the moment was something else entirely.

Point two was admissions. Interview time was round again. Lilly said, 'I've got sixth formers coming in from schools. More than five hundred to see this year.'

'*Five hundred*, Werner,' she emphasised.

'So what?' Koenig said.

'They've got nowhere to sit is what.'

'Nowhere to sit? Nowhere to sit?'

Lilly waggled her finger about to the assembled staff.

'Admissions are falling,' she said. 'Not as bad in Maths as in other subjects I know. Our applications aren't down as much as elsewhere either. I know that too. But we want to make a good impression, don't we?'

'Do we?' Koenig yearned for a department with no under-graduates at all.

'I'm not asking for much,' Lilly said. 'Just a place they can sit while they're waiting to be interviewed. A few easy chairs, a coffee table, something to read.' She didn't see a lot of sympathy around so she added, 'Well otherwise it's the corridor outside my office.'

Koenig said, 'Lilly. We've got a committee for this. Somebody just mentioned it didn't they? This is surely a question for the rooms' committee, not a departmental meeting.'

'You've just abolished that, Werner,' a voice said.

'Did I?' Koenig said blandly. 'How remiss.'

That was when Lilly got the froth.

Kane faced it. Norm was drifting away into something with this girl. It was more than a mere table-end job, the fool was getting stars in his eyes. Whatever he was getting up to with Elaine was going to make their relationship difficult, wasn't it? He was going to have to do something about it, wasn't he? And quickly. Was that going to be a problem or just a pity? Or neither? Or both?

'Jack?' Al said, after obviously thinking a little bit about it, 'why don't the Chinese mix the rice with the rest of the food. Like in Indian restaurants, where they pile the curry on top?'

'Boiled rice is easier to eat with chopsticks if you take it on its own,' Jack said, demonstrating.

'Uh?'

'Indians don't use chopsticks, Al.'

'Oh, hell, yes,' Al gushed. 'Yes, of course.'

Stupid girl, stupid girl, she told herself.

She watched Jack bobbing about the dozen or so little dishes he had in front of him, stabbing away with the sticks, a bit here, a bit there. She'd stopped eating already.

'Thanks for the performance, Jack,' she said, wrinkling up the old nose.

'Enjoyed it,' Jack said, truthfully though. 'Your father's a gen guy. But your mother's a worrier.'

'I know, I know.'

Lamarre kept eating, while his sexy sergeant sat opposite with her elbows on the table and her hands clasped and her chin resting on the backs of them. The hair was down, twice as long as in the office, miracle of miracles.

'I'm very fond of you, Al,' he said, and he said it suddenly and matter-of-fact, so that there was no hint whatever, none at all, of the effort and courage he had needed to muster to say it. Even as it was he was already thinking that he'd made a real pig's ear of it. Very romantic that was, he was thinking, what with a mouthful of curried bloody limes as well.

But Al knew, she just knew, and she said so. 'I know,' she said, without moving.

Lamarre coughed. 'I was really freaked with that phone thing. He was rubbing it in, I reckon. Making mugs of us, I mean.'

'Definitely,' Al said. 'We were all going on gold. I was even looking for the chemical symbols for it, you know, the letters as it were. I mean it said *literally* . . .'

'Yeh, right,' Jack said tiredly. 'I was going for foreign languages.'

'. . . I thought it might be pointing to a jeweller or something,' Al finished off, helplessly.

Silence. Medium length. Not strained.

'We'll get the Reaper, Jack.'

'I know. Sooner or later.'

'Sooner. This can't go on.'

Lamarre pulled himself out of what looked like gloom coming up, and shoved the bowl away from him. He started waving for a waiter.

'Been meaning to drag you in here,' he said 'the boss is a friend of mine. Nice old guy, you'll like him. I think he's got some kind of problem at the moment though, but you've got to be careful with these people when it comes to . . .'

He nearly missed it.

'. . . fond of you too Jack,' was what she'd said.

Later on, after some more work in the Yard, Al legged it home to her flat on the tube. Just recently she'd been wishing she had a car and she'd been researching prices and looking at models. Of course, she'd have to go for the economy end of the market on her pay, but she hadn't been able to resist buying a couple of the big glossy mags that were full of page after page of the big, long, flat, wide, shiny executive jobs. You could look, after all, and you could dream.

First thing she did when she got in was mix a drink, drop into a chair and think through a glossy. There was a long article in this week's issue about how much they cost and how you can get a thou off here and there if you shop around. Of course, there's availability to consider on jobs like Maseratis but according to this jive here the people who deal in these things were making vast sums, wondrous to the mind. Look at this kid here (photo of dashing young man in double breasted Saville Row threads, fondling a phallic Porsche), heir to a chain of dealers, a *chain* if you like. Bet he wouldn't be thinking about buying a Mini if he was a lady copper, Al concluded in a sort of Freudian cul de sac. Then she tossed it aside and stripped off.

Five minutes later she was steaming in a hot bath, blissfully unaware of much at all but the smell of the Badedas and the tiny crackling of the foam bubbles that came up to her neck. After the bath it would be the hair, then the deep cleanse (*just* for the sake of it, bath or no bath), then the toenails, then the change of sheets, the record, the book, the cocoa, the bed. Then tomorrow she'd bounce in and mop up Jack's killer, no problem. Aaaahhh . . .

About then, Jack was running all the way to Wandsworth.

PART THREE

Here comes a candle to light you to bed,
Here comes a chopper to . . .

Tommy Thumb's Pretty Song Book

TWENTY-NINE

Jack woke up stiff. He had slept deeply after the long run home and the large quantity of Scotch that he had poured down, so he didn't *know* he was stiff till he tried to get up. But God, he was stiff.

It was a fine morning, with the sky an unbroken flat blue all the way across to the rooflines. You get that in cities, he had noticed, a constant colour sky because the buildings stopped you looking too far towards the horizons where the blue always faded and changed. It was just gone eight thirty.

Jack made himself some hot, sweet tea and took it out onto the doorstep of his flat to drink. You wouldn't have taken him for a copper then, with his white sweatshirt that he slept in and the pale and battered jeans he had slipped on to come out in. Looking at him, you'd have thought he was just another of the locals relaxing before going in to work.

That's the trouble really, he would have said, it's the way people think that's wrong. Because he *was* just another local waiting to go to work, right?

Across the cracked street was a tarmaced area surrounded by a high wire fence to stop balls flying about. It was marked out inside for all kinds of things; cricket, football, basketball, tennis, but round here it was always football or cricket and right at this moment it was football. There were twenty of them in there, screaming and yelling and fighting, burning some off before they went to school, or before they were *meant* to go to school. Jack knew that half of them just wouldn't.

Go on, Jack told himself. It's been a while.

Leaving his half empty mug on the step, he bounded down the half dozen steps and went over to the game.

'What side am I on?'

A black kid looked at him suspiciously, clutching the ball.

'You ain't playin'.'

'Like who says,' Jack challenged.

171

'Ah fockin' do, man, that's 'oo.'

Jack glanced at the others. He had played ball with most of them before. They knew he was a cop but they didn't care one way or the other, he knew that. They were watching this confrontation with nervous interest, waiting to see what he'd do. It looked like Tarzan here was the new king of the hill and he didn't like goody-goody chummy coppers that tried to be one of the gang. So he was changing things.

Fair enough.

Jack took one step to his right as if to start walking away, but really it was just so he wouldn't be facing the kid any more but would just be a little to one side of him. Then, not exactly slowly but with a kind of studied leisure about it, he bent forward, snaked his left arm behind the kid's back and then seized him by the waist, hoisting him up horizontally in one hard pull.

The black boy was too astonished to speak. Suddenly he was dangling in midair looking down at the policeman's heels. Jack took one look at the tight rump he now had under his arm, another one at the other boys all around him and then started whacking.

Very hard. Very fast.

The boy under his arm bellowed his outrage while the others guffawed at the spectacle. Lamarre just kept on belting him until his hand started to get sore and then he laid it on harder. Gradually the kid's tone changed and took on a hurt sound. Tears would follow soon, so now it was time to stop. He put the boy down.

'Nobody talks to me like that first thing in the morning,' he calmly told the hate-filled little face. 'Not you, not your big brother, not the King of Siam. Nobody. I wouldn't play football with you if you paid me a thousand quid. Now my phone's ringing an' I'm going. Goodbye.'

Full of dignity, the Clint Eastwood of Wandsworth, he strode off. Don't mess with the man, see.

'Half your people are in already,' Tickle sneered down the line. Then, there was a pointed gap before he added 'As am I.'

'You rang me up to tell me that, did you?' Jack inquired lightly, deliberately omitting his 'sir.'

'No, I bloody didn't,' Tickle said. 'I rang you for the same reason I did the last time I rang you, when you were having a meal out. The same reason we were trying to get you the time after that, when you were having another meal out. Remember?'

Lamarre was caught between being annoyed at Tickle for deciding to get on his back, now, this morning, by phone, not man to man, and being startled at what he was saying.

'Another note?'

'Yes, another bloody note. PO did a special collection in Kensington last night, just to try and catch it hot and we scooped one.'

'What does it say?' Jack asked.

Tickle breathed heavily into the phone, like he was trying to uproot the desk at the other end or something like that. 'Why don't you come in and bloody read it, Jack?'

'Right,' Jack said. 'You can save it as a surprise.' Watch it, watch it.

'Right,' Tickle said. 'And by the way, your girl reckons she knows who it is this time. How do you like that?'

Tickle dropped the phone before Lamarre could say anything, which left Jack incredulous because the whole call had been leading up to that, hadn't it? That's why he'd rung up instead of Al. That's why the carping preamble.

'The pillock,' Jack muttered, to the wall.

THIRTY

It did work. Without money. And as for them playing ball quickly, well . . .

Koenig coming down a corridor was like a close-up of a cannonball looming down a gun barrel; unstoppable, leaving no room for anything else. Halfway down he stopped before the notice board at the head of the stairs and cast his mad eyes across it in search of some new monstrosity. But there was only one new thing and that, though certainly non-mathematical, could stay, he supposed. It was a bright orange strip of paper bearing the heading 'Metropolitan Police' and then the urge for help concerning this Reaper creature that seemed to be slaughtering people just about all day every day. There was a big telephone number at the bottom of it, for communicating one's help.

Koenig went, 'NNNNrhhh' and plummeted on to his office.

'There's a man to see you, Professor,' called Dorothy as he flashed past her open door.

'Me?' he said as he came back. 'What about? Has my mail arrived?'

Koenig had this confusing habit of thinking more than one thought at the same time, though unhappily he had but the one mouth for communicating them.

Just then, the lorry driver peered round the edge of the door and then emerged into the corridor to confront the formidable Professor of Pure Mathematics. Koenig surveyed him with huge malice. Having just arrived for the day and being already late for his eleven fifteen lecture he was in no mood for trivia. Koenig had no patience, even at the best of times, having been constructed without the faculty.

'Sidel Electronics, Guv'nor,' the driver said, proferring a scrap of paper. 'The equipment you ordered.'

'What equipment?' The Prof grabbed the invoice sheet and glowered at it. 'I ordered no equipment.'

The driver nodded at the sheet.

'Professor Werner Koenig, Mathematics Department, Imperial College,' he said, grossly mispronouncing both of Koenig's names. 'That's you, 'ennit?' He was about to go on, but after taking in Koenig's face he elected to shut his mouth.

The Prof read his name, address, department and phone number as if they were all beyond his comprehension and then started to read out loud the list of items on the sheet.

'Electromagnet. X-ray spectrometer, oscilloscope . . .'

There were about a dozen items in all but by the time he had read these three, the mathematical part of his mind had raced to the bottom and noted the total price. Immediately it ordered his mouth to stop functioning. Fourteen thousand six hundred pounds. Several thoughts materialised at once, going in different directions.

'There's clearly a mistake here. Have you tried Physics?' He looked at Dorothy. 'I'll be late for my class.' Back to the lorry driver. 'Who are you, did you say?' But before the man could repeat his earlier ID, Koenig added menacingly. 'This is very annoying, very annoying.'

'Listen, don't get on at me mate. I just deliver the stuff.' He put his grimy finger over the top of the invoice. 'Are you this bloke 'ere?'

'This *is* the Mathematics department.'

'I know that. But are you . . .'

'Yes!' shouted Koenig. 'Of course I am. But this is riduculous. We need no . . . no . . . (eyes down) *electromagnets*, here.'

'Well I don't know nothin' about . . .'

By then, Koenig had managed a rational thought.

'Dorothy. Will you please go along to C29 and ask my class to wait. I shall have to sort this out.'

Dorothy fled the room, choking with suppressed mirth and thinking, 'just wait till I tell Margaret,' Margaret being her friend and confidante from Computing and Control.

Professor Koenig never did get to give his eleven fifteen lecture, nor his twelve fifteen lecture either. It took him twenty minutes to ask the same set of questions and get the same set of denials from three Physics professors and two Engineering professors (both chemical, it seemed like a fair try) about the responsibility for a van load of apparatus standing at the entrance to the Huxley building. It took him another twenty minutes to convince the exasperated lorry driver that there really had been some ghastly error *somewhere* and that he could not and would not permit the articles to be left in his care. Unable to shake the man off even then he resorted to a rather more forceful suggestion as to what the driver might care to do with them if he did not wish to return them to his employer.

It was about five minutes after that when, cursing eloquently, the driver climbed into his cab and drove off, load still intact. And about an hour after *that*, Koenig got the call from Sidel Electronics in Chiswick, in the person of a Mr Jameson.

Jameson inquired politely as to the nature of the Professor's complaint regarding the equipment he had ordered, but of course, Koenig was ready this time.

'I ordered nothing,' he informed Jameson smoothly. 'I am a pure mathematician. I have no use for electromagnets and indeed, I would not know one if it fell upon my head.'

Jameson figured he was ready for this because he reckoned he'd done all right with this one on the whole. Hellfire, the frigging order only got to him last thing yesterday but he'd seen Imperial, he'd seen Professor, he'd seen Urgent, so he'd gotten the stuff on the lorry, right, no messing. If people like that wanted gear urgent they got it, because that was what got you more orders and you never had money problems with *them*, so what the hell was all this?

He coughed up his flash voice.

'I have checked carefully, Professor,' he said. 'In fact I have the order form before me now. There has certainly been no mistake on our part. The order is marked urgent and appears to be from your address in, er — Willis Jackson House, Evelyn Gardens, South west seven, and the delivery address is *definitely* the Mathematics department, Huxley Building, Queen's Gate, South West seven. Really, I don't . . .'

'Just a moment please,' Koenig said. 'Just wait one moment will you?'

That couldn't be a mistake, he was thinking. You couldn't mistakenly think a person like him lived there.

He leaned backwards, slid open a bookcase and extracted a copy of the Imperial College prospectus. This had crossed his mind of course, but it had other things going then. As he flicked through the index he reflected on the weird fact that Jameson seemed to be under a false impression here, namely that the only thing wrong was that it had gone to the wrong department, not that it had been ordered at all.

Ah, yes.

'Are you there?'

'Yes, Professor.'

'Ahem. You aren't going to like this and neither do I, but I believe I smell a student prank here.'

'I beg your pardon?'

'A prank. A joke, a practical joke. You see, Willis Jackson House is a student residency in South Kensington, maintained by the college. Clearly someone's been using it as a fictitious address. It begins to look rather elaborate, doesn't it? Perhaps you should have used it, or at least phoned.' There was a silence then before Koenig added vacuously, 'Efficiency can be costly.'

Jameson was stunned. In his business this didn't happen. Jokes got people strappado'd.

'But our advertisements and order forms are not sent to students. Only to departmental staffs. I fail to see . . .'

'My secretary assures me that your literature was indeed sent to me although I personally don't recall it and we can't find it now. We get such things all the time, from lots of firms. I must say, I could never fathom out why you people send these things to everybody, irrespective of their department. It would seem to me intuitively obvious that a Mathematics department would have no use for scientific equipment!'

'We send them out by computer,' Jameson muttered dumbly.

Koenig barged on.

'Not to put too fine a point upon it,' he said meanly, 'your advertisements, with their order forms, frequently end up as useless scraps of paper floating around secretaries' offices. It's quite possible that a student picked one up with my name on it. As provided by *your* computer, of course.'

'But the order looks so very official,' Jameson said. 'It's typed. There are college stamps all over it, and . . .'

'All lying about in secretaries' offices,' Koenig repeated.

There was an embarrassed little yelp from the man in Chiswick then, followed by a gurgling and what sounded like a conference between him and somebody else. Koenig waited patiently, fiddling with his pipe and a tin of Erinmore.

'I'm sure you'll appreciate that we are hardly in a position to view this as much of a joke, Professor,' Jameson finally said. 'This little affair will certainly cost us a tidy sum of money.'

The Prof didn't care if it bankrupted them, but the inconvenience to him was something else again.

'Indeed I do,' he purred reassuringly. 'And I shall endeavour to get to the bottom of it. Now if there isn't anthing else?'

Over in Chiswick, Jameson replaced his phone and wished a plague on all students. Covered in boils was what they should be. Or something.

Koenig was still riled when he got back from a late lunch. He sat in his padded chair wringing his big mitts as if crushing the invisible larynx of some seedy miscreant scholar.

Dorothy didn't know how to put it.

'There's another man to see you, Professor.'

Koenig stared up insanely.

There were two actually, one right behind the other. The man from General Automation had an SPC/16 minicomputer and a bill for eleven thousand quid, whilst Calcomp's driver came bearing galvanometers to the value of seven grand and a half.

This time, Koenig went out of control.

He stamped up and down the corridor shouting like a battery sergeant major. He swore rustication and death upon the perpetrators when he found then, and find them he would, he bawled at the GA man (who took up a slightly defensive posture) yea, though it took him an hundred years.

In C29, thirty-six undergraduates missed out on prime fields yet again. Dorothy rushed to the loo to release her merriment unobserved. It went round the building like wildfire. Peals of glee rang from every office and down every corridor.

And everybody, but everybody, was hooting at Koenig.

Ergo, somebody had to catch a cold. Now.

This time he had been shown an order form and he observed furiously that the signature on it was a tolerable imitation of his own. It wasn't that the Maths postgrads were the *only* people who ever saw his signature on things, and it wasn't that they were the only ones that ever roamed in and out of his secretary's office, but it was as good an excuse as any. So, after smoothing out a couple more marketing managers, Koenig rounded up as many of the scum as he could find and lined them up in rows, two deep.

'Now I'm not saying it was any of you here present,' he hissed, as his beady, porcine little eyes glinted up and down the lines, 'I'm not even saying it was anybody in this department. But I wish to make it crystal clear to the student body as a whole, that

I will tolerate no more of this outrageous behaviour, or I assure you, there will be very dire consequences indeed. And I mean dire.'

No, Norm thought, what you mean is very. Monk's face was a mask of serenity. So was Elaine's.

'Please be so kind as to spread the message,' Koenig told them. 'I want no more cars towed away. I want no more depredations on the computer. I want not more fleets of vans bringing things I have not ordered. If anything *remotely* like this happens again, heads will roll.'

This has got to stop, he thought, as they filed out. Whoever it is must be mad.

While all that was raging, Al was pulling it apart for them. What it said was:

Five down
Mix up bits of this gloomy little bird
and he won't need limousines.
        Reaper

'So let's have it again,' Tickle ordered, 'for the Inspector's sake.' He eyed Jack truculently.

'All right,' Al said to Jack. 'The victim is a young bloke called Nigel Renwick. He belongs to the Renwick family who own the Renwick chain of car dealers. Rich as hell, they are. They flog everything from Rolls to Ferrari, but nothing cheaper. This Nigel is a sort of heir to it all, but he's also a noted jetsetter and society type. Get's in the gossip columns from time to time, though I read an article on his firm only last night. Bit of luck, sir, had to happen.'

'How's it work out?' Jack said, though he felt as if he didn't give a damn for some reason not to be wondered at.

'Renwick is formed from bits of Wren chick, right; Al explained, writing it down by way of help. 'Take out the ch and mix up bits you've got left and make Renwick, see. A wren chick is a little bird, right?'

'A gloomy one?' Jack said, sniffing.

'That's the Nigel,' Al said. 'Nigel comes from the Latin word for black. Or is it Greek? Anyway black's gloomy.'

'I suppose the mixing up also refers to the bomb that we assume the bleeder's making out of the dynamite,' Tickle put in.

'And as for the limousines, that seems like a clincher doesn't it?'

'If you say so,' Jack said. 'We'd better get him covered, hadn't we.' He was reaching for the phone. 'This killer moves quick. Probably planning to get him tonight.'

'He *is* covered,' Tickle said, clearly delighted to be saying it, putting as much of the 'who's supposed to be running this operation?' into it as he could.

Jack squirmed. If he ever packed in the force, he was going to thump Tickle in the mouth on his way out.

'He lives in Kensington,' Al told him quietly.

'Another clincher, eh?' Tickle gobbed.

'Queen's Gate Gardens,' Al added.

'Uh,' Jack mumbled. 'Well it better be a low profile, that's all. Anyway, I want a word with him.'

'It's low,' Tickle said. 'Lower than a cat's belly. Your man Taylor's handling it.'

Should be low enough for anything, Jack thought, very spiteful at everybody just now, though he'd had a few thoughts about Taylor in particular recently.

THIRTY-ONE

Norm wished Daph would sod off, frankly.

He'd gotten Elaine down into the Sheffield common room for a cosy little chat about how the Shilluks of the White Nile used to collect testicles as trophies when up turned the rotten flatmate with a paper.

'Brian gave me this,' Daph was saying. 'This reporter reckons the Reaper actually rang him up.'

'Ooooh,' Elaine said, 'Gosh.' She perused the other night's *H & R Gazette* avidly, downing Harold H's outpourings in a sweep. 'Clues,' she exclaimed. 'What kind of clues do you think he sends?'

'Don't know if it's a he,' Daph said. 'They don't know anything for sure. Hey! Do you know that Bruegel picture he's on about?'

'No,' Elaine said quickly. 'No, I don't know anything about art and that.'

'We should send one,' Daph said. 'Tell them we're going to do the Mayor.'

'Don't be daft.'

Daph *was* daft — wasn't she?

'One thing's for sure,' Norm decided to say, 'they can't stop him. Just seems to kill who he wants, at random. Quick, too. Can't have been going more than a week, and how many is it?'

'Four now,' Elaine said. 'That they know about.'

Neither of the others knew what that meant, but neither of them wanted to ask either.

'Wonder who it is?' Daph pondered wistfully, still refusing to go and leave Norm and Elaine alone, which made Norm glower, which Daph noticed, so she said, 'I bet it's Norm.'

'Or Norm and Brian,' Elaine giggled.

Monk almost told them what a shit he thought Brian was, even as a potential partner in crime, but he held off because that would have upset Daph, and that would have annoyed Elaine and that would have queered his own pitch, as it were.

Sod off, he thought, sod off.

Fancies himself, Lamarre had decided instantly, as soon as he met the Renwick kid, thinks he's the Great Gatsby or something. Lamarre was still in a foul humour, so Taylor and Prendergast were giving him a bit of a berth.

Nigel Renwick was about twenty, suntanned, black haired with a parting down the middle like Robert Redford in the afore-mentioned saga, and had a mouthful of even, white teeth and a shine in his eyes that caused them to twinkle fetchingly in unison with the glittering of the ivories below. What really threw Jack though was the dressing gown. Very ham, that; dark green satin with velvet lapels, worn over his clothes, and if Jack wasn't mistaken he had the trousers of a dinner suit on, because he definitely had a bow tie up top. All that was missing really was the two-foot-long cigarette holder and the floosie draped over the settee. Al was seated upright in a chair.

'Really, Inspector,' (Reahleah, he said), 'you don't really think this person will attempt to harm *me*, do you? What on *earth* have *I* done to the beastly fellow?'

'It's nothing personal,' Jack told the man. 'This person is clearly insane. We can only guess his motives, but so far the victims have been random. Choosing you is a random act, almost certainly.'

Even as he was saying it, Jack was recalling the psychiatrist's remark. Psychopaths don't have to be insane. How the hell was that possible?

'Well how do you know,' purred Renwick, 'I mean how do you *know* it's me he's after?'

Lamarre winced at the *knayw* and the *ofter* and tried to keep it general.

'We have received a very specific clue as to his intentions,' he finally said. 'I really would prefer not to say more than that if you don't mind, sir. But we are pretty sure it's you he's lined up next, and we're pretty sure of the method he'll try to use.'

'What's that?' Nigel wanted to know.

'Again I'd rather not say,' Jack insisted. 'But it will require some ingenuity on his part.' (Was that right? Not going to make a grenade was he, and just sling it through the window? — don't even think it.) 'Judging from previous form the whole thing will have been carefully worked out in advance so the killer will be ready to move as soon as he er . . .'

Sent the clue, Jack suddenly didn't want to say.

'. . . as early as tonight, we think.'

'Tonight? I'm having people in tonight.'

'He may well know that,' Jack said. 'We've learned not to underestimate this murderer.'

Originally Renwick had been all smug, though now it was ninety per cent smug and then maybe a few per cent fear.

'You mean he's actually *researched* me?' the heir to the family fortune said incredulously.

'Certainly,' Jack said. 'The killer has probably observed you closely. That's why the Sergeant and I came separately. It looks less suspicious that way, less so than arriving together.'

Renwick glanced over at Al, who just smiled, as if she didn't want to say anything, but then she said, 'Probably not out there now, though. We think he hides in some regular job around here during the day.'

Shut it, Jack's look told her.

'Well, hang it all Inspector, er . . .'

'Lamarre.'

'Yes, Lamarre. Look here, I hope you've organised some protection for me, even though I have guests due, as I say. I mean . . .'

Jack was patting the air, and beckoning Nigel over to the window of the flat. They were downstairs in the ground floor lounge, though the flat extended right the way up through all three floors, nobody else in the whole house. The entire terrace was like that, very expensive places, very big.

'Stand back from the window,' Lamarre said, pointing. 'You see the place opposite. One floor up.'

Renwick looked out to the white front across the street, followed Jack's finger up the steps and then to the first floor window. It was lace curtained and white from reflected cloudy light. Lamarre pulled out the handset with it's thick little wobbly aerial on top and put it to his mouth.

'Front man,' he said. 'Give us a wave. This is Lamarre.'

Taylor's face appeared briefly at the window with a stupid grin on it and a hand blipped up by the side of it before it vanished again.

'He has a handset like this,' Jack said. 'And a telephone link to our headquarters. He'll be there, or somebody will, continuously until this is over. He won't take his eyes off your place for an instant. There's another one out back doing the same, and tonight there'll be one at either end of the street, they'll be in contact with each other all the time. If you go out, both of them will tail you, but you won't know it. You're as safe as a tank, Mr Renwick, but just as an added measure I'm going to leave this handset with you as well.'

Jack put it down on a coffee table.

'I just press that button do I?'

'Yes. And just speak. They'll all hear you.'

Renwick the young dash looked fairly happy about it by then, though the fear was still there, so you had to start wondering how he'd feel when it went dark.

About eleven p.m. after the inevitable, Jack lay on his back and Al lay on her front by his side running her fingers around in the hair on his chest. The bed, her bed, was warm now, and suffused with the smell of her perfume, heightened by the body heat of their love making. Jack's mind was cooler after this. He let his finger trickle down the hollow of her back to where it started to rise again and divide.

'Tell you what I think,' he said.

'Go on,' Al said. 'Tell me what you think.'

'I think it's somebody very clever and academic and highly qualified who isn't getting paid a lot of money.'

Al went, 'Uh? Why?'

'Well, look at it,' Jack said. 'Look at who he hits. If you think about it they're all people who've got success without talent. They're all people who've got this high opinion of themselves, or seemed to have. Chat show man, disc jockey, fashion designer, pop singer, none of them had anything special, but they'd all landed on their feet and they were all cocky and self-admiring as if *they* thought they *were* clever. Must be very irritating if, you're a genuinely clever and unrecognised genius and a psychopath as well!

'Narcissistic,' Al said.

'What?'

'Narcissistic. Self-admiring.'

'Right. Anyway, I can almost see his point, if that is his point.'

'Think it could be a woman?' Al said. She was giving the hairs on his chest a few playful little tugs now.

'Possible,' Lamarre said, after a while. 'The methods could be used by a woman, even the hammer. Anybody can kill with a hammer, all the weight's in the weapon, no real strength needed. And that lance was so sharp it wasn't true, no muscle needed to shove that through a bloke.'

'Sorry about what I said to Renwick,' Al said, after a pause to remember it. 'It was a bit too much.'

'It's OK,' Jack told her, though technically it wasn't. 'You're right anyway. The killer does hit either early mornings or late at night, as if he's got a job during the day where he'd be missed if he wasn't there. Anyway, forget it. Oh, by the way, I rang the shrink again and he reckoned the killer *doesn't* do crosswords.'

'Doesn't do them? Why's that, Jack.'

'He said there's no style to them, no consistent pattern. People who know about crosswords, like the solvers and the setters right, well they all get to think in certain ways. If you like anagrams you buy the paper that uses a puzzle with a lot of anagrams, see, so you think anagrams. Anagrams are your style. But these clues have no style. They're descriptions of names that look like crossword clues. Probably just the first thing he thought of.'

'I don't think I buy that,' Al snorted. 'Not all of it anyway. I reckon those shrinks guess too much.'

'Not what you said before,' Jack retorted. 'You once said they always played it safe.'

'I never!'

'You did. In the pub once.'

She punched him on the chest and then bit his ear and got her bottom squeezed as a punishment. After another few things they rolled apart again.

'Taylor on it now then,' Jack checked.

'Yes. Till midnight. Then he's off till noon. Twelve hours is a long time to sit in that room, Jack. Maybe you should have had three shifts front and back instead of two.'

'It won't kill 'em,' Jack scoffed. 'Anyway, it won't be for long if we're right. Either tonight or tomorrow should see it happen.'

'You're the boss, Inspector.'

There was a cloud on Lamarre's face then.

'Anyway,' he stated gently. 'I'm the one who's going to kill Taylor, not the twelve hours of surveillance.'

'Why?' Al seemed really surprised.

'Because he's feeding that bloody reporter,' Jack said, grinning cheerfully. 'Didn't you know?'

'You mean the *Hounslow Gazette* bloke?'

'Right. They probably set it up early on. Now Taylor's on the take. It won't be much, because he's not giving the guy much and it's not exactly the *News of the World*. Probably thinks he can swing it for a bit of pin money, down there in a local rag. But I'm going to slay him for it, when I'm ready.'

'But Higginbotham said he was rung up,' Al said. 'He said . . .'

'That's what Taylor said he said,' Jack told her, 'that's what they agreed to say because we can't nail him for protecting a criminal source if they say that. Only it's too thin. All that stuff about a high-pitched voice with a phoney Welsh accent just doesn't wash.'

'Come on Jack. It could be true, couldn't it?'

'Of course it *could*, but it's not. Listen, before I got that laughing noise played at me down the phone, somebody asked for me by name. The voice was probably synthetic, according to the chap that heard it. You know, words recorded and pieced together. The name, my name, was kind of whispered right, so we still don't know anything about this person, neither sex nor age, but I'm telling you this, it wasn't high-pitched, and it wasn't Welsh.'

'Well all right. Maybe he used piecing on one call and a disguised accent on the other.'

'Balls,' Jack spat out.

'All right then,' Al was challenging now. 'If the Reaper *didn't* ring Harold Higginbotham, then why *doesn't* he contact somebody with the details. I mean, it's in his interest to confuse us with imitators, isn't it?'

'We haven't got any imitators because Taylor didn't give the reporter enough. He's got enough to him to stop at giving the guy everything. And the reason the real Reaper doesn't do it is because he doesn't *want* to be imitated. He's too bloody conceited.'

'Maybe it's Sergeant Taylor himself?' Sergeant Prendergast said wickedly.

'If it is, then Nigel won't cop it tonight, or any other night, will he? Like I said, it's somebody very clever. That's why it's not one of the members of the cabinet that live in Kensington, or Tickle, for example.'

Al squawked at it, causing the sheet she had over her bosom to slide down and give Lamarre an oscillating eyeful, though even as she was shaking, she wasn't all that sure if he was still kidding or not.

THIRTY-TWO

Archie Chatwin finally came downstairs at about eight or so, feeling great. Even after a late night in town he didn't need what he still called a long lie in, with or without some popsy half his age, though last night that hadn't been possible.

Never mind, Archie thought, there's time. Where there's brass there's boobs.

Feeling hungry, he wished he'd told his woman to come in this morning and knock him up some breakfast. Archie liked a good breakfast, plenty of bacon, sausages and eggs, the whole thing, none of that bread rolls and coffee rubbish. In his years in the clubs he had moved from one lodging to another and had frequently gone without breakfast or, at best, prepared it himself.

That was before he became a star of course. Now Archie never made any meals for himself. Not breakfast, not dinner, not tea, not anything. He was through with that. He was also through with washing up, making beds, cleaning cars, ironing shirts, and so on and so on, because stars didn't do that kind of thing, not in Archie's book anyway. That was for second raters, not stars like Archie.

Sometimes, Archie would walk round his beautiful house in Chesham Bois all by himself, imagining that he had a couple of admirers behind him, or an interviewer perhaps, hanging on his every word. He would stroll through the plush lounge pointing things out to his invisible worshippers, usually quoting a price and saying that he'd 'picked it up' or 'found it' somewhere and thought it would look OK in his place in Buckinghamshire. Imagining his admirer to be a woman he would linger in the huge kitchen, with its superb imported fittings (German they are, he'd say, the best) and its fabulous views over the woodlands beyond his three acres or so out back.

If you think the view from the kitchen's good, he would say out loud, you should see the view from the dining room. He had had the floor raised to take advantage of it, so when he dined he was on a kind of pedestal looking down through the big French window to the side. (Architect's idea, not Archie's, of course.)

Then he would amble out into his "grounds", if the weather was fine, lost in his conceit and his stupidity, smiling like an ecstatic monk.

Archie often did this, but nobody knew. Archie loved being famous. He found it natural. Archie Chatwin, the famous wit.

But what about this breakfast, then?

Dammit, if he wanted breakfast he was going to have it. He'd slip into Amersham, eat at the coffee house and after that, the pub. Tell 'em a few jokes, have a few pints. Archie pulled on his two hundred quid check velvet jacket (exclusive, no other) and left the house from the back patio, heading for the garage.

The garage was in fact an old converted stable, fully fifty feet from end to end, into the front of which brick pillars had been added to take the up and over double doors which, when shut, gave the appearance of a row of four double garages. Inside it was all just one long box with windows at regular intervals along the rear wall. Archie had two cars in there at the moment, the Bentley and the Jag. He honestly didn't know which one he liked best, was his usual line in that situation.

His visitor liked them both too, in a purely academic way though the black figure had no great love of cars really. They both had to be wired to be sure so that was what had been done.

Archie swung up one of the middle two doors and went in to the Bentley. He failed to notice the fact that the window behind the car was very slightly ajar and that a plank of wood which had been on the floor yesterday was now leaning against it. The plank was hiding the cable that snaked in over the window ledge and down the wall behind another heap of debris on the floor. There it split into two lines, one running along the wall to the Jaguar, the other going under the Bentley, emerging under the rear nearside door. This one made a brief appearance under the sill then disappeared behind the lip of the rear door on its way up to the slightly open rear window where it went inside the car and down the centre pillar, then along to the device under the driver's seat. The one going to the Jag did something similar.

Even if Archie had noticed any of it, he wouldn't have done himself any good, because in that eventuality the figure who was watching at this moment from the firing box forty yards away in the trees, would have just set the thing off there and then.

By the time Archie had dropped into the Bentley's luxurious

real leather seat, nimble fingers hooked the correct wire to the box and the figure was crouched behind about seven feet of elm trunk. A black leather gloved thumb slid over the side of the box, on to the flat red button there and pressed it gently.

There was a double bang, one just behind the other, merging together into a good solid explosive roar. The roof of the garage, substantial though it was, oak beamed and tiled, bulged momentarily in two places before splitting and erupting into bits and soaring up into the air. The doors and walls similarly vanished in their respective directions so that an entire chunk of the garage, everything bar the remote ends in fact, just *went*.

A hundred yards down the leafy road, Archie's nearest neighbour was hosing his lawn after a sprinkling of moss killer. He stared in disbelief at the flying fragments of automobile and converted stone stable and comedian that came twirling down through the trees around him and skittering on the roof of his own house behind him.

'Oooh, Bernard,' his wife mewled from the greenhouse, 'whatever's that?'

'Get an ambulance,' Archie's nearest neighbour said, throwing down his hosepipe, 'and the others. Get 'em all.'

The figure waited obligingly by the side of the road, along with a few other motorists heading into town, as the emergency vehicles went honking and ringing by. Not bad, it thought, looking at the watch again, not bad at all.

Should have guessed that the other car would go as well. Pressure wave did it, obviously. It was bound to trigger the other charge in sympathy, unavoidable at that distance. Should have worked that out in advance, not that it mattered in the least, of course.

Somewhere underneath this scientific ice layer the other mind was working now. It felt curiously deflated because only one more victim had been scheduled after this one, although there had to be at least one more after that, as yet undecided, though there were plenty to choose from.

The next one was the car dealer.

There was a blazing cold hatred of car dealers in the black figure's mind, ever since the idle calculation of how easy/difficult it would be to afford a thing like a new Jag, which *they* always had (always the best, always the latest) and even more so since the discovery of the kind of mark-ups they made on new cars.

They all stank.

Snigger.

This one was going to be stinking all right, because he was going to soil himself during his last few seconds, out of sheer fright, no doubt about it.

And then it would be the axe.

Oh yes, the axe had to have its day. There was no need to worry about the mess now, and the terror stories of cops hanging people on the strength of microscopic specks of blood you could never wash away and so on, because it wasn't such a big thing, blood; after using a hammer you could feel a lot easier about blood, a lot easier all round. Blood was no sweat if you were careful. It was just a matter of dressing sensibly, that was all, and watching where you put your hands and feet.

Either an axe or a knife anyway. A blade, certainly.

But that wasn't all, of course. The eyes and the teeth and the wig were a great idea too, a great idea, though you had to put yourself in the victim's mind to really appreciate it.

Detective Chief Superintendent Tickle had a standing order out about explosives. He wanted to be told, without delay, at once, immediately, or else. He was there before Lamarre.

First of all he gaped in blank disbelief at the devastated outbuilding and the scattered bits of two big cars, both now little more than diverse engine blocks, axles and the more durable lumps of chassis. Then he went and looked down at the firing box they'd found, still there on the ground behind the tree with the flex coming from it.

'That got a number on it?'

'Yes sir,' spake a Sergeant with stripes. He was Met though.

'Right. Get it to the quarry firm or blasting firm or whatever. Get them to check it. What's wrong with him?'

The Sergeant looked over to the Constable that Tickle was glaring at. The Constable was heaving softly into a laurel bush.

'He found the victim's head, sir. Not a pretty sight.'

'Get him out of the flaming way.'

Gives us an ID easier, Tickle thought callously, wonder how much more of him they've got yet. Him? Them?

He wound his way between two passing firemen and over to Leech, who was bent over the remains of the Bentley's roof, though you wouldn't have guessed. The pathologist's car was backed up towards the shell of the garage, with its boot open. Leech was pulling a strip of something off the edge of the metal sheet in front of him, with a large pair of forceps.

'This is a bit more of him,' he said to Tickle's legs. 'Any idea who he is?'

'Resident is a comedian name of Archie Chatwin. Seen him on TV. His place, his cars. I see you've got my lads shovelling him up.'

Leech looked up.

'I don't know if they're your lads or not, I don't really know what I'm doing out here myself, except that it's another of this Reaper's efforts in all probability. I just handed out some plastic bags.'

'I'm not complaining,' Tickle said hurriedly. 'You're taking the remains in yourself then?'

'Might as well,' he pointed over to his car, with its bootful of plastic bags peeping up. 'There's a head in there. Why don't you try and identify him now if you're in a hurry?'

'Thanks,' Tickle said, choking on it.

Taking a deep breath he went into the house to look for a photo of Archie Chatwin that he could give to somebody else.

When he came out again, Lamarre was waiting, peering into the nightmare of Leech's boot, hands in pockets.

Prendergast was standing well back from it.

Right, Tickle thought. Right.

'Long way from Kensington, Jack,' he opened.

'Twenty miles or so,' Lamarre said, eyeing Sergeant Prendergast, 'give or take.'

'Got it wrong, didn't we,' Tickle said, raising his voice, and using the 'we' as people do when they don't mean to include themselves. The Superintendent had a triumphant relish in his eyes, which Lamarre thought inappropriate considering (a) all that garbage about clinchers, (b) the killer was still on the loose and (c) they were all standing among numerous chunks of his latest victim.

'It's a bloody imitator,' Tickle shouted. 'You were supposed to prevent that.'

'It's him,' Jack said, bristling up.

'Wrong victim, Jack. Wrong victim.'

'Doesn't prove anything. He changed his tack that's all. Probably saw the watch team.'

'Nobody sees watch teams, Jack.' Tickle was really in this for a row. 'They're not meant to be seen.'

Lamarre sneered at that. 'Leave it out,' he said, pulling back his lip.

Leech looked up from his scraping, that half amused lilt in his expression. Tickle pulled Lamarre away to one side.

'That's leave it out, *what*?' Tickle repeated it for him.

'Sir,' Jack hissed back, 'leave it bloody out, *sir*. Now get off me. Now.'

'What does that mean, Inspector?'

'It means I'm getting fed up with your attitude to my handling of this case, Superintendent. If you don't like it, take me off it. Otherwise I'd appreciate a little less interference.'

Tickle actually stepped back a pace.

'Interference? What the hell do you mean by interference?'

Lamarre gave himself a breathing space of a few seconds while he fought his emotions.

'When I got here,' he said quietly, 'there was a lad putting a firing box into a patrol car. I asked him what he was doing with it, and he said that *you'd* told him to get it checked against the one nicked from the quarry.'

'So?' Tickle asked, suspiciously.

'There was a lump of cable attached to it. I asked him what he was going to do with that. He said nothing. He hadn't got any orders about the cable. He'd just screwed it up in a ball.'

'Listen, Jack.'

'No, you listen, sir. There was no cable pinched from the quarry. He's provided that himself, so it could be useful. Very useful. I want to be in control of possible evidence. I don't want it treated like that, sir.'

The Detective Chief Superintendent could have assaulted Jack Lamarre for two pins. No, one. He breathed, very deeply before he tried to say anything else.

'All right Jack. That's it. Your office at the Yard, let's say three o'clock.'

Jack watched Tickle mince off for a second and then looked down at Leech. My oh my, the pathologist's eyes were saying, dear oh dear.

'Where's your young oppo these days?' Jack suddenly asked.

'Brian? Oh, he's got a couple of days off I believe.'

Jack went 'Hum' and turned to Al, but he was smiling now, as if to say, not going to bite, Al.

'Taylor?'

'Not on till twelve.'

'All right. You'll have to get this started. This happened at about eight right, and he had to be here to press the button, right?'

'Right?'

'So if he works in Kensington then he's got to cover twenty miles in the rush hour before work time starts.'

'I'm with it,' she said, dawning.

'OK. So it's a case of checking every single person on all our lists Al, and I mean all of them, however many. We want to know who was late for work today.'

'It'll take a while, Jack.'

'So what? We aren't any nearer now than we ever were. Nothing's changed has it? Tickle's right to be getting warm.'

'OK Jack,' she said. 'I'll get on it.'

Leech was starting to whistle some Bach.

THIRTY-THREE

Later, at the Yard, in Jack's office, at three, Tickle had some egg on his face.

'Play it again, Sam,' Jack said to Prendergast, as soon as the Superintendent was through the door.

'What?' Tickle said.

Lamarre just pointed at Al and leaned back in his chair, giving her the stage.

Al coughed. 'You aren't going to believe this, sir.'

'Believe what, Sergeant?' Tickle looked perplexed.

Al took the pen again (she'd done this for Lamarre already) and wrote the word *Whinchat* on the pad in front of Tickle's fly.

'What's that?' demanded the Chief.

'It's a bird,' Al said. 'A little bird. A small member of the thrush family in fact. Drop the first h and rearrange the bits remaining like the clue said and you get Chatwin.'

Tickle said 'Oh.'

Al said, 'I think the gloomy bit is a sort of pun on comedian'.

Jack said, 'And he collected limousines, though he won't need 'em now, will he, not now his bits have been rearranged.'

Tickle went a kind of grey colour, like that of his socks.

'Are you telling me it was the comedian after all?'

'I never said it wasn't,' Jack told him. 'You did.'

'No I didn't, *she* did,' Tickle said.

'Sorry sir,' Al said. 'It was the article I read. It . . .'

Al held up both of her hands, as if the walls were closing in.

'Forget it, Al. You weren't going on about clinchers. You weren't going on about imitators.'

Tickle went from grey to jet black. Small quantities of smoke began to puff out his nostrils. His teeth started to sprout beyond his lips.

'You're still no nearer, Jack,' he said hoarsely. 'I'd still like a result in this case, sometime before the end of the decade.' He was starting to back out.

'Try and oblige, sir,' Jack grinned openly.

When he was gone, Lamarre relaxed visibly and beamed at Al as if everything was wonderful, which Prendergast thought was wrong though she just smiled wanly back.

'Well?'

'Well what, sir?'

'Well what, Jack.'

'Well what, Jack?'

'We'll get the surveillance team off, that's what. They're wasting their time aren't they? Better things for them to do. Call 'em off now. And tell Mr Renwick he can relax.'

So what was wrong with her all of a sudden?

The note was in the post, just like all the others, more or less. Of course, the cops would be getting them almost immediately by now.

The figure stood in front of a full length mirror, having first put the room into half light for extra effect.

The black cloak was an afterthought. Actually it was a black groundsheet that had been in the boot of the car when the vehicle was acquired so it was untraceable and could be discarded afterwards. But it seemed to go with the rest.

Not overdoing this, am I, the figure asked itself critically, but then it threw on the cloak and thought no, no not at all, you look fab.

The wig was black and more than shoulder length, coming down on either side of the face at an angle, so the hair line just skirted the eyes and took off half the cheeks. The false teeth which, like the eyes and wig had been obtained a long time ago from a shop in another town, were long Dracula-type fangs that stretched down below the upper lip when in place, even when the mouth was closed, but leapt into full, horrible length as soon as the mouth was open.

No doubt my mouth will open, the figure thought, as I close in for the kill, like.

But the real thing was the eyes. These were, in fact, full contact lenses that covered the whole eye, but apart from a little clear bit that went over your pupil, they were completely black, so when they were in place, your eyes just disappeared, and what were once eyes became just empty black holes. It was scary as hell, honest.

The figure stood and preened itself for a long time. Then it picked up the hatchet from the table and admired its glittering brand new edge before holding it in front of itself and looking at the blade in the mirror as it caught the light and threw flashes across the room.

Then the figure opened its mouth and hissed.

Elaine decided. No she didn't. But then she felt she ought to. After all, if Kane was keen then what the hell was she doing with Norm. She wasn't responsible for Norm's feelings was she? She wasn't his nursemaid was she? And she had given him some fun hadn't she? No she wasn't and yes she had was all you could say to that, so why shouldn't she please herself for a change? Well? Why not; Dammit she *wanted* Steven Kane, right?

THIRTY-FOUR

'Where the hell have you been?' Lamarre demanded from his open office door. There had been nobody there but him and Prendergast.

It was almost ten p.m. Taylor had been due in after the surveillance team was called off almost five and a half hours ago.

'Out and about, guv'nor?' Taylor replied, glancing at Al Prendergast.

'Out and about where? Down in Hounslow?'

'Pardon?'

Al kept her eyes down on her desk. She didn't want to watch this.

'No,' Taylor said, 'I haven't been in Hounslow. I been quizzing a few folks about why they were late for work today.' He looked at Al. 'That was the brief, wasn't it?'

Al nodded.

'So what's in Hounslow, guv'nor?'

'You're a canny little sod,' Lamarre told him, ticking like a bomb. 'How'd you like to come in here and pick a bone with me.'

Hell's teeth, Al thought, where can I go?

'I was just about to nip out again,' Taylor said with a shrug. 'Be back in an hour.'

Lamarre nodded slowly, like a presiding judge. 'Oh aye? Got an urgent meeting with a friend, like?'

Sergeant Taylor put on this puzzled face, as if he didn't know what the man was getting at. It was very good, very cool, and Lamarre seemed to be in the mood for it, so sure was he of his ground.

'Listen, guv. I don't know what you're on about with Hounslow and meeting friends like, but I was just going over to South Ken that's all.'

'Why?'

'The radio-phone's still in opposite Renwick's place. It's not been picked up. I said I'd do it.'

'Not your job, cleaning up after the watch team.'

'Then I won't do it.'

Al thought Taylor looked just a little bit warm now. Jack was being incredibly nasty, playing him like a fish.

'No, no,' Jack said. 'You go and get it, eh. I'll wait here for you, shall I? And when you get back, we'll have a chat, shall we, Sergeant?'

'If you say so, Inspector. But what about?'

'Just go,' Jack said. 'And be back in an hour, sunshine.'

Lamarre let him go then, but he sat there in his chair looking at the door of the incident room, with his fingertips touching under his chin and his knees crossed, rocking himself from side to side in his swivel chair, with a malicious look in his eyes. After a while he broke the position and went to work again.

Al didn't say anything for a while, but then she reckoned she'd chance it.

'Perhaps you're wrong, sir,' she said. She didn't have to speak loudly because Jack's door was still open and there was still nobody else in the room so it was very quiet.

'I'm not,' was all he said.

'He didn't seem to know what you were on about.'

'He knew.'

'Why let him go then? Why not have it out while he was here.'

Jack Lamarre dropped the pen with an exasperated gasp and looked straight at Al, though patiently maybe.

'All right, he's gone to pick up the link to the flat outside Renwick's place. If that's what he said then it'll be true. Why not let him do it. But he's also going to Higginbotham and warn him to stick to their story because he knows what happens when he gets back. And that's something I can check when I burn Harold.'

'You're just going to let him hang himself, aren't you?'

'Yes.'

They both went back to whatever they were doing again, though Al was thinking that Jack was maybe more of a rotten animal than she used to think before she stopped thinking it and started to think he was different, but she was confused so she tried not to dwell on it.

Neither of them spoke for ten minutes or so, which was when the policewoman came in with an envelope from the Post Office, marked

Inspector J. Lamarre. Urgent and then left again without saying anything.

Al couldn't see what it was from where she was sitting but she recognised the WPC that had come and gone as the one doing the running to and from the PO's sorting office and she saw the look on Jack's face when he opened it, so she got up and went in and stood behind him. Same old thing . . .

Six down
This wheeler dealer confuses a worn engine
click and takes out half a conrod.
  Reaper

'Oh God,' Lamarre lamented, stroking his weary brow. 'Why couldn't it wait till bloody morning. The last bugger isn't cold yet for God's sake.'

'Wheeler dealer?' Al said, suspiciously. 'Wheeler dealer?'

Lamarre looked almost desperate.

'I reckon he's guessed that we've got the PO running for us,' he said. 'He knows we're getting them special delivery. He must do.'

'Worn engine click?' Al said. 'Click? What rhymes with click?'

'We aren't any bloody closer than we were on day one,' Jack keened. 'Either too many suspects, like the whole frigging country, or none at all.'

'Jack . . .'

'Goddam, he'll be coming at us once a sodding day at this rate. I just . . .'

'Jack, it's Renwick. It's *Renwick*!'

'What?'

'A worn engine click. Start with that,' Al was saying breathlessly. 'Now take out the letters a,c,o,n. — that's half a conrod. Then rearrange what's left.'

'Nigel Renwick' Jack said. 'Almighty God.'

'Right.'

'The wheeler dealer.'

'Right.'

Inspector J. D Lamarre was beyond belief. Freaked wasn't the word. Disarrayed wasn't either. After nearly choking on it for about ninety seconds, he said:

'Did Taylor take a handset?'

'No,' she said, counting those in the room.

'Got an RT in his motor?'

'Possibly. No, wait. No, he hasn't.'

'Can you get him on that opposite Renwick's place?'

'That' was a big box of tricks they'd installed in the corner of the incident room when the RT link was set up for the surveillance on Nigel Renwick's door. It had a receiver/transmitter for talking to the telephone that Taylor had gone to remove. Sergeant Prendergast tried it once, twice.

'Buzzing,' she told Lamarre. 'It's still live. He's not there yet.'

'OK. Keep trying it. I'll get some more arm on this, just in case our boy's on the move.'

He's not covered, Al kept telling herself, feeling sick all the time, Renwick's not covered, oh God. She kept shoving in the call sign and getting the no-reply buzz from the surveillance phone.

'Superintendent Tickle's office,' Jack was saying into his phone. 'No. I know he's not gone yet. Find him please. Now.'

Al kept on trying — Click — buzzzz, click — buzzzz.

'Get him to call me back, this is Inspector Lamarre. Tell him it's urgent. Just *tell* him!'

Click— buzzzzz.

Click — buzzzzz.

Jack had another number now.

Click — buzzzzzz.

'Jack Lamarre. Listen, I want that squad back outside Nigel Renwick's place pronto. I mean fucking *now*. Never mind why, let's just say we might get a vist from our boy after all. I said never fucking *mind*! No, use the same men, they won't need briefing. Same set up. What! No, Renwick hasn't got the WT still . . . Yes, yes, I said *yes* . . . OK, thanks.'

Click — buzzzzzz.

'Yes. Well *find* him. I don't want to call again. Get up off your arse and *go and look for Superintendent Tickle*.' Slam. 'Like watching bloody grass grow sometimes.'

Click — buzzzzzz . . . HUMMMMMMM!!!

Al stared at it, a weird feeling dawning softly.

'It's been cut off, Jack,' she said, firmly and calmly as she could. 'It was ringing and then it was cut off.'

For one stupid slot of about three seconds, Lamarre wondered why Taylor would disconnect it whilst it was ringing without answering it first, but of course he wouldn't, would he?

Why he grabbed his coat he'd never know. You just do that when you leave a place. Maybe he didn't realise he'd done it, maybe neither of them did, because they both had nightmares sprouting then.

'Come on,' he said. 'We'll pull some help in on the way.'

It was closing on eleven p.m. then.

Nigel Renwick had dined alone, enjoying a whole bottle of St Emilion to himself, and was taking a small break from his Proust for a brandy. The remnants of his meal were in the dining room, waiting for his staff to come back in tomorrow and clear up. Now he was alone, as the horror entering the rear of his house knew perfectly well. Nigel had his housecoat on over his dinner jacket. He had already stopped thinking about that surrealistic little episode with the police. At four p.m. this afternoon he had described it to a constable as being rather like the cars he *didn't* sell, horrible but quaint. The constable had looked no less idiotic than before.

The double doors of the lounge burst open with a bang and Renwick spun around. When he saw it, he dropped both glass and decanter and tried to speak, but no way, not possible, because this thing had a woman's hair, a white face, a cloak, fangs, and an axe, any one of which would have rendered most people lost for a phrase, but what really clammed up poor Nigel was the obvious and undeniable fact that it had *no eyes*! No eyes, for the love of God, it had no eyes, a thing which numbed your mind, because such a thing was beyond human, and even when it leaped forward and came over the coffee table with its cloak flying out and its mouth open, and that long *Waaahh!* erupting from its mouth, even then Nigel didn't have the conscious control to move, not even when the axe swung around in a great looping arc, even then Nigel was still transfixed by those empty eyes, even when the blade crashed into his face . . .

THIRTY-FIVE

Queen's Gate Gardens was deserted when Jack dropped the car into the end of the street and stopped it. He turned off engine and lights and then they both sat there, he and Al, just looking.

'Can't see the watch team,' Al said. 'I don't think they're here, Jack. They've not arrived.'

'Nobody's bloody here,' Jack breathed gently. 'Just us. Is that Taylor's car?'

It was parked opposite Renwick's place, across the street, facing the same way they were.

'Yes, I think so,' Al said, straining to see in the dark. 'Jack. Renwick's lights're out downstairs.'

'Yeh, right. Maybe he's got no guests tonight.'

'Maybe. Probably.' Jack gave it a second. 'Go check Renwick, Al, but take it casual, in case our boy's about. I'll see what the hell's going on in there.'

As Prendergast walked slowly down the street towards Renwick's door, Lamarre went smartly down the other side, getting ahead of her. He reached the white fronted house where Taylor's car stood and hopped up the steps to find the front door ajar. It was dark inside, pitch dark.

Jack pushed the door to behind him and stood in the hall, looking at the stairs in front of him. There was a window halfway up, letting in some moonlight from the yard behind, giving a faint glow to reflect the banister. He knew the rest of the house was empty.

'Taylor?' Just a whisper, nothing more. Almost no point to it, but the place seemed to be frowning at him just for being there. 'Taylor?'

Jack went up the stairs, sliding against the wall, craning his neck to look around the bend halfway. He was going faster than he thought. When his head reached the upper floor level he saw the door of the front room wide open, and by the light streaming in from the street lamp just outside he could see Taylor's face against the floor, with the eyes open. He could see the bloody gashes from here, glistening in the half light. Jack jumped the rest of the way.

The man was finished, slashed with something. God it was a mess. The RT set's power cable was hacked through, otherwise it was undamaged.

That was when Jack looked out of the window into the street below and saw Al going up the steps of Renwick's place. She was right at the door when the face appeared at the window not three feet from her shoulder, one white featureless face, suspended over a black garb as if hanging on its own like the sudden materialising of some nether ghoul, there but not to be believed.

Jack didn't think. He just put an elbow through the window to stop her and then threw himself down the stairs. He made Renwick's door in about three and five thirteenths of a second, give or take.

'Jack,' she said, shuddering, he could feel her shuddering with his hands on her shoulders, 'Jack, I saw it.'

'So did I. That's why I smashed the window.' Lamarre stopped for a second and bit the back of a hand. 'Listen Al. Taylor's dead up there, hacked to death by the look of it. This is our chum, Al, and he's on his way out the back. Al? *Al*!!!'

'It wasn't human, Jack,' and she thought, *What* to death?

Lamarre gripped both her shoulders and squeezed, 'It was human, Al, right? *Right?*'

'Right, Jack.' She was shaking her head as if to clear it. 'OK Jack. I'll go in the front.'

'Sure you can handle that?' Though he was backing off and starting to turn before she nodded, and then he spun away and began racing for the corner of the street forty yards distant to get around the back of the place because (a) it *was* him wasn't it? and (b) he *wasn't* going to come out the front and (c) he wasn't going to wait to say hello and (d) funny though it might have seemed to be thinking this right at this moment there was this certainty pushing its way up that if he wasn't caught now he'd be gone for ever. Jack nearly broke his neck around the corner.

Al Prendergast kicked open the door after smashing the glass and unlocking it, soldier style, then reached in quickly and swiped on the light in the hall. She was ready to fight then (and she *could* fight), or run maybe, or scream or bite or faint or anything but when nothing batlike flew out at her she went in and looked up the stairs and stopped because there's something about stairs and already in her mind's eye she was seeing Martin Balsam coming up the stairs in *Psycho*, straight into the butcher knife, but then she thought that was stupid, he wasn't up there, was he, so no point charging up, she'd just wait here for Jack.

Or maybe put a light on for him. Oh *hell*.

Al staggered into the lounge . . .

Around the back of the terrace, Lamarre had located the rear of the place by number and crashed over the gate into a cursing heap on the stone path. Stumbling about in pitch dark he groped his way to a door, fumbled his way to his left and found a window. There was a hole in it. Jack could feel the curved edge of the hole and the faint stickiness around it where the tape had held the glass in place while the cutter worked. So the door was open, right?

Right.

He clattered into the blackness and through to the front, banging on lights, heading for the glow ahead and shouting for Prendergast all the time with this sick cloying feeling growing in his belly when she didn't answer right off. But when he came through into the hall he found her, leaning against a wall with her palm against her mouth. She didn't look at him, she just kept breathing long and hard and deep and stared wide eyed at the wall opposite. In her other hand she was holding a black cloak or cape or some such thing and what looked like somebody's scalp though you had to think wig, obviously, this being Kensington and not the wild west.

'Al?'

It took her a beat or so.

'I'm all right Jack. I'm all right. It's Renwick . . .'

'Stand still, Al.'

Lamarre went into the lounge and looked at it, or at least the nearest bit of it. Then he went further in and looked at a few more bits of it and then he came back out.

'Blood all over the cloak,' Al said, holding it up in front of him so he could see the wet streaks on it. Lamarre stood and studied her, wondering how it had hit her, walking in on that, and of course she knew what he was thinking which was why she was waving it about and talking at him, to show him she was back on line again, or something. 'It's long, Jack. Must have covered him from head to foot nearly. He just left it.' Jack just stared. 'And the wig, Jack. Look how

204

long that is, too.' Jack was shaking his head as she burbled on, 'Jack, he came in disguise, see, and then he did *that*, and then he went out *clean*, Jack . . .'

'Relax, Al.'

'*You* fucking relax,' she almost bawled. 'He's a raging psycho. We've got to get him. *Now!*'

'All right. Now.'

Jack cursed. He could jump back into the car, but where then? And dammit, there should have been car units here by now . . .

But shit, he couldn't be far. You had to try.

'Got a weapon?' Jack said.

'A weapon?' Al told him, 'I'm not even wearing a bra.'

'Any good without one? Never seen you in action.' He had time for a smirk, even now, the shmuck.

'I've stopped a few clowns,' she said, trying to sound indignant, though whatever he had in mind she wasn't all that keen on.

'Good girl. Cromwell Road, right?'.

'Right, Jack.'

Wrong, Jack, she thought, but where was she going to get a choice? Rat-piss, she thought in her amateurish style of cursing, sod-knob-shit.

A man being chased generally did one of two things, or so the police were wont to contend. Either he ran like hell for a short distance to put some distance between himself and his pursuers and then he started walking slowly, or he stood still for a while hoping his pursuers would put a distance between themselves and him *then* he started walking slowly. In either case he ended up walking slowly and casually and looking around a lot and generally working too hard at being one of the crowd. The trick was to guess which way he'd gone and then cover more ground than he had and then *wait and watch* because if you're lucky you'd spot him when he came walking by. Nothing but horse manure, of course, because obviously it hardly ever worked, but when you had nothing else that was what you had to do.

Jack had guessed on the general direction of the Cromwell Road because that was where the way out of Kensington lay, that was where the people would be, and that was the first thing that came into his head. It took them both two minutes to reach it, Al by way of Grenville Place, Jack by way of Queen's Gate and when they got there they were a hundred yards apart. It was eleven thirty p.m., dark and wet, a little cold, some people about, too many from one point of view, not enough from another.

They both watched. Every face. Every coat.

Lamarre waited on the south side of Cromwell Road for about five minutes and then started to work his way gradually west to where Al was lurking at the corner of Grenville. When she was in sight he stopped again, looked at her, got looked at, nodded, got nodded at, started looking at the passers-by again. They were nearly all couples dammit, hardly a loner among them and what there was looked either too old or too drunk or too fat or too damn something, not a maniac to be seen and, hellfire, supposing he was in a car? It was possible, probable even, because although Jack had never associated this killer with cars and no positive traces of one had ever been found, it still stood to reason he had to have one for carrying his goodies around; his spears and his hammers and his bombs and whatever the hell he was packing tonight.

Already he felt stupid. Across the road Al shrugged her shoulders and started stamping her feet as if they were cold or maybe she ran into a swarm of ants so Jack flicked his head to the right and they both started walking east now, with Jack leading on his side by twenty yards or so. This wasn't going to fucking work, he decided, it was just going to be a case of making his mind up when to give up and call it off. He was right to have tried, of course, you had to give it a throw and oh boy was he going to twist this up Tickle's nose because but for that prat there'd have been *somebody* hanging about at least. All right so they might not have got him anyway, but they wouldn't have lost a cop either, and at least that poor sap back there would have had a ch . . .

The figure came out of Gloucester Road just as Lamarre came to it. Jack stopped like a gun-dog.

The pale features and the black coat clanged up in the detective's consciousness like the bell of some sinister cash register or the dinging of some mental fruit machine registering a kill. Looking back and across he saw that Prendergast was moving hard now, closing on the shape, waving and pointing. The thing in black had seen neither of them yet; it was strolling average to slow, shoulders hunched up, looking dead ahead. Jack let it get in front a little in case it looked over and then he signalled Al to move in. He still couldn't make the face. That was important, the face.

Somewhere in his mind Lamarre asked God to let this be him. Please, he said. Please.

Just beyond Queensbury Place, the figure stopped right under a street light and turned to cross the road. It could have been a few seconds later and that might have been enough, or there could have been traffic to distract it and that could have been enough too, but none of those was to be, which is the way fate sometimes has it, because as it went through some kerb drill, right left right again, and Lamarre looked at the face, it lifted its head and stared right into the cop and Jack knew immediately and for certain what was going down because it didn't hesitate, it didn't go rigid or anything, it just swung round, picked out Prendergast, gave one more look to Lamarre, and started running which meant, obviously, that the chase was on.

Prendergast could have screamed but she was wise enough to save her breath and she just went with it. God, she hated running, just hated it.

The black coat was streaming slightly, but not impeding it any as the figure dashed across the Cromwell Road, head down, arms pumping. Thirty yards behind, Lamarre dropped his topcoat and started yelling to Prendergast to stay with him as the figure flew around the corner of Cromwell Place and out of sight, going south now, though Jack was ready for this and he was thinking, oh no, oh no, not enough corners in this whole city for you, pal, and he drove himself into a dead run, pulling in all the air he could on each breath, working his hips into the stride, trying to eat up the ground, minimise his contact with it and just kind of *float* above it like he sometimes imagined himself when he wasn't suffering in an actual run because it's always easy to imagine yourself doing it and Ryan and Ovett and Coe and so on made it look so rotten simple though this probably wasn't how they trained, really. Looking back he saw Al come round the corner on two wheels behind him, still mouthing something, flapping her arms like a chicken dodging a truck, and ahead the figure was in sight again now, still sprinting. It was heading for the tube, Jack decided, going for Thurloe Street. Well he could head where he fucking liked because he's got a real ace behind him now, if anybody drops it'll be him, not me, I'll chase the creep into frigging Croydon if I have to, right? This time he's coming in.

Couple of hundred yards at this pace, was what Prendergast was thinking, give or take a few. Then I burst.

The figure crashed into South Kensington tube station head-long, with its arms out in front of it like a rugby forward and took an old tramp full in the chest with them and sent the man flying, scattering a bundle of newspapers up in the air in a kind of cloud. Bouncing off the man, the doll-face gave an angry and bewildered and what could have been a painful look as it spun around on the run and then it was away again, into the tunnel only now it was slower. Lamarre piled in maybe three point five seconds later and all but floored the tramp again. The cop stopped and gaped at the choices because South Ken is like that inside, full of choices — trains (Circle, District and Piccadilly lines), underpass to museums, exits to various streets, you've got to know what you want — and then he grabbed the hobo by the throat and started shaking him like a rag doll.

'Where did the runner in black go,' he shouted, 'A runner in black.'

'Bloody young 'ooligan,' wailed the knight of the road. 'Nearly broke my neck. Come bargin' in 'ere.'

Al wheezed in then, saw Lamarre pulling at the tramp, and, like, took in the situation as it were at a glance. Without stopping she ran hard into a ticket box where there was this Pakistani youth with a shock of black hair sticking out under his London Transport cap, smoking a Benson's and watching the scene on the tiles with philosophical detachment.

'Which way did he go?' yelled Jack with the tramp's teeth all but coming out now and God he stank like a fish and Jack was naturally breathing hard still. The tramp seemed to have clammed up in terror.

'Jack,' Al shouted in his ear, 'Down there.'

Lamarre let go of the shaking itinerant and followed his Sergeant into the pedestrian tunnel. At that moment he didn't know if the tunnel was a good thing or not, and if so for who. At that moment he didn't know anything.

The South Kensington tunnel is for pedestrians only. Normally they close it about nine p.m. on weekdays and eight p.m. on Sundays, but if there's some kind of thrash on in South Ken, like the Albert Hall maybe, then they'll leave it open for the late tubes. The tunnel is twenty feet wide and twelve feet high and it runs from the tube station in Thurloe Street, under the streets of Museumland fairly straight apart from a couple of kinks for a distance of four hundred or so yards to a point underneath Exhibition Road. It is a concrete chute with tiled sides for people using the underground system into South Kensington. Leaving the tube station you walk the tunnel northwards, passing exits here and there, until you reach the end somewhere near the Science Museum, which is where you either come out to the surface or you turn around. In the daytime you will usually pass a busker or two filling the gloomy echoing space with the sound of a guitar or a harmonica or a piece of brass, and if you use the tunnel a lot you'll find that the buskers get younger all the time.

At eleven thirty it was just plain gloomy, because it had been Queen at the Hall tonight, but by now the crowds had gone.

The figure was thirty yards ahead, walking.

Jack and Al got that down to twenty five before it looked around and broke into that streaming run again, and this time Lamarre went flat out for it, because with little or nowhere for it to go but dead ahead it had to be right for a try. Dropping behind again, Al tried to hold on but couldn't, she just kept pounding along as best she could, panting and sucking in the echoing hollowness of the tunnel, their three pairs of shoes clattering disjointedly on the concrete. The gap closed. Lamarre started to hurt now, though through the rasping and gasping of his own chest he could hear the breathing of his quarry, and it was heavy, labouring, full of pain like his own. And then the figure turned.

It was so quick, so unexpected, a mere flying spin of a movement that Lamarre had no time to dodge or duck or cover his head or do anything, so if the axe had been on target and coming on edge-first he'd have picked up a split face but as it was it just flashed in his eyes, banged off his shoulder and skidded metallically away to one side. Ignoring it, he kept on going, just a belated flinch was all it earned as it grated along a wall, the sound falling behind him as he went and he thought what the sweet fuck was that, something nice no doubt, something pally.

Twenty yards back now, Al Prendergast stopped and scooped the hatchet up and tore the picture from around the rubber grip. Reaper smiled and grinned again and she felt herself go sick with anger and heard herself saying very calmly and out loud 'It's him' before she started to run again, only this time there was a hatred inside her and it freed her legs and her lungs and her throat and it let her fly and it made her shout what she did which was 'Stop him' two or three times. 'Stop him. Stop hiiimmm!'

Which was all the yobs heard.

Well all right, they probably wouldn't have even needed that much anyway because they'd been horsing their way up out of Chelsea for most of the night, one pub after another, and now they were tumbling down the steps of the second side entrance (Natural History Museum, Victoria & Albert) like a crowd of babbling apes with shaven heads and gold studded earlobes slapping each other in that sloppy way that so characterises the chimpanzee, so when Lamarre went bounding by the sight of him alone was probably just too much in itself, given the average yob's highly developed sense of waggery and slapstick, just too much to resist probably, so out went the boot and down went the cop.

Hard.

He got his hands out as he plunged, enough to save his skull from fracturing but the concrete found his face and it tore up his palms and when he hit he took a winding. Some of his teeth ended up loose in his mouth too and as he rolled he could feel the blood springing out of his nose. He knew he was all messed up before he stopped scraping along the floor, before he started to pain even, and somewhere somebody was laughing like a drain, which was about as much as Jack thought for a short while. Hooting their rings up, he thought, as he faded out.

Al knew better than to stop.

The figure hadn't, and the end of the tunnel was all that there was in front of it now so she had to stay on it, had to be near when it hit the street again, so she kept pumping and gasping and gulping for the next hundred yards until the end of it started to show and then she made a like suicidal spurt as the figure disappeared left up the stairs to the Exhibition Road. And when she came up seconds later, it was gone.

The big wide street was almost deserted, like the set of some giant outdoor play, bathed in the street light, strangely quiet because she'd caught it brooding, minus traffic for a moment, breathing on its own. She walked north, looking around like a cat and God but she felt bad, with her throat burning and her god-damned tits hurting (so in future she must be sure to always wear a bra for chasing killers on demand, OK?) and her legs shaking like jelly. She nearly walked right past the young couple by the wall but she saw them in time.

They just stared at her as she darted up to them and asked if they'd seen a person run by, a person in black, and they probably wondered what the hell the poor sap could have done to have this wild woman after him with an axe but they didn't risk any comments like that, they just told the truth and said yes, yes, went down there, pointing down Imperial College Road, at the corner of which thoroughfare they were having their goodnight grope. Down there, they said, respectfully.

Down there was the main entrance avenue to Imperial College. Nothing but rows of parking spaces, a few trees, and buildings to the sides, (Chemistry on the left, Engineering and Libraries on the right). Al sprinted another sixty yards down it to the corner of a little street called Wells Way before she stopped again and bent for breath. It was darker here, the street very narrow, just an alley really with no lights of its own, just what streamed into it from the surroundings, and it was deadly quiet, like a tomb. Even so, when she stood up again it was her eyes that found it and not her ears because there was no sound when it moved, it just moved. Just one movement, that was all, down there under a great slab of a building lurking in the dark at the far end of the narrow street, totally dark, the back of somewhere or other rather than the front, and it was the dim glow of sodium yellow catching the black coat that picked it out and just for a second before it was gone. Al swallowed, painfully, and started to run again and suddenly she was splashing through a puddle and the water soaked into her favourite slacks and if she'd had the mind she'd have cursed because hellfire it hadn't been raining that hard had it? This was frigging rainwater, this was, and a bloody blocked drain, and this was a door, a small stainless steel door, the only one for a hundred miles so this was where he went, right? Get a grip, get a grip.

Al stepped inside what was, unbeknown to her, the Physics department basement and looked up into a dingy stone stairwell, lit by watery bulbs about every three flights. New, fresh, wet footprints went up into the gloom and Al knew she had to follow them. She wasn't scared yet, exactly, but there was this voice in her head now asking her what she was doing here anyway and what was wrong with modelling anyway, it paid well didn't it? It didn't get you mixed up with homicidal paranoiacs did it? Well did it?

Al went up the stairs, kind of on the alert.

She didn't estimate that carefully but it was about three floors before the footprints left the well, and they were very faint by then so she was having to look very closely at the steps and when they came out onto the wooden floorboards on what she didn't realise was the Mathematics entrance hall they disappeared completely so she'd have been stumped then and there but for the lift lights.

Tell tale lift lights. Four, five, six, they said, and then they stopped, and for a few seconds Al just stood there and looked at the little red six above the doors, feeling maybe like a person with an invitation, but to what and for what she didn't want to think. Then she went on up, naturally.

Well, she had to, right? Sixth floor.

She was in a half lit landing area in front of a pair of swing doors, over which was a sign that read 'Level 6. Mathematics' so Al realised only then she was inside Imperial College and she thought, yes, oh yes, this was what we wanted to think all along, it really was. And then she went through the doors into a carpeted corridor. She followed the corridor round a bend or two, taking the corners wide and watching the walls and listening to the silence. Every other bulb in the ceiling was lit so the light was bad, and it kind of unnerved her eyes as if it was making them work too hard without them really wanting to do it. The carpet absorbed the sound so even her own breathing was damped and that made her feel choked as if she wasn't breathing at all.

Which was all what we'd call fear of course, though the word alone is never enough of course and Al was frightened now of course.

From what seemed far away, a door slammed.

The room at the end was wide open. The light was on.

Somewhere a lift hummed up its shaft.

God Almighty, Al thought, I'm shit scared.

She approached the door along the opposite wall. Before she reached it she stopped, waited, listened, tried to squint through the crack by the hinge. Nothing moved. She edged forward again until she was almost level with it, with her back against the door opposite the open one. She needed that, her back to something solid because if some person, some *thing*, came out of that open door she didn't want to be stumbling backwards over her own feet. She could read the sign on the door now. 'Postgraduates' it said, in white on black, and the number underneath it was C42 which was all that Al logged in before the door behind her sprang open and she nearly fell in before animal electricity took over and she went leaping into 'Postgraduates' like a startled frog without even thinking about whether Count Dracula was in there because if anything was lurking inside C42 it couldn't be as bad as whatever was breathing down her neck right now.

She nearly froze when she turned though, because the young man in black was coming in behind her and he was making no sound, just coming straight at her with his hands out like claws and his face blank and expressionless and those empty eyes like two big black pods of mad hate so that Al almost screeched when she saw the face, before she got control, and then for another few moments while her feet moved on their own her mind went through some strange contortions, like *hot shit*, it thought, *it is the Reaper, the actual Reaper, I always thought there were horns* . . . She scrabbled for room and kept her right arm dangling out of sight by her side as she fished in her pocket for the warrant card with the left. She didn't honestly expect a response from this, but then you never knew, so she said like a drip, 'Calm down,' dropping the card on a table by her side and backing away from it. 'Look at that. I'm a police officer. Calm down. It's all right.' But of course he didn't say anything, he didn't even lower his hands or blink his black eyes, but he picked up the table, all six feet by three of stainless steel tubular frame with a stout melamine top and he hurled the thing over to one side, so that gave Al a fair idea of his state of mind, and she thought, not coming quietly then? Ah well.

'Not got another spear or anything,' she said, to psyche him up, taunts being breeders of carelessness.

He kept coming.

'You missed my boss by the way,' she added, and thought two more steps.

He came on.

One step, two steps, and then Al went to him. Not a charge, nothing frantic, just a smart clean step like the instructors showed her and then she brought up her right arm and laid the blunt back side of the hatchet across his temple, lashing him with it to snap his head round and jar his brain. He recoiled and she gave him another, two handed, in the opposite direction across the other temple, whipping his face the other way.

Awfully cool, Jack would have been delighted.

The man crumpled to his knees like a drunk and then sagged back and rolled and lay still with his legs bunched up behind him and his hands on his belly. Al looked down at him and wondered if he was dead because no way was she giving him mouth to mouth, that was certain. She'd tried not to kill him. She'd tried to knock him out without smashing his skull like they wanted you to and as far as she was concerned that was bending over backwards, considering the circumstances. God, but he hadn't even said a word. What kind of voice did he have?

Well anyway, she just stood there for a couple more minutes until she got some of her breath back and she could look at her hand without it shaking too much and then she glanced around for a telephone she could use. Seeing none in this room, she went across the corridor to the other office and found one there. Once upon a time cops blew whistles and crowds of other cops came running. Al had only seen a police whistle once, and she only blew it once. She was pulling a strand of hair into place as she dialled, even though the whole thing had to be a mess after all this, because the gesture was subconscious and mechanical by now, she just did it.

That was when the arm went around her neck . . .

THIRTY-SIX

Elaine walked into the common room and saw Kane straight away. He was practically the only person there. Punching out a hot chocolate from the machine, she went over.

'Steve,' she said breathlessly. 'Steve, the department's full of police.'

'Is it?' Kane looked to be distracted.

'I couldn't get in. Wonder what's going on.'

'No idea,' he said testily.

'Seen Norm?' she said, sipping. 'He said he'd meet me upstairs, but he's not there.'

'No,' Kane said. 'No, I haven't seen Norm.'

'We were going for a row in the park.'

'That's nice. So why don't you go?'

Elaine felt stung. There was no call for that, she thought, puckering. What was his mood all about, anyway?

'Well, what're you doing here, Steve?' she said, trying to sound silky and seductive.

'Listen Elaine. That's my business, all right?'

'Well I was just asking.'

He turned away, but as he did so he said something *very* mean.

'Throw yourself at somebody else, Elaine.'

Straight off, Elaine didn't quite lock on to that, but after about two point seven instants she got it and felt immediately sick. Two emotions tumbled over each other, with hurt running first because she had been just a little bit afraid, deep down, that shacking it with Norm could backfire on her Kanewise and here it was, borne out, just like she feared, he was calling her a trollop. But dammit, she thought, and this was where anger caught up, he had no right to speak to her like that, had he? He had no right to judge. She'd never been anything but sweet Elaine with him, the rotten stuck-up louse. Elaine boiled up.

Deep red, she jumped up from her chair and turned on her heel and stamped towards the swing door. Approaching it, she flung her half-full cup of cocoa at a flip-bin and then pushed the door instead of pulling and ended up struggling with it and rattling it like hell before she got through it.

And it was during that fight with the common room door that she glared at the orange police poster that was glued to it, the one like the one they had on the Maths board upstairs. And when she finally got out on to the balcony, she was still seeing it, in her furious little mind's eye, though she wasn't thinking anything, not until she'd stamped another ten yards or so. Then she stopped dead.

Lamarre sat in his office with his mouth full of cotton wadding and his nose covered in Gentian violet. What with that and the bruising he looked like a plum and what was more he was aching. God oh God but he was aching. Later he was going to slowly kill four yobs, though that could wait.

Jack was thinking, at that exact point in time when the phone rang, that he would never in his life ever say that thing again, the old line about getting used to it when people asked you about the sour side of the job, the dirty, cruel side of it. The one where you said you just got hard because you couldn't avoid it and it helped anyway. (Let's face it, you usually added.) It was a stupid macho lie though he had used it often enough, said it often enough, without a thought.

He'd said other things too, without having a conscience about it, like please believe me, Mrs Prendergast, there's no danger, Mrs Prendergast. Jack squeezed the bridge of his nose until it hurt, and choked on his own thoughts.

He had just got back from looking at Al's body, even though it had meant struggling out of the hospital again to do it, and now he was just thinking it out. What he was thinking out was that it was OK that he had come back here and wept, that it was all right. He was thinking that it was just normal.

Nothing else was, but that was.

Tickle was outside, trumpeting to the assembled press, though the poor guy wasn't enjoying it any more than Jack would have done. They just had to be faced, that was all, if only for this one last time, though even that was unlikely. Yes, he was telling them, we have the man. He committed suicide after killing a police officer, but there is no doubt he was the Reaper. Yes, he threw himself from a building. No, we cannot give his name yet.

Yes this, no that, yes the other. Jack just listened numbly as it came through the glass of his office wall, and he was thinking savagely, oh no, don't give them the name, Tickle, old pal, don't give them that, because we've had the damn name all along, haven't we, bit by bit, and sooner or later it'll dawn on one of those wolves and then you'll have a question to answer won't you, oh my yes. Why didn't you realise this Superintendent, one of them will say, could you not have saved a life or two?

Was that fair? No, not really, it was just grief talking, lashing out. We never had it really.

Lamarre fingered the bit of paper he'd scribbled it on in the student's flat. Jack had gone there direct when they told him what had happened, even though he was having the inside of his nose sutured with a long needle at the time, even though he could hardly see through the swellings over his eyes. There was no note this time; the message had been sprayed across the wall of the kid's bedroom with a touch-up can, in metallic grey. Jack had jotted down a copy with his pen on the back of a letter he found in the inside pocket of his jacket and as he looked at it again he realised that the letter was one he had written months ago but never posted, and for some reason that crazy little thing made him hurt very badly now so maybe his mind was bending a fraction too. Anyway, he'd figured the message out all on his own this time, because 'their endings had a common theme, names naming a name' wasn't all that cryptic, whatever cryptic meant after all this, it was just a statement. You just took the endings of the victims' names, all the last letters, starting with N from Hogan and O from Mayo and all the rest and you shuffled them a little and you came out with your killer's name, you came out with N.D. Monk, and it wasn't hard because (i) it was a short name, so it was easy to spot and (ii) they'd just shovelled its owner up from a sidewalk in South Kensington so he was on the tip of the tongue in a way and (iii) they'd come across it already along with the thousands of others in the files though you couldn't honestly say they'd had it all along, not if you wanted to be fair, not on reflection, though on reflection, who was ever fair to the cops anyway? It was just the poor little raver's suicide note, right?

Wasn't it?

Al was dead.

The old boy in Queen's Gate was still in shock, apparently. Understandably too, because if one minute you're waiting for a taxi to come along and the next minute this kid lands on the pavement behind you from six floors up, splashing the backs of your legs, well that's a shock. From that height, the Reaper had spread a little.

Jack felt bilious. He wanted to get out somewhere, anywhere, but that damn phone was ringing.

He slid out to the far end of the incident room, behind the howling mob, and picked up the phone, ignoring the sorry-I-should-have-got-that sick look from the young dick nearby.

He didn't catch it at first. He was just answering mechanically. Somebody or other was squawking at him.

'What?' Pause. 'Oh yes. Do you really?' Jack listened for a second, not caring. 'No, we don't need your name. Go on then . . .'

He wasn't interested really, he thought as he put the receiver down. In fact he didn't give all that much of a damn any more but it was another name that was scheduled anyway, sooner or later, and right now he needed to get out, anywhere, anywhy. He nodded at the nearest face as he went by.

'What park?' Brian said, after he got fed up of the atmosphere.

Daph turned her face to him dead slow, as if she couldn't believe he was real.

'Well what's the nearest park, Brian?' she said, all saucy. 'I mean what's the biggest park in London, about fifty yards from this spot?'

'Hyde Park,' Brian said. 'No? OK, I give up.'

'Oh piss off, Brian,' Daph ground, reaching for a fag. 'She said Norm was taking her in the park for a row and they'd meet us here.'

Here was the common room, but Elaine and Norm weren't here.

'Maybe they got shipwrecked?' Brian said.

'Piss off.'

'Pirates?'

Daph lit up. 'Piss off, Brian.'

Higginbotham felt like he'd been stood up as well, because the man was late, very late. At least three drinks late. Harold H started to sip half of bitter number four.

Every so often the newsman would reach into his inside pocket and finger the envelope there, as if an envelope with fifty quid in it acquired a kind of mobility that caused it to be continually slipping away from whoever was unconsciously worried about it slipping away.

Taylor was late, that was all. Couldn't be anything else, could it? Couldn't have gone to the wrong place, could he? And if he did get the place wrong he only had to ring the paper to find out where to go because Harold H always left his whereabouts with them whenever he could, just in case something incredible happened like a Martian landing or something, and they wanted him to get over and cover it, *toute suite.*

But the cop wouldn't do that would he? He wouldn't risk that, would he?

Harold craned his neck around and looked out of the pub window, seeking the detective's car, and to his huge surprise he did see the variety in question but there were two of them and they were in a big, marked squad car and they had uniforms and when they got out they strolled over to *his* car and started eyeing it up and down before they came towards the pub door.

And Harold thought 'Uh-uh?'

THIRTY-SEVEN

Kane put the last picture on the sink top and then he put the little pile of newspaper and magazine cuttings down just next to it and then he put the other plastic capsule of Aconitine on top of the cuttings. He was about to turn around and walk out of the kitchen and go through to the front of his flat for the final check, but then he stopped by the open back door and looked down at the picture. He would burn it in a few moments, along with the cuttings and the capsule, and then all the traces would be gone. The door was open to dispel the smoke. The matches were in his pocket. Something like affection was in his eyes as he gazed at it.

I shall of course return, he told it, when the time seems right, though not as you, not as Reaper. It will be something else then, though the message will be the same as far as they're concerned, the self-esteemers and the do-nothings, and I shall find another Norman however long it is, because there are many of us around, for every self-esteemer there are ten of us. Or a million. Poor Norm, he was rare though not unique. He was found once and could be found again.

One final check then, though these few things were surely all there was. There could be nothing else then, but one final check before the fire.

Steven Kane went down the hall of his flat and left into his study and started to go through the drawers of his desk, one by one. Tidy by nature, he put everything into one or other of these drawers, everything he wrote, or researched, or noted or named. Every time he had worked out a clue he had used a piece of paper from these drawers. They were all destroyed by now, burned as he had gone along though there could just be something, just something. A line, a word, an imprint on a blank sheet, anything. Drawer by drawer he looked, closing each one afterwards with a final, certain, confident slam.

Poor Norm had flipped his lid, slam, as the poets say, though it had been a manageable thing in the end, given a little retuning of the dials, so to speak. Kane had planned a little scene worthy of Marlow last night had not poor Norm turned up dressed like Hecate with a cop in tow. It would have been a quiet little meeting at midnight, like all the others, and Kane would have gone for the coffees from the machine and given one to Norm with the contents of the other capsule in it and if Norm hadn't asked who the seventh picture was for then Kane would have asked him to guess, as a prompt, just so he could say 'for you Norm, poor Norm, for you' just as he took a sip. It would have been an electric moment, wouldn't it? Kane would have kept it to himself forever, to be relished in silence every day, when life got boring and people even more so. Still, you couldn't have it all ways, poor Norm had really blown his dome, dressing up like that and leading the lady in behind. Pure psychosis had taken over so the suicide had to match didn't it? Something dramatic it had to be, like a last leap into oblivion, though you can't make an unconscious man take a drink anyway, come to think of it. Still, all things considered, the message sprayed on the wall seemed to fit the end rather better than a final note in the post, though one had to be in quickly there, before the authorities came bearing down because Norm had well and truly bounced by them. Slam. Nothing in there. Slam.

Ex-Reaper Kane floated upstairs to rifle through some pockets, though he knew there'd be nothing there either. But still, thorough makes for secure, as somebody may once have said.

You see the trick was to let them think they'd been clever, so they get the idea that they'd *earned* the result instead of it just kind of happening. Just putting the transformer and the perfume spray into Norm's flat wasn't enough (I'll get rid of them, Norm, leave them here) you had to give them something to do as well. That was why they had to have the first capsule (don't carry it back, Norm, it's lethal once it's open, just drop it there and leave it) because that gave them a chance to track something down and once they'd done that they'd claim the conclusion for their own, and then they would guard it like a dog with a bone, a thing inviolate. The cable was a bonus, same source they'd say, it's the student all right, oh yes, they . . . Hello? Kane was holding up a receipt for a hammer and slicing one thought with another, just goes to show he was suddenly telling himself, another little look is never wasted, burn it, burn it . . . they what? Was that all? Yes, of course it was, they were desperate for a result by now, weren't they?

Definitely nothing more to burn now.

Kane went back downstairs in a kind of wistful fog, folding the receipt into four neat parts as he went. By the time he reached the kitchen again he had it into a little arrowhead, like when you start to make a paper plane, and with that and the matches he didn't catch the shabby figure in the yard outside, and for a second or two it didn't see him either, so softly did he tread.

It was in the doorway when he looked up, and he looked up because the picture wasn't there anymore. He had a match in one hand and the box in the other, about three inches apart, and now he looked the man right in the eyes.

'Doctor Kane is it?' Jack said. 'My name's Lamarre. I'm a detective.'

Kane stared at the picture in the cop's hands. He just held it in front of him, carelessly, as if he hadn't connected it with anything at all. His face was all messed up, with stitches in his nose and forehead and mouth . . .

'I did knock at the front,' Jack said. 'But there wasn't any reply.' He hesitated for a second and his eyes flicked down to the thing in his hand for a fleeting instant, less than a beat, 'So I came round the back here.'

Kane began to breathe, but so far he hadn't blinked even.

'Copper's habit,' Jack added. 'Sorry 'bout that.'

Slamming drawers, Kane thought finally, crazily, was that possible? He knocked while I was slamming the godforsaken drawers? But all he said was, 'Elaine,' and he said that in a whisper.

'Is that the lady's name,' Jack said. 'All I got was a voice on a phone.'

Kane just kept on smouldering, so Jack Lamarre began to wonder if they were talking about the same thing here, not that it mattered now. There was something unearthly here, like a scene from a dream, none of this made an atom of reasonable sense.

Kane lowered his hands and then opened the matchbox and very gently put the match in his other hand back inside, so it looked very symbolic of something but only he knew what, or maybe even he didn't, or maybe it just wasn't. It was then that the policeman nodded at the picture he was holding, as if he was suddenly stuck for something to talk about and had only just remembered he had it.

'Busy, are you?' Jack said.